HYDE

THE DEVIL'S BIBLE

Justin Hyde

For my daughter,
Kailyn

"His rea[lm] is above the powerful mighty
before the might of his power all are terrified,
they scatter and flee before the radiance of his dwelli[ng]
of his glory and majesty.
And I, the Sage,
declare the grandeur of his radiance
in order to frighten and terr[ify]
all the spirits of the ravaging angels
and the bastard spirits,
demons, Liliths, owls and [jackals...]
and those who strike unexpectedly
tray the spirit of knowledge,
to make their hearts forlorn and...
in the era of the rule of wickedness
and in the periods of those defiled by sins
not for an everlasting destruction
but rather for the era of the humiliation of sin [...]"
—Dead Sea Scrolls, 4QSongs of the Sage 3-8

"But who prays for Satan?
Who, in eighteen centuries, has had the common
humanity to pray for the one sinner that needed it most?"

—Mark Twain

Prologue

1229 A.D. — Bohemia

The smell of dusk and dew rode atop a night breeze and slowly filled the small stone cell. The Black Monk stood shivering near the far wall, pulling together tightly on the front of his flea infested wool habit. He looked down at his bare feet, now black and swollen from the dirt and the cold, and listened as two sobering voices echoed through the chamber behind him.

"Is vota affor abbatis," One of the guards whispered in Latin.

He wishes to speak with the Abbot? The second guard slowed his stride. "Sit morior. Quod quis is fatur of est *impossible*."

Beyond the rusted metal bars to his right, Hermann could see the faint flicker of animal fat burning dimly in an oil lamp. The torch was one of few that hung from the monastery's inner walls, barely illuminating the damp dark passages running beneath the abbey's sacristy.

Slowly Hermann turned to kneel before a

small wooden cross that set atop a lone shelf. Although the misericord of the monastery was a place of discipline, the abbeys elders allowed a single crucifix to be kept with those monks who had fallen. But the deprivation of food, isolation, and the truth of tomorrow's comings, tore violently at his faith in God.

The monastic rules governing a Benedictine monk were extreme—chastity, patience, obedience, poverty. Falling ill to these temptations consequented in harsh punishments—starvation, flagellation, being stripped of the ceremonial black robe. But for Hermann it was to be worse. His sins had been deemed to unholy to speak of. Not even *he* dared to speak of his crimes. A monk succumbing to greed, wrath, and sexual aberration, damaged the sanctity of the monastery, and by order of the Arch Bishop would be put to death.

A final footstep scuffing the stone walk beyond his cell door preceded a familiar voice. "Vos es Hermann contineo?"

"Yes, I am Hermann Inclusus." His voice was faint. The man behind him lurking beyond his confine was the abbeys Claustral Prior, second only to the abbot himself on the totem of hierarchy at the monastery.

As one of the guards turned an iron key into the cell door, Hermann began to turn and face the man. The Prior stood deathly still while the heavy bars creaked open. Behind him, the dim light reflecting from the passageway sparkled off the gold leafed koukoulion atop his head as he entered — flanked by both guards.

"Child of God," the Prior began to say. He stopped his walk and lifted his chin and palms toward the sky. "By order of the monastic brotherhood of St. Benedictine, he with sin shall..."

"You're Holiness, No!" Hermann pleaded as he fell to his knees before the Prior. Trembling on the ground, he inter-weaved the fingers of both hands tightly together and held them up for mercy.

His cries fell on deaf ears as the Prior continued, "Da, quaesumus Dominus, ut in hora mortis..." *Grant, we beseech Thee, O Lord, that in the hour of our death....*

Hermann struggled to his feet, keeping both hands clenched for forgiveness. "Father," He cried. "I beg you. I cannot repay my sins in the afterlife. Spare me, so that I may show penitence to God."

The two guards stepped forward and grabbed him by each arm. Effortlessly they drug him backwards away from the Prior. And as the final words of the holy prayer for the dead chorused through the chamber, a revelation entombed itself into Hermann's mind.

Suddenly he stopped resisting. The guards, still holding firmly to his arms, set him down onto a stone table in the center of the room. "Your Holiness," Hermann pleaded again. "If you shall spare my life on this night, I in return shall scribe for you a great book, a book that will contain all the knowledge of man and beast. I will glorify you and our monastery forever in the writings of God our Father."

"Ha!" The guard on his left laughed. "Such a feat would be impossible."

Hermann, un-phased and trance-like, looked deeper into the Priors eyes. "I will scribe for you the greatest book you have ever seen. The greatest book *the world* has ever seen." He paused. "And I will complete it for you by morrow's first sun."

The other guard to his right grinned devilishly. He had only chosen life in the abbey to please his father when he was a boy. Upon growing into adulthood, he realized that sin brought with it the joys and pleasurable things in life. His deception and wickedness was known only by his father, but as a Dean in the monastery, his father could not will himself to denounce his only son—for it would surely destroy them both. And now the guard indulged himself in the amusement he received, knowing that this old monk he held captive would soon face execution.

"Tell me," said the Prior. "Tell me of this book." He moved a step closer to the guard on Hermann's right and looked him briefly in the eyes, a reflection of candle flame danced over his gaze before he returned it to the condemned monk. "Tell me how you would accomplish such a task."

With his upper arms still restrained, Hermann spread his hands over the tops of his knees. "I shall repent that my sins be stripped of me. This shall be the redemption for the crimes of my temptations. Should my endeavor fail, then I too shall fail." With his head still raised in certitude, he finished, "And await my judgment."

To the guard's surprise, the Prior stood in meditation. His lips moved quietly and his eyelids trembled. Moments later his right arm raised, and with the tip of his thumb he motioned the sign of the cross over his body. "In the name of the Father," he touched his forehead, "The Son," his chest, "The Holy Ghost," both shoulders.

Each guard looked down at Hermann who remained undisturbed in his new-found accord.

"My son," the Prior said humbly. "You shall have till the morning sunrise. If you complete this book which you speak of... your life shall be spared."

The guard to Herman's right, in disbelief, stepped forward. "Vestri venia. The Arch Bishop will not be pleased."

The Prior ignored his concern. "Licentia him ut suus negotium." Then he turned and slowly walked from the dark cell and into the subterranean passageway that led to the night-stair and up to the abbeys warming room.

With no choice, both guards followed.

Hermann only watched a moment as the three disappeared into the shadows. He then turned, walked slowly to the beeswax candle set atop the farthest corner of the stone altar, and held an open palm behind the flame. A dozen stained white trails of melted wax slithered down the last remainder of the wax stick, over the edge of the large stone tablet, and onto the floor. With his free hand, he reached   behind a small rock near his foot and picked up another candle from the dwindling supply the monastery had left for him. Cautiously, he picked up the melting candle and set it on top of the fresh one, forging the hot wax into a single structure with his fingers, then set it back down on the table.

"Hermann contineo," another voice called from behind him.

He turned, and standing just beyond the bars of his cell was brother Letholdus — named after a knight from the First Crusade in 1099. He stood with an arm outstretched into Hermann's dungeon. "Supplies for you," he said.

Hermann saw not only the outline of the goose feather in Letholdus' hand, but also the immense pile of scribe tools and parchment paper resting by his feet. He forced a smile before walking over and taking the feather. "Gratias ago vos."

"You're welcome my friend," Letholdus answered.

Hermann hauled the material over to the stone table. But before he could begin work, he scooped a small pile of sand onto a flat rock and held it over the flame of the candle. Once the sand became hot, he buried the tip of the feather deep into it. The steady heat would harden it, making it less brittle, so he could then sharpen it slightly by working it against another stone.

Once satisfied with the quill pen, he looked absently at his source of ink. It was of poor quality and quantity. Without access to metal, he had only one other option to improve and add to the supply. Scattered all around his cell were various insect nests. By crushing them into a paste, they would make a sufficient form of filler to the ink.

He spread the first giant sheet of paper across the table. Dipping the tip of the goose pinion into the insect ink, he touched it down onto the page. Carefully, he watched his hand guide the pen slowly around the top of the paper. It took nearly ten minutes, but after that time he stepped back and judged the quality of the elaborate letter that he had just created.

Content with the penmanship, he bent down into the flickering light and began the strenuous task which he had bestowed upon himself. Hours past. Deeper and deeper into the night, he furiously scribed line after line, page after page.

But as the darkest of hours continued to pass, Hermann began to grow frightful. No matter the dedication or concentration that he devoted, there was just insufficient time. *What have I done?* Furiously he grabbed the top sheet in front of him, tore it in two, and threw it to the floor. He fell hard onto his back in the center of the room.

"My Lord!" he cried out. "What hath Thou done to me?" Desperate and rabid, he rose from the floor and began violently ravaging the room and all its contents. The sheets of parchment paper, the remaining candles, the loose stones, all destroyed in his rage until he finally collapsed again from exhaustion.

"I have sinned," he confessed. "But You…, *You* have abandoned me."

A soft breeze, one no longer filled with the scent of dew, gently wafted into the room. Hermann noticed the airs odorless and unusually dry features. Despite its warm touch, it gave him a chill and he picked his head up from the floor. "Who's there?" he called.

As quickly as it came, the draft was gone. But it had left a strange feeling in him. A dark feeling. An — *evil* — feeling.

Uncontrollably, he rose back to his feet, spread his feet apart and thrust his hands high into the air above him. The Book of Revelations burned in his head and he screamed out, "And if any man shall take away from the words of the book of this prophecy, *God* shall take away *his* part out of the book of life, and out of the holy city, and from the things which are written in *this* book."

His head thrust backward and his body stiffened. "He who was banned from the mountain of God, cast down to earth and reduced to dust in the sight of those who look upon you. I bathe in the midst of your fire. You are a horror to me no more. I welcome you, oh fallen arch angel, and offer upon you my soul. Speak through me, Satan. Guide my pen along these pages."

The two men standing post at the foot of the night-stair heard none of Hermann's cries. A demonic presence cloaked his evocation. But as the final words were expelled the devilish wind surged through the halls, extinguishing the oil lamps and torches hung from the inner walls.

Both men shook.

—

As the first rays of morning light began radiating over the eastern hillside, the abbey Prior adorned his funereal black robe and gold leafed koukoulion. Calmly he draped a small crucifix around his neck and walked out from his private dorter.

The Prior felt unusual this morning, and as he walked past the scriptorium, he saw an eerily strange expression on the faces of two clerics who were studying one of the monasteries manuscripts. Without speaking he continued past the refectory and began his decent down the spiraled night-stair.

Half asleep, the pair of guards forced their attention as the Prior appeared next to them in the passageway.

"Has is universa libri?" The Prior asked.

"We don't know your Holiness. We have not left our post."

The Prior nodded. "Insisto mihi."

At his request, the two guards followed close as he began walking down the stone lined corridor. Reaching the metal bars of Hermann's cell, the three men stopped abruptly.

"Deus in Olympus!" One of the guards cried.

"Non possible!" The other whispered.

In the farthest corner of the dungeon, Hermann stood statuesque in the murky light from a dying candle. But there—on the large stone altar in the center of the room—sat an enormous book.

1

79 miles north of Eugene, Oregon — 2010

The thin blade easily penetrated the tough flesh of the lower abdomen. With a single rapid motion, it sliced open the belly from navel to sternum, exposing a bloody tangle of entrails. Beneath his grasp, the body struggled violently as each major organ began getting carelessly ripped from it.

"Eeeewwwww! Daddy, you have blood all over your hands."

He smiled at his little girl before turning and washing off the remainder of the small rainbow trout in the bank of the North Umpqua River. "That's how you clean a fish, baby."

She watched in wonder as her father wiped each edge of the blade across his pant leg before sliding it into a sheath on the back of his belt. But as he stood and tossed the fish into the creel hung from his shoulder, she perked up in excitement. "My turn, Daddy? My turn to fish?"

"I don't know," he said in slow drawn out

words. Before continuing, he tilted his head at her and raised the eyebrow over his left eye. "Only big girls get to..."

"But I'm *five* already!" she demanded without hesitation.

Playfully, he slapped his forehead with the open palm of his right hand. "That's right. You *are* five now aren't you?" He bent down and rested his pole against a dry rock, then turned, scooped her up by the arms, and held her in front of him. "Can you believe I forgot how big my little girl's getting already?" Then he gave her a quick kiss on the forehead and set her back down.

"I just had my birfday party, silly," she said, having some difficulty still with pronunciation. "Remember."

"Yep, it's all coming back to me now." He began scratching the rough salt and pepper stubble on the bottom of his chin. "I think maybe I forgot to give you one of your presents though."

Her little blue eyes grew in excitement. "Another present!" she screamed in joy.

"I'm not sure. I think I might have seen something in the back of the truck." He paused for a moment to let her soak in the anticipation. "Maybe we should go have a look."

A tremor of delight shook over her body. "Yaayyy! Another present!" She grabbed for the bottom of his shirt and began tugging in the direction of the truck parked at the top of the hill. "Let's go see, Daddy. Can we go see? Can we?"

"You bet we can. Wait one second okay." He un-clipped the leather strap holding the creel around his neck and set it on the ground near his pole. "Hold my hand," he said before starting the walk up the hill. "Remember — leaves of three...?"

"Let them be," she sang, finishing his rhyme and taking his hand.

"At'a girl." Aside from the areas poison oak, he kept a close watch for the less notorious stinging nettle plant as they began the short hike up the hill. Once the narrow trail opened up to the dirt plateau where he had parked the truck, he released her hand and watched as she ran quickly to the back of the Chevy. "I'm coming," he called, when she had turned back to see that her father had not kept pace.

"Hurry, Daddy."

Reaching the pickup, he pulled the keys from his front pocket and unlocked the back window of the camper shell and lowered the tailgate. "Now where did I see that present?" She struggled to look above the rear of the truck. "I swear I thought it was in here," he continued. But before allowing too much disappointment to set in, he threw back the corner of an old blanket to reveal the edge of a long box wrapped in brightly colored paper.

"I see it," she cried happily, then pointed a small finger to the words "happy birthday" written on the front face of the gift. "There it is!"

"Yeah, I think you might be right." He dusted off the back of her little pants before picking her up and setting her down into the back of the truck. "Why don't you go check it out."

She scrambled over to the box and pulled the rest of it free from under the blanket. "Can I open it? Can I?"

"If you don't, I'm going to."

"Nooo!" And without further delay, she tore through the paper like there was a bomb inside, and its timer was about to hit zero. "A Barbie fishing pole!" she shouted. "Daddy look, it's a Barbie fishing pole." She hugged her new toy to her chest, then looked up at her father. "Can we try it?"

I wish your mother could be here. Kate would have been so proud of you. He fought off a tear before answering his daughter. "Of course we can try it."

While his daughter wrestled with the plastic packaging around her new fishing pole, he began collecting some of the shredded wrapping paper and crumpled it up into an empty bag. As he was about to reach for the final piece, he noticed a faint green light flashing and beckoning him from inside the cab of the truck. His satellite phone.

"Be careful, baby," he said. "Don't cut yourself on that plastic. I'll be right back, okay. Stay in the back of the truck."

She nodded in agreement, but was clearly only paying half attention as she continued to fight with the packaging. He smiled, then looked up at the sky and shook his head disapprovingly at the thought of being targeted by one of the United States' 66 low-earth orbiting satellites, then walked around and unlocked the driver's door. Inside the cab, the Iridium 9555 satellite phone was blinking in repetition through its transparent aqua-pack. He unzipped the bag and flipped up the auxiliary antenna. "What is it?" he asked into the receiver.

"Colonel Skull," the man answered. "General Kestner has asked me to contact you."

Nightcorp International, although borrowed its system of ranks from the U.S. Army, didn't use any of its subtitles — no Major Generals or Lieutenant Generals separated Colonel Skull from his commanding officer.

Similar to Blackwater or G4S, Nightcorp was licensed by the United States Department of Defense as a Private Military Contractor. But unlike Blackwater or G4S, Nightcorp operated much more covertly and unpublished within the Pentagon. As well, Nightcorp dealt more with overseas operations and intelligence rather than combat.

With a minimal full time staff of only 6

officers, 4 administrative personnel, and one "muscle," Nightcorp outsourced many of its operatives through its ties with the NSCC — the NATO SOF Coordination Centre, SOF referring to Special Operations Forces. In fact, NATO often relied heavily on Nightcorp, as they had in Kosovo back in 99 when Colonel Skull and Ethan Price were "quietly" requested by NATO's ground surveillance division commander to provide interim security assistance.

"What is it Frank?" he asked, immediately recognizing the voice. "I told Kestner I was spending time with Kendall this weekend."

"How's she doing?" Frank asked.

Francesco Ferrari, better known as Frank, was a Captain with Nightcorp. At just 41 years old, Franks face was already beginning to show signs of stress wrinkles beneath the eyes. He was of average height and weight with jet black hair and olive skin. But to meet the man face to face was an experience to say the least. In typical Italian fashion, Frank spoke with his hands as much so as his mouth. His friendship with Cameron Skull was nearing 15 years now, ever since they had worked together at the Savannah River Nuclear Site in South Carolina back in the mid-nineties. Frank had been a new scientist there, fresh out of Cornell University. He had been heading up a division for nuclear "cleanup," when Cameron Skull was sent in by Nightcorp to investigate an internal breach of security at one of the facilities plutonium reactors. Soon after, Frank was recruited, and their shared passion for river fishing quickly spawned a friendship.

Cameron looked through the back window of the Chevy at his young daughter play-casting with her new hot pink fishing pole. "She's doing good Frank. Still misses her mother." He paused. "But then again... so do I."

"It's only been a year, Colonel. It's gonna take time."

Cameron squinted his eyes and rubbed his forehead. "Anyways. What is it that Kestner wants?"

"He didn't brief me on the details," Frank said. It still surprised him that Colonel Skull never addressed his superior as "General." But he also knew that Skull's friendship with James Kestner predated even his own. "I've been instructed to inform you of a plane leaving tomorrow morning for the Czech Republic."

"So, what?" Skull questioned. "Even if there's something of interest on that flight, he can have one of his local agents check it out. Where's it flying out of? I'll get someone over there myself."

"It's leaving from Chicago O'Hare."

"Fine, I'll get someone over there. You both owe me for this."

"Colonel," Frank said calmly. "The flight is for you. General Kestner has already arranged a 47F cargo helicopter to take you from the Coast Guard Air Station in North Bend, to a connecting flight out of Seattle. It's the best he could do on such short notice. It leaves at..."

"No way!" Skull yelled into the phone. "He's lost his mind. I'm not going to the Czech Republic." He looked out at his daughter again who was still playing with her Barbie pole, but quickly growing impatient. "Even if I wanted to, I've got no one to watch Kendall."

"Actually," he hesitated, knowing that Cameron was about to get very upset at what he said next. "I'm on my way to the airport right now. I should be there in about 4 hours. Kestner asked me if I would stay with her till you get back."

Are you fucking kidding me? "What? Now he's making parenting decisions for me. This is ridiculous. Don't board that plane yet. I'm going to call him, then I'll get back to you."

"Cameron, wait. General Kestner is meeting right now with Parkinson."

Parkinson? "The CIA guy?"

"The one and only."

Soon the overwhelming reality that there was going to be no way out of this created a lump in his chest. He rubbed again on his forehead. "God Damn It, Frank."

"Sorry, Colonel. Believe me, I tried talking

him out of it."

Skull let out a deep sigh. "What time does the chopper leave?"

"O three hundred," Frank answered. "I'll be there before then to take you to the airfield."

"I can't wait." He hung up the phone.

"Can we go fishing now, Daddy?" Kendall asked when she saw him close the phone. "I'm ready to try my Barbie pole."

He smiled at his beautiful baby girl before looking down at his watch. Fortunately, it was still fairly early in the day. *Priorities.* He had lost track of them before Kate passed away. But not with his daughter. Not again. "Yes baby. We can go fishing now."

2

The large airliner taxied up to the gate at terminal two—Ruzyne International Airport; Prague. The flight in from Chicago had been a rough one. Fortunately for him though, the first-class seats on a Boeing 747-400 handled turbulence substantially better than the G22 Transports he was accustomed to.

Immediately upon exiting the plane, Colonel Skull powered on his recently upgraded iPhone and searched for a signal. Nothing. He tossed the phone into his coat pocket and began scouting for any directional signs written in English that could help navigate him towards baggage claim. He had not checked any luggage, but logic assured him that that would be the quickest route out of the terminals.

So far he was having no luck. All directories and information monitors were so far written in Czech. Deciding to follow the crowd, eventually he found himself looking down a long row of glass windows and doors—baggage claim to his right, and a surprisingly busy passenger loading and unloading curb waiting for him to his left.

Eager to check his messages however, he pulled the phone from his pocket again before exiting the airport. A series of bars along the top of the display indicated the recently obtained satellite signal. With one hand holding the strap of his small duffel bag securely over his shoulder, he entered his unlock code and hit the button to retrieve messages.

One new voice-mail.

"Cameron." The message started. It was Frank. "Glad you made it there safe. Don't worry, Kendall is fine. I knew the first thing you'd do after landing was check your voice-mail, then call and check on her."

He knows me to well. Cameron thought.

"Anyhow... two things. First, don't call to check on her right now. I checked your flights arrival time. It should be just after five a.m. there, tomorrow morning. WHICH MEANS," he yelled, "that it's after eight o'clock here, so I've already put her to bed for the night."

Cameron smiled a loving smile at the thought of his baby at home sleeping. "And second," Frank's message continued. "General Kestner has also arranged a car for you. A guy by the name of Jake Evans. Some Englishman Kestner recruited to document your progress. I guess he's going to be like your sidekick... or whatever you want to call him. Anyhow, if I know you as well as I think I do, you're probably still standing somewhere in the terminal."

Jesus! He knows me much too well.

"So, take a walk outside," Frank continued. "He should be waiting for you. Of course, don't ask me how you two are supposed to recognize each other." Skull turned his head towards the street outside. "Good luck buddy. Arrivederci!" the message ended.

"Jake Evans, huh," Cameron muttered to himself. He switched off the phone and returned it to the pocket of his coat, then took another look outside. A scrawny blonde-haired man, dressed in stained blue jeans and an un-tucked green flannel shirt was waving at him and walking quickly in his direction. "What-the-ffffff." He cut himself off to avoid shouting obscenities inside a foreign airport.

"Captain Skull," the man called.

Cameron looked all around him. *No way.* What the hell was this guy thinking? And what the hell was he wearing? In twenty years Cameron had never seen anyone associated with Nightcorp dressed so casual, and dirty, when on assignment. *Has Kestner lost his mind?*

"Captain Skull," the man said again as he neared him.

Cameron grabbed the man's outstretched wrist and threw it down to his side. "First of all, it's *Colonel* Skull. I assume you're Jake."

"Jake Evans, Sir."

"Keep your voice down for Christ's sake. What's the matter with you?"

"Sorry, Sir. Can I take your bag, Sir?"

"No, you can't take my bag. Matter of fact... just start walking. I'll follow. You can relay any information to me once were in the car."

"Yes Sir."

"Go, go," Cameron said, shooing him away with the back of his hands. *Unbelievable!*

—

Once finally situated in the passenger seat of the car and heading east on E67, Cameron shifted his feet around and heaved the heavy duffel bag from the floor to his lap. "So much for remaining inconspicuous," he mumbled as he began trying to unzip the bag in the cramped quarters.

"How so?" Jake asked, not paying nearly enough attention to the road.

Skull didn't look at him, but instead looked at the brightly lit and impressive dashboard of an Audi R8 luxury sports car. "If you hadn't noticed, we're not exactly in the wealthiest neighborhood. What are we doing driving around in this thing?"

"Pretty bitchen, huh?" Jake said, satisfied with himself. "It was my idea."

Skull just turned his attention back to the duffel bag and muttered sarcastically, "Why am I not surprised?" He then pulled a mini-cassette out of a side compartment, inserted it into a player, and pressed a small ear-bud into each ear. Although he had already listened to the recording twice on the flight over, he knew it was nearly 70 kilometers from the airport to their destination. And anything to occupy the time was going to be better than listening to Jake Evans rambling on about whatever precarious thought happened to enter his mind.

"General Kestner has made accommodations for us at Hotel U Vlasskeho Dvora," Jake said, oblivious to the Colonels lack of interest. "I've been told to take you directly there."

This last part however did get Cameron's attention and he pulled the ear-bud out of his left ear. "Ohhh no. We can check into the hotel later."

"Well actually, Colonel, Kutna Hora is a relatively small town. Much of it still resembles its medieval heritage. I'm afraid the hotel is actually about as close as we're going to get by car."

"You're kidding me? How the hell are we supposed to get to the ossuary then?"

"Going to have to walk it, I'm afraid. Don't worry though. It's very close."

Perfect. That part had been left out of the pre-recorded message Kestner had had Frank deliver to him. *Conveniently* left out, Skull suspected, was a little more appropriate.

Acknowledging that conversation with Jake was going to be unavoidable, Cameron removed the second ear-bud and slipped them, along with the mini-cassette player, back into his bag. "Fine. But I left the States on short notice and need to find a currency exchange." He leaned his head down and looked out the passenger window. Morning sun was beginning to brighten the landscape on the horizon. And despite its reputation, the hillsides and architecture were rather breathtaking. "Something tells me we're not going to find a Wells Fargo out here though." He pulled the iPhone from his pocket to begin a search for nearby financial institutions. "Hopefully we can find one of their international partners."

"I have a couple hundred Euros on me," Jake offered.

"Which would be great if we were in England. They use Korunas here." He went back to looking at his phone when he realized, "Wait a minute. How long have you been here? Haven't you had to buy anything? What about putting gas in this thing?" He pointed a finger at the Audi's dash.

"Nope. I took a train from London to Dresden Germany last night. Rented this there."

Rented? Cameron thought. *I'd better not find out that Nightcorp paid for this.*

3

Stockholm National Library — Sweden

Iris Wilhelmsson stood in the entrance hall looking up at the impressive figure before her. The statue—simply titled, "Man reading"— somehow bore an astonishing resemblance to her father. Back when he was a young man anyhow.

She pulled up the sleeve on her right arm and checked the time on her new wristwatch. 11:04 am. Unfortunately, she wasn't scheduled to meet with the library's head of National and International Cooperation Department till noon.

With nearly an hour to kill, she knelt down and sat on her ankles to retrieve her portfolio and extend the handle of her leather laptop case. She draped the sling of her portfolio over her shoulder and kept a cautious hand on her rear as she stood, to assure the seat of her skirt didn't decide to reveal more of her upper thighs than desired.

Content, she straightened out the bottom

of her jacket, ran a quick hand through her long blonde hair, and took hold of the rolling case by her feet. It had been years since she had been to the library, but after a brief look around she remembered that there was a restaurant one floor down.

"Excuse me," she said to the guard at the information desk. "How do I get down to the restaurant?"

The man only slightly raised his eyes from the newspaper in front of him and pointed behind her. "Sumlen restaurant?" he said in a tone that didn't imply either question or statement. "Just down the staircase behind you," His Swedish accent much thicker than hers. "Prova quiche," He kissed his fingers.

She smiled at him. "Thank you. And I will definitely try the quiche."

"Ursakta," he said, before she got herself turned around. "Apologies. Excuse me, but you will have to store your bags in a locker at the coat check area. Electronics are only permitted in the Main Reading Room—that is, with exception to the far end."

"Oh, sorry. Here you go." She stopped and reached into her jacket to pull out her credentials. This got the guards attention away from his newspaper and onto her top, and she gave him a scolding stare. Once unveiling the badge, she held it up to her chin and waited for the man to retract his last verbal *and* visual statements. Instead, he nonchalantly reclined back in his chair and raised the paper back above his face.

She shrugged it off and turned for the staircase. Her laptop case sounding off in loud *thuds* two steps behind her as she made her decent. Upon reaching the hostess kiosk at the front of the restaurant, Iris held out her badge again before the young woman could interpose.

The woman smiled. "How many?" she asked.

"I'm afraid it's just me for the moment," Iris answered.

"Right this way."

Iris followed her to a quiet table towards the back of the restaurant. "Thanks," she said, before hanging her portfolio off the back of the chair and taking a seat. She took a minute to look at the different faces sitting around the room, then picked up the menu and began scrolling through this week's specials.

"Miss Wilhelmsson?"

Startled, she turned to see who was speaking to her. It was an older man wearing a dark gray suit, white shirt and maroon necktie. The jacket of which appeared to be made out of wool. His overall appearance, she thought, resembled the look of a U.S. President during the 1950's—sort of a young Eisenhower. "Yes. How can I help you?"

"Pardon me." He held out his hand before

continuing. "My name is Guy Olsson. I oversee the libraries domestic and foreign affairs."

"Mr. Olsson." She started to get up from her seat but was interrupted.

"Please, if you don't mind, I have not eaten either." He pulled out the chair across from her and sat down. "I thought perhaps we could talk here."

She wasn't exceptionally comfortable discussing foreign policy in a public restaurant. "Mr. Olsson, I think it would be better..."

Again, he interrupted her. This time it was not with words, but with a head gesture to his left and right. She followed his motion. As it were, the table to her right was empty, and the table to her left was occupied by a family of Asian tourists who didn't appear to speak much English.

"So, you are the famous American translator I've been hearing about," he continued without waiting for her response.

Sensing that she was only going to have her words cut short again, she waited for him to continue. She almost spoke up however, when he began unfolding a cloth napkin and laying it across his lap. "Welcome to Kungliga Bilblioteket," he said, formally greeting her. "As you can see, I arrived a little early. I hope you don't mind me joining you. Security informed me where you were."

"Not at all, Mr. Olsson."

He grinned at her.

Is he scrutinizing me? She wondered. *Or is he actually trying to be friendly?*

Guy folded his hands on top of the table. "Forgive me for saying, but I was surprised to learn your name. And now I am even more surprised by the sound of your voice."

Judging by the look on his face, she suspected that her appearance could also be playing a part in his speculation. It wasn't the first time she had been judged by her looks. Most people expected a representative of the United States embassy to be a man, or at the very least, an *unattractive* woman. "I understand your surprise," she told him. "But I'm actually native to Sweden. I was born in Gothenburg, but now I hold dual citizenship with both Sweden and the United States."

"But your accent is nearly nonexistent."

"Well..." She had to think about it herself. "I guess when you're fluent in as many languages as I am your accent begins to adapt naturally to each."

He leaned slightly forward in his seat. "And how many languages are you fluent in, Miss Wilhelmsson?"

"Four." She returned a grin similar to his. "Four... that both countries agree upon, and permit me to disclose anyways."

Both Iris and Guy noticed the young waitress holding a pen and notepad approaching their table. He leaned back against his chair and held up his menu. "Hus sallad grunder," he told her.

"And I'll just have a strawberry pastry and decaff coffee, please."

Once the waitress left with their orders, Guy leaned forward again. "As you know, Miss Wilhelmsson, some of the books in the library have gone missing over the past few days."

She did know. "Yes, but... well, you'll have to forgive me Mr. Olsson. This *is* a *library*."

"The Swedish National Library," he corrected, "does not operate in the same fashion as an American library. Books here are non-circulating. They must be requested from a library official and retrieved from a closed stack. They are also only to be read in one of the four reading rooms, based on the nature of the book. The research room, the microfilm reading room, and so on."

"Okay. But I still don't understand how I can be of assistance."

"The missing books are, shall I say, of a sensitive nature. We didn't recognize their connection at first, but one of our historians found it immediately. The Ambassador of Prague is scheduled to arrive here for a conference this afternoon. That's where you come in."

Iris sat back confused. She spoke Slavic — an older form of the Czech language, more similar to Polish. "Sir, admittedly I have to ask why I was chosen instead of a direct Swedish-Czech translator."

"I can only answer that to the best of my own knowledge," he told her. "I *do* know however that finding a Swedish-Czech-*English* translator is slightly more difficult. As well, you are here at the direct request of one of your fellow Americans. Who? I cannot say."

"Why not?" she asked him.

"Because, I don't know."

"I still don't quite understand though. What is the affiliation between the books and these countries? And why is it being treated like a matter of national security?"

Guy softened his voice to a whisper. "There's more, Miss Wilhelmsson. It seems that our facility is no longer secure. We found the body of one of our restricted level security guards in a storage closet down in the lower level. Perimeter cameras and surveillance have so far been less than helpful."

"I assume you've notified Swedish National Guard."

"Of course."

"And?"

"The man was found nude. Forgive me for speaking of such vulgar acts... but his face and right hand were also missing."

What? "His *face* was missing?"

Guy held a finger to his lips, now

rethinking his decision to have this conversation in the library's restaurant. "Yes. And according to the coroner, the man was killed last Tuesday."

She sat silent, fighting with everything she had to not envision a naked body, stripped of face and hand.

"But..." he continued. "Our cameras and access cards show him reporting for his shift Wednesday afternoon."

"But why...?"

Guy silenced her again with a finger to his lips. "That area is the most secure wing of the library. And the missing books, they all link to the Czech Republic as well as to our restricted sub-basement."

"What's down there?" she asked quietly, almost afraid to know the answer.

He leaned farther forward across the table. "Miss Wilhelmsson. Have you ever heard of the *Codex Gigas?*"

4

It was nice to get away from the obnoxiously bright orange walls of the hotel room. However, the early afternoon sun seemed an almost identical shade.

Stepping out onto the cobblestone street, Cameron instantly took a step back under the protection of an awning that shaded a quaint outdoor dining area. He pulled a pair of classic wire-framed Ray Bans from the front pocket of his shirt and put them on, ran the fingers of both hands through his light brown hair, then looked over at the much-improved appearance of Jake Evans.

Although he didn't pull off the look as well as Don Johnson from Miami Vice, his belt-less slacks, tight t-shirt, and cheap jacket, were still an improvement from yesterday's Beverly Hillbillies costume.

At least his suit is dark blue, and not white. Cameron thought.

After Jake finished fishing around in his pockets, he looked up at Colonel Skull. "What?" he asked.

Cameron just shook his head. "Nothing. Let's get going." He checked the time on his watch. It was just a little before one o'clock. Jake had been right about one thing at least; the ossuary was less than two kilometers from the hotel. "Roll down the sleeves of your coat," Cameron muttered as he began walking away from the hotel. "My God, man." — He almost laughed.

"So, Colonel," Jake called, jogging to catch up. "What exactly is this place that we're going to?"

Cameron now wished *he* had chosen a different colored shirt. The black combination of cotton and polyester was growing exceptionally hot directly exposed to the elements. He un-buttoned the top two buttons and squeezed quickly on the necklace that hung over his chest. "It's called the Sedlec Ossuary," he answered. "Or, sometimes more commonly referred to as The Church of Bones."

"The Church of Bones?" Jake repeated. He was about to continue with some eccentric comment when he caught sight of an ominous Czech man crawling on all fours along the walkway to his left. Cameron had noticed the man as well, but paid little mind to him. Written in Czech, English, and probably a hundred other languages, the word BAR held the same meaning. But the man's dirty appearance, along with the rundown and vine covered facade of the building, unsettled Jake's nerves.

"Yes, the Church of Bones," Cameron reiterated. "It's a small ossuary and chapel built here in Sedlec back in the twelfth century. It... what happened?" He turned to face behind him.

Jake was brushing off his knees and looking down at the ground behind him. "Nothing, I just tripped over one of these bloody cobblestones. I can't believe these people walk around on this all day." He joined back up with Cameron. "What's an ossuary?"

Skull stood motionless with a dumbfounded look on his face for near a minute. *Wow. This guy is something else.* He thought. *Good job Kestner.* "Anyways," he continued, turning back to finish their walk. "It's one of the largest burial sites in Europe, outside of the Paris catacombs anyhow. And an ossuary is just a term used to describe anyplace that stores the bones of the dead."

Jake thought about it for a few brief seconds, giving Skull a moment of peaceful silence—a very short-lived moment of peaceful silence. "This isn't the same place I've seen on the teli is it?" he asked. "The one with human heads and bones all over the walls?"

Cameron inhaled then blew out a long breath of air that inflated his cheeks before answering. Like breathing into a brown paper bag—without the bag. "Yes Jake. It's probably the same one you've seen on the discovery channel, or whatever channels you get in England."

"I once heard that..." Jake stopped talking when he saw Colonel Skull raise an arm and point up a small hill in front of them.

A tall dark building loomed hellishly over the horizon. Dark brown stone walls—stained the color of rotten wood from centuries of war and weather, were crowned by a black roof and three towering steeples. Despite the clear September day, a fraction of gray cloud imposed upon the blue sky and cast a dark shadow onto the southern edge of the church. And as they drew nearer, the forced perspective of the branches of a dead oak in front of them appeared to slowly grow and consume the front of the medieval cathedral.

Seeing it for the first time, both men, including Cameron, felt an icy chill run through their bodies.

"Wait here," Skull said without taking his eyes off the building.

"What! Wait here? Why?"

Cameron turned to Jake. "We passed a small bakery on the way up here. Meet me there in two hours." He checked the time on his watch, then spoke again quickly when he saw the protest about to come out of Jake's mouth. "JUST GO! Look, its one o'clock right now. I'll meet you there at three."

Disappointed and irritated, Jake walked

away.

Cameron suddenly felt half bad for not including him. But from his current distance to the ossuary he could see that local Czech law enforcement were already patrolling and investigating the surrounding cemetery. Unfortunately, Jake's clumsiness and inability to blend in made him a liability. County and district police agencies were never informed of Nightcorp's involvement. Actually, according to General Kestner's audio recording, the only man outside of Nightcorp and the STB who *was* aware of Colonel Skull's involvement was a priest by the name of Father Matousek. And more unfortunate, the STB was a plain-clothed secret police task force that since 1990 the Czech government has denied existence of.

Trying to play the role of a curious tourist, Cameron took the iPhone out of his pocket and walked slowly up to the cemetery gates. The tattered sign out front was written in Czech, but he already knew what it said. *Cemetery Church of all Saints.* However, standing there pretending to translate the sign gave him an opportunity to inspect the area.

He saw the officer before the officer saw him, and as soon as the man turned to say something, Skull raised the phone to his right eye and snapped a quick picture. He then shot the man a quirky smile and waved before walking towards the front entrance.

Surprisingly, while the cemetery was quarantined by a barrier of yellow tape, the church remained open to the public. Cameron followed the trail of tape till he reached a point where it was tied off around the base of a granite statue. The tall memorial appeared to be a representation of the pope, but Skull wasn't sure, nor did he care to spend time finding out. He maneuvered himself between the statue and another man who was exiting the building and walked through the large wooden set of double doors.

Inside the main entrance, two opposing bone chalices, each several feet tall, adorned the right and left walls. Between them, a wide but short staircase led down through an incredible archway to the room below. An archway like Cameron had never seen. The masonry inside the cathedral remarkably mimicked the dull white complexion of human remains, and at least a hundred empty eyes stared down at him as he passed beneath the giant arch.

Once stepping off the bottom stair, he scanned around the room trying to capture a mental layout that he could reference back to later. The task proved to be a difficult one. In every direction there was a distraction. To his right, he noted a connecting room with what appeared to be a large coat-of-arms displayed on one wall from floor to ceiling—made entirely of human bones.

He let his body follow his head as it turned slowly clockwise around the room. Scanning over the steps which he just came down, his eyes stopped at the next alcove that stretched out from the main chamber. Another adjoining room—this one strongly resembling a dark cave. It contained a meticulously arranged stack of human skulls, femurs and tibia's.

Cameron continued to turn. The corridor opposite the staircase was perhaps the most bizarre yet. Against its back wall was a narrow window, and in front of that window was a life-sized replica of Jesus himself crucified against the holy cross. To each side of him, an arrangement of bones was sunk into depressions in the walls — displayed in a pattern that Cameron couldn't recognize a symbol in.

He turned back around to the center of the room. Other visitors were walking around and pointing. Some were making comments about the incredible craftsmanship while others shunned at the gruesome and macabre artwork.

Starting to feel a little less cadaverous, Cameron took one last 360-degree spin of the room before sensing that he had missed something. But what?

Slowly he picked up his chin and looked toward the ceiling. Hung from the center of the room was perhaps one of the largest chandeliers he had ever seen. But like everything else, this chandelier was not made from crystals and diamonds, but from the last remaining pieces of at least a thousand men and women.

Actually, he found it to be quite remarkable.

"It contains at least one of every bone in the human body," a friendly voice said behind him.

Startled, he took his gaze away from the ceiling. "Excuse me?"

"That chandelier you're admiring," the older man said. "From the navicular in your foot, to the tiny stirrup in your ear."

The Colonel wasn't sure what to make of this man. He was very short and probably somewhere in his late fifties.

"I'm sorry," the man said. "Sometimes people don't recognize me without the white collar." He held out his hand. "My name is Father Matousek."

5

Trying to manage both her portfolio and laptop case while wearing high heels was difficult enough, but now a hot cup of vanilla cream coffee and a brown paper bag containing her strawberry pastry greatly increased the burden. Guy Olsson had been gentlemanly enough to assist her with the cup while on the stairs, but quickly returned it to her once reaching the upper landing. And now Iris found herself struggling to keep up as they walked down one of the libraries long hallways.

"The library," Guy said softly as they neared the midpoint of the hall, "is built on top of two separate underground depositories. The smaller of the two is carved deep into the bedrock, and has the highest security level of the facility."

"You mentioned *Codex Gigas*," Iris said. "Giant Book."

"That's right, Miss Wilhelmsson. Giant book." He looked over at her, too proud of himself for getting her to reveal another of her foreign talents. "The smaller depository is reserved for only two things, the Codex Aureus of Canterbury, and the Codex Gigas."

"Is the Codex Gigas one of the books that was stolen?" she asked.

"Ha! Not at all." He turned around and almost forcefully backed her against the wall with his breath, his voice kept to a whisper. "You've never heard of the Codex Gigas... have you?"

She shook her head from left to right. "No." *This doesn't intimidate me, Mr. Olsson.*

"It may translate to "giant book," he continued. "But most people around the world call it by another name."

"And what name is that?"

He leaned closer to her. *"The Devil's Bible!"*

As she was about to comment, Guy turned and continued the walk down the hall, speaking louder as he went. "Giant book is not an expression, Miss Wilhelmsson. No single man could ever steal it. It far surpasses anything you've ever seen—thousand-page dictionaries, stacks of legal documents, other bibles, *et cetera*." He turned and smiled at her. "That means, *"And the rest."*

Iris looked down the hall to her right before continuing behind him. She knew the translation before he had said it, but the term *Devil's Bible*, was a disturbing combination of words that she was unfamiliar with. Traditional

Latin was worldly considered a dead language, mainly used by scholars and historians. However, as a young girl she had once overheard her father talking with her mother after he had lost his job at the fish hatchery. "How are we going to survive?" Her mother had asked him. His reply — "Aut viam invenium aut faciam." She never forgot it, and later learned that what her father had said was, "I'll either find a way, or make one."

Already being fluent in Swedish and English by age fourteen, her father's response that night triggered a love inside her for the knowledge of foreign language — Latin quickly becoming the third in what would eventually grow to the impressive size of eleven. But with all the religious, spiritual, and conspiracy connections that were tightly wound around the Latin language, both the U.S. and Swiss governments agreed that it should be omitted from her resume and kept secret for the exclusive use of each countries "private litigation's." Unfortunately, she had mistakenly just revealed it to Mr. Olsson.

As they neared the end of the long hallway, Iris took one last sip from her coffee and threw the paper cup into a trash bin. "How big is it?" she asked.

Mr. Olsson paused briefly before inserting a key into the elevator control panel. Clearly, this elevator was not intended for use by the public. "It is without question the largest medieval manuscript in existence," he said. "It stands over three feet tall and weighs over 160 pounds."

"Wow," Iris commented. The elevator chimed and the stainless-steel door slid open. "Is that why it's called the Devil's Bible?" she asked, following him into the cramped elevator.

Guy held open the door while she pulled the laptop case in behind her. He then released it and selected one of the three buttons on the inner panel. Unlike typical elevators, Iris noted that none of the buttons here were numbered, and it surprised her when the car began moving. *I thought it was kept below ground. Why does it feel like we are going up?*

"That's one reason," Guy answered. "But legend has it that the book was written by a possessed monk who sold his soul to the devil. It is said that he created the book for his monastery in a single night. As an exchange for his life."

"Well most legends..."

Guy cut her off. "Obviously that would be impossible. We have learned recently that the name of the monk, Hermann Inclusus, is actually his pen-name. Inclusus, we now know, comes from the word inclusion. But the correct translation of his name is actually Hermann the Recluse, meaning — someone who separates themselves from society. He probably devoted his entire life to the book. Purposely chose a life of isolation just to complete it."

"So, you're telling me," Iris challenged. "That you think people have been mistranslating *their own* language for hundreds of years."

Clearly Guy had forgotten that he was suggesting this to one of the country's leading translators.

"What makes you think," she continued. "That for centuries, the same people who developed the language, were incorrect in its translation? Are you aware Mr. Olsson, that the word recluse comes from the Latin word recludere? Why wouldn't he have chosen the pen-name Hermann Recludere if that's what he meant?"

The elevator came to a smooth stop and the metal door opened to another hall. This one however, was nowhere near as elaborately decorated as the one they had just left. The walls were bare and windowless, and the ceiling height was pushing seven feet at best.

"Honestly, I tend to agree with you," Guy said as he stepped through the door. "Although, our mutual feelings are not shared by many of my colleagues."

Iris looked to the end of the narrow hallway before stepping off the elevator. "Where are we going?"

Guy ignored her and began walking. "And what else is baffling," he continued, "is that whoever scribed this book showed no signs of age or fatigue in his writing. Our paleographer determined that the book would have taken anywhere from twenty to thirty years to complete. But detailed analyzation of the handwriting shows no abnormalities in its consistency." He looked over his shoulder at her. "It truly looks as though it was scribed overnight."

"Mr. Olsson. Where are we going? I thought you said the book was kept in an underground depository."

"It is. But the room it's held in is under high alert right now. As well, the sub-basement is climate controlled. So we try and keep visitors to a minimum." Again, he looked quickly over his shoulder. "Besides, there's no reason for you to go down there. I am taking you to the security control room. I want to give you a chance to review some of the surveillance tapes before the Czech ambassador arrives this afternoon. I met the man one time, and let's just say…, well, he's rather impatient."

Iris stopped next to him at the second to last door in the hallway. He raised his right hand and gently tapped his knuckles against it, then lifted the tail of his coat and stuck both hands in his pockets as they waited for the door to unlock. A few seconds later it opened and a thin pale faced man wearing thick bifocals held the door as they entered.

"Guten tag."

"Miss Wilhelmsson, this is Mr. Fischer. He's our head of security operations in the library."

"Pleased to meet you, Mr. Fischer." She held out her hand.

"Mr. Fischer, I need to see surveillance tapes LLC - 6, 7, and 9 from last Wednesday." Guy instructed.

"What about eight?" Iris asked him jokingly.

"Lower level camera eight is located near the storage closet." Guy turned to face her. "For our immediate purposes, I think we can skip that one."

The dead security guard. She remembered, and then simply nodded her head in agreement.

"Why don't you have a seat," Guy offered. He pulled a chair out from under a desk and held the back of it for her.

She accepted and set her bags on the floor before sitting. In front of her was a row of four 13-inch closed circuit security monitors, the one on the far right slightly larger.

Once Mr. Fischer located and retrieved the tapes, he handed them to Guy Olsson who flipped through them like they were a deck of cards. Placing them in a specific sequence, he put a hand on Iris's shoulder as he bent down to insert them into the old-school VCR's mounted under the desk. From left to right, the screens in front of her began to illuminate and display the recordings of last Wednesday's depredation.

"These all appear to be video from the sub-basement," Iris said, leaning closer to the monitor on the left. "What about the other books that were missing from the main room?"

Guy stood behind her fumbling around with a handful of remote controls. "Jesus! Why the hell aren't these things labeled? How am I supposed to know which one controls what?"

Mr. Fischer walked up and took one of the remotes from him. Without saying a word, he flipped it over and handed it back. On the back of the controller was a white piece of tape with VCR #3 written on it.

"Oh. Thanks." He found controller 1 and hit pause. "The video from the main library had nothing useful on it. We still don't know how he was able to steal the other books." Locating controller 2, he hit pause on the second tape.

"Then how do you know it's the same person?" Iris asked, looking up at him.

"We can only assume it was the same person," he admitted, "judging by the contents of each book and their relationship to the Codex Gigas." He hit pause on controller 3.

"But that doesn't necessarily mean that..."

"Fischer!" Guy yelled. "Where is the fourth remote?"

Iris turned from him and looked at monitor 4. It was showing video of the man as he entered the vault and approached the large book. This was the first she had seen of it, and found it difficult to turn away. Not because of the man in the footage, but because of the book itself. It truly was a formidable sight. Just as big as Guy had described, it sat alone on top of a solid table, its pages opened up to what appeared to be a giant illustration. She leaned closer. *That picture. Is that...the Devil?*

Fischer walked over and looked quickly under the table at the VCR's, then turned his attention to the larger monitor on the far right. Undoubtedly a man of very few words, his eyes grew big beneath his thick glasses and he pointed a shaking finger under the monitor.

"What's wrong?" Guy asked, as his eyes began to follow the trail of Fischer's finger to another piece of white tape stuck to the bottom of the screen. Except this time the piece of tape didn't say VCR on it. This piece of tape said, *Live feed!*

"Vad I helvete?" Guy shouted. "That can't be live footage. That entire area is under lockdown. Even security..." Suddenly he realized that he had only inserted 3 tapes into the VCR's—not 4.

The three of them watched the monitor closely. The figure on the screen, now resembling more of a monster than a human, suddenly stopped its walk. It stood motionless for what seemed like minutes.

Then—as if it knew it was being

watched — it quickly turned its head and looked directly into the camera.

6

Cameron Skull had followed Father Matousek up a second flight of stairs to the main chapel. Unlike the lower floor of the ossuary, the chapel itself was not decorated in bones. Instead, it simply resembled any other Roman Catholic Church that he had been to. But standing now among the pews, Cameron realized that this was the first time in over a year that he had set foot in a church.

Slowing his walk, he looked up at the eternal flame burning steadfastly next to the altar. Fifteen months ago he had stood similarly inside Saint Peters cathedral back home in Oregon. Christmas Eve 2008 — he remembered clearly the sound of Kendall's voice as she tried to sing along with the congregation. He also remembered looking over his baby's head and seeing the smile on Kate's face when their eyes met.

A tear escaped his eye today, standing inside the church of bones, the same way it had back then. Suddenly he envisioned the inside of this church decorated with the festive wreaths and bows that he remembered from that night. After mass the three of them had packed into the family Suburban and drove home. He and Kate tucked their excited little girl into bed, then went downstairs and quietly took the wrapped gifts from the hall closet and set them neatly beneath the tree.

Christmas morning in the Skull household was entirely devoted to Kendall, so before going to bed that night, Cameron had sat next to his wife on the couch and handed her a small box. She smiled and kissed him before opening the gift, and cried when she saw what was inside. It was a small alabaster stone in the shape of a heart. Not carved into a heart shape, but perfectly formed by the gentle touch of Mother Nature. With it was a folded hand-written note.

My dearest Kaitlyn. I found this stone nestled in a spring running beneath a limestone cavern in southern Italy. Immediately I knew that it was the second most beautiful and perfect thing I had ever seen. You are my true love, and I knew that God himself must have guided me to this rock, for there is no one else on earth that would be deserving of such a treasure, and I thank him every day for letting me spend my life with you. You are and forever will be, my best friend and my angel. I love you.

She had leaned over and kissed him again. "I love you," she whispered. Then she reached beneath a cushion on the couch and handed him a tiny box in return. He unwrapped it slowly and found a small necklace inside. Hanging from its chain was a little silver medallion with the word *Knight* etched across it. Kate had always called him her knight in shining armor. She said he was "brave but humble, strong but gentle."

They fell asleep together on the couch that night next to a warm fire. In the morning, Kendall had come running downstairs, filled with all the joy and holiday spirit of any three-year-old on Christmas morning. Cameron had got up to make a pot of coffee, then sat back and watched with Kate as their beautiful little girl happily opened her presents.

After cleaning up that morning, Kaitlyn had decided to go to the market and pick up something for lunch. Cameron objected, suggesting that all the stores would be closed, but she was persistent. And so she had walked out the door that morning with no kiss goodbye. Not even a hug.

That would be the last time they ever saw each other. Two blocks from the market a drunk driver ran through a red light and hit the side of Kate's Toyota at over 60 miles per hour. The paramedics had said that she died instantly.

Forever now, Christmas day would never be the same. Last year, when Kendall had asked about her mommy again, Cameron had to tell her that on Jesus' birthday, the only thing he asked for was for mommy to come and fly among the angels.

He reached into his shirt and squeezed again on the necklace that hung over his heart.

"Sometimes the best things in life are the memories that live forever inside of us," Father Matousek whispered softly.

Cameron released the necklace and wiped the back of his hand quickly across his eyes. He was embarrassed showing his emotions, but took comfort in the priests' words. "Thanks Father."

Matousek nodded. "Shall we go?"

Skull looked briefly at the altar one last time before agreeing and following the priest into his chamber. He closed the door behind him and watched as Father Matousek opened the door to a small closet in the back of the room. "How did you recognize me?" he asked.

The priest kept his back to Cameron, fishing through the coats and shirts hung from the closet. "James Kestner sent me an email two days ago," he said. "He told me that you were coming, and he was kind enough to include a picture of you with his letter."

"What else did he tell you?" Cameron asked.

"Only that you were here on an investigation. But he wasn't specific about the details." He turned around and was holding a decorative white scarf and a strand of rosary beads. "He did ask me however, to please be discreet about your identity." He walked over and handed the items to Colonel Skull, then looked up at him and smiled. "He was very convincing and polite, and I agreed."

Cameron took the scarf from him and looked confused at it. "Why?"

"I suspect," Matousek continued, "that your purpose here may be a sign of good fortune. And although I am not clear on your intentions, I sense that they are noble."

Cameron nodded his head again then took the rosary beads from him.

"Perhaps it is God's will," Matousek said. "that I can even be of some assistance." He motioned to the scarf and beads in Cameron's hands. "I told my parish yesterday, along with the Czech police, that an official from Vatican City would be joining us today. So, when we leave this room, you will be from the office of the Congregation for the Causes of Saints. They are the department of the Vatican that deals with the preservation of relics."

Cameron looked up at him. "But I've already blown that cover. Before I came in, I was seen by an officer outside. I tried to make him think I was a tourist."

"Do not worry, my son. The Czech police can sometimes be a little corrupt, but they are never quick to disregard or question the Catholic Church."

"Okay," Cameron agreed dubiously. "But why would I be here concerned about the preservation of relics?" He set the scarf and beads onto the priest's desk in the center of the room. "Look Father, you seem to be an intelligent and trustworthy guy, so I'll tell you vaguely of some of my business here."

Father Matousek stood patiently with his hands held together in front of him. The look on his face, although a kind expression, made Cameron suspect that perhaps he indeed knew more than he was letting on. But Colonel Skull was no stranger to extracting information from people simply by remaining silent. A technique not licensed by Nightcorp, but one that he found particularly effective, and so utilized the game of ignorance on more than one previous occasion. Still, he let himself continue.

"There was an occurrence," he began, "at the Swedish National Library a few days ago. Some of their books were stolen. *I* am here because of the timing between their disappearance and the desecration of your cemetery." Matousek nodded but didn't speak. "The books in question have particularly interesting contents," he continued. "As well, they were discovered to have unusual connections to each other, *and* to this ossuary."

"I see," said Father Matousek. "And I'm imagining that perhaps our cemetery was desecrated only shortly after their disappearance."

"The next day," Skull admitted.

"Did you know?" Matousek asked as he walked passed Cameron and opened his chamber door. "That the unusual artwork you see below us wasn't created until 1870 by a local woodcarver." He held the door open and waited for Cameron to exit the room before continuing.

Cameron picked up the scarf and rosary beads from the desk and walked past him. "All the more reason," he said, entering back into the chapel. "That I don't understand why I would be here for the preservation of relics. If the displays of bones are only a little more than a hundred years old, then why would the Vatican even take interest in it?"

Matousek shut the door behind him and together they began walking back through the church towards the staircase. He noticed Cameron's stolen glance at the eternal flame next to the altar as they went. "It is not this ossuary that is of interest. As with your missing books, it is our cemetery that is of high religious concern."

Cameron stopped and faced him. "I understand my interest in it. But why do I feel as though there's more I should know?"

The priest smiled. "There is always more to know, Mr." He paused and emphasized the next word. "Skull. But what a person thinks he *should* know, often times gets confused with what a person *shouldn't* know."

The Colonel put his hands on his hips and was about to argue. But before he got the chance, Father Matousek raised his right palm to him. "Have patience my son. I have no intentions of hiding anything from you."

He turned and walked to a window next to the staircase, then gave Cameron a moment to join him before continuing. Below them in the outer courtyard was the Cemetery Church of all Saints. Both men gazed out and watched the commotion as Czech police scattered themselves about like a colony of ants across the cemetery. Thick marble headstones were crumbled to the ground by some unimaginable force, and the graves left covered by only earth had been exhumed, and all remains inside what was left of the wooden coffins had been thrown forcefully about the cemetery.

"This cemetery contains earth from Golgotha," the priest said softly.

Cameron looked at him for an explanation.

"That is why the Vatican considers it a relic." Still looking out the window, Father Matousek placed his right hand against the wall and leaned his forehead to the glass. "The Golgotha," he continued. "Or, Skull Hill, is one of the holiest sites in Christianity. It is the burial mound where Jesus and the two thieves were crucified." He inhaled a long breath through his nose. "In 1278, the abbot from the Cictercian Monastery here was sent by King Otakar to Jerusalem. When the abbot returned, he brought back with him a handful of dirt from Golgotha and sprinkled it over this cemetery."

Skull was becoming intrigued and wanted to ask questions, but decided to wait until the Father finished his story.

"Shortly after — in 1347 I think it was, a terrible plague fell over this land — the Black Death. And as more and more people began dying, word spread of this cemetery and how it contained Holy soil. People from all over Europe began descending upon here, requesting — *demanding*, to be buried here."

"That's quite a collection of bodies that must have built up."

"It's estimated that this ossuary holds the remains of nearly forty-thousand men, women and children." Father Matousek looked up high into the sky, then turned from the window and faced Cameron. "The day is passing quickly. Why don't we head down? I imagine you're anxious to get a closer look."

—

A cobblestone walkway, one matching the street outside, ran a path through another archway and into the church's cemetery. Cameron kept the rosary beads in his hand and draped the scarf over his shoulders as he followed Father Matousek through the wrought iron gates.

What the hell could have broken a piece of marble that size? "These headstones don't look like they're seven hundred years old," Cameron said before they got too involved in the flurry of Czech police.

Father Matousek turned around. "You have a sharp perception. Indeed. Most of them are not." He walked back a few steps to Cameron and took the scarf from around his neck. "Wear this draped over one shoulder only."

"Uh, okay. But I've always seen them..."

Matousek hung the sash over Cameron's left shoulder and smoothed out the wrinkles over his chest. "Yes, traditionally the stole is worn around the neck. Deacons are the only ones who wear it as a sash. But you are not wearing a cassock, and I think this would be better when dressed casual." He stepped back a step to get a good look at him. "That's better. I'm glad you wore a black shirt."

Me too, Cameron agreed silently.

"This cemetery has gone through many changes over the centuries," Matousek continued.

Skull followed on his footsteps deeper into the churchyard. A brick wall surrounded the property but was barely visible through the thick vines and dead leaves that covered it. In the center of the grounds stood a large cross, which too had nearly been consumed by the weaving grasp of an evergreen vine.

They walked further, past the first of the exhumed graves. Fragments of shattered wood from the coffin and earth covered bones laid scattered over the surrounding plots.

To Cameron's ease, most of the Czech police seemed to ignore them. A few of the men looked in their direction, but hesitated to make contact. "Have you spoken with them?"

"Only briefly," Matousek answered. "To one of the detectives."

"And how 'bout the STB? What can you tell me about them?"

The priest slowed down and kept his voice low. "They are... were, a ruthless and violent group. Originally they were organized back when this was still Czechoslovakia to combat anything considered anti-communist."

"I know they're still around, Father."

"So do most people," Matousek admitted. "But Czech parliament has kept them hidden for the past twenty years. It's not always wise to speak of them. Beyond lawful persecution, the STB has been known to practice horrible things. Even going so far as to torture or kidnap people who get in their way." He paused and looked Cameron in the eyes. "Be careful around them."

"How can I recognize them?"

"That I don't know. I imagine that you are in a better position to reveal that secret than I am."

True enough. If anyone could infiltrate the demeanor and disguises of secret agencies, it was Nightcorp. Cameron made a mental note to get Kestner working on that as soon as possible. *Maybe that'll be a good assignment for Jake.*

"Father Matousek," a voice called.

"Ah, detective Novaka. This is Father Cameron. The Vatican official I spoke to you about. He flew in this morning from Rome."

Colonel Skull shook hands with the man who eyed him suspiciously. *Shit!* This was the same guy who had seen him take the picture earlier. No doubt about it. Novaka stood a good six inches taller than any of the other officers, and he had a dark purple ring around his right eye. *Probably a boxer in his spare time,* Cameron thought.

"Velcome to the Czech Republic Father Cameron," he said, still grasping the Colonel's hand.

The way he rolled his R's caused sprays of saliva and Cameron had to resist the instinctual urge to pull away. "Thank you, Detective."

Matousek noticed the tension between them and intervened. "How is your investigation coming along?" he asked Novaka.

The detective finally released Cameron's hand and turned to Matousek. "It's looking like this was just another case of vandalism. Perhaps a group of teens. But because of the age of these graves, we are unable to determine what they might have stolen."

"Is there anything we can do to help?" Matousek asked.

Detective Novaka looked back at Skull. "Ne. Not at the moment."

"Please let us know if things change," Colonel Skull replied.

"I will be sure to do that." He looked to Matousek one last time, then turned and walked over to one of the other officers.

"That's the same guy who saw me this morning," Cameron said when Novaka was far enough away.

"Don't worry. As I told you, the Czech police will not rush to question officials from the church."

Cameron wasn't as optimistic as the priest, but he let himself forget about the detective for the time being. He checked the time on his watch. It was getting close to three o'clock and he still needed to look around some more before going back to meet Jake.

Father Matousek began walking further down the stone path and Cameron followed slowly behind as they made their way to the far end of the cemetery. But the walkway didn't end as he thought it was going to, but swept around the rear of the building.

"Hang on a sec, Father." Cameron walked off the trail and over to a rusted gate surrounding a tarnished stone angel. It didn't appear to be a headstone, but yet the ground inside the gate was large enough to accommodate two, maybe three graves. The angel, once a bright shade of white, was now nearly black from dirt and age. Its wings were outstretched behind it, and its face was looking to the ground in front of it. "What is this?"

"That is a garden angel," Matousek answered.

"Yes but... is it a headstone? Is anyone buried in there?"

"Not to my knowledge. This angel is one of the oldest statues in the cemetery, but there is no inscription on it. And I don't believe that it marks a grave. If you look, the gate surrounding it has no entrance."

He hadn't noticed that. Cameron leaned back and looked all around the metal fence. Sure enough there was no way in, no way for a loved on to leave flowers or offerings. He grabbed hold of one of the bars on the gate and shook it gently. It swayed. "This isn't very sturdy." He turned to the priest. "Why wasn't this vandalized? One hard tug and this gate would collapse. But it wasn't touched." He scanned again over the cemetery. "In fact, it's the only thing that wasn't touched. Why?"

"I have no answer for that," Matousek

admitted.

Cameron thought a moment. "I'm starting to think that this was no random or un-meditated act of vandalism. I think someone might have been searching for something." He thought harder, then took a few steps back and studied the position of the angel. "No, this wasn't just a bunch of teenage grave robbers." He turned to Father Matousek. "This was an excavation."

7

"**FISCHER!**" **Guy yelled.** "Code 7. Get on that phone right now and lock down the entire building. No one moves. Got it? NO ONE!"

Iris inhaled a frightened breath and covered her mouth with both hands. Unable to take her eyes from the screen, she stared back at the monster looking up at her. Its face appeared wrinkled and deformed under the shadow of the pillaged security hat atop its head.

The lights in the security command center suddenly darkened to a nearly black shade of purplish red — and by looking at the rest of the library's live surveillance cameras, so had all the lights in the facility. A quick siren sounded off, followed by a computerized female voice coming over the facility's loud speaker. The message played first in Swedish, and then repeated itself in English.

"Attention. The National Library is now under code seven alert. Would all patrons please remain where you are. This is not a test. Should you require assistance, raise your hand and security personnel will aid you shortly. Repeat.

This is not a test. Please remain in your seats."

"Lock those doors," Guy shouted as he searched frantically for the correct button on the control panel in front of him. "Fischer, how do you lock those damn doors? Seal that son-of-a-bitch in there."

"AHH!" Iris screamed.

At the sound of the libraries alarm, the man on the screen opened his mouth wide, lunged toward her, and chomped down furiously onto his own teeth. She could almost hear the sharp crack as his upper and lower jaws snapped together. A strange action, but the figures aggressive bite out of the still air sent a jolt of terror through her body and she jerked back in her seat.

Fischer hung up the phone in his hand and ran the few steps over to Mr. Olsson. "Here! But it won't do any good." He reached around Olsson's shoulder and hit a large button on the wall forcefully with his open hand.

"What the hell do you mean it won't do any good?"

The computerized announcement coming over the building's intercom was repeating itself again, this time in Mandarin Chinese, and Fischer had to raise his voice to speak over it. "The underground vault was built in the sixteen hundreds. It was originally constructed as a safe room—not just for valuables, but also for people in the event of an attack. You can lock people out of it, but you can't lock someone in."

Guy's shoulders raised and his hands went up in dumfounded amazement. "In four hundred years, we've never changed that?"

"No. We wanted to keep the room accessible in the event of a fire or other natural disaster without worrying about..."

Iris interrupted. "What is he doing?" There was fear in her voice.

Fischer and Mr. Olsson each turned to the monitor. The man on the screen looked away and then bolted towards the Codex Gigas resting on top of its large pedestal. Without hesitation, he grabbed the top corner of the open page and tore it from the book—the same page that contained the two-foot-tall depiction of Satan. Then, one by one he began slowly tearing out the pages that followed.

"Can't you override it?" Olsson asked. "There's got to be a way to seal those doors."

"I can," Fischer confirmed. "But not quickly. It'll take a few minutes." He turned and ran for a computer on the desk next to Iris.

Guy looked back at the screen. "Never-mind. There's no time. Grab a radio and let's go!"

Fischer let go of the mouse next to the computers keyboard and stood up, Iris quickly following his lead. She snatched her portfolio from the back of the chair and took hold of the handle of her laptop case.

"Stay here, Ms. Wilhelmsson," Olsson instructed. "Lock this door behind us when we leave."

"Stay here! Are you crazy? I'm not staying here by myself."

Guy looked at her frustrated but had no time to stand and argue. He shook his head and swung open the door to the outer hallway. Fischer ran past him first, followed by Iris. But before she made it over the threshold, Guy stuck out his foot and kicked the rolling case out of her hands and back into the room. She paused and looked at him.

"Go," he commanded. He grabbed her by the arm and pushed her out of the room. "Your computer will be fine." He exited the room behind her and ran to catch up with Fischer. "Over here," he called.

Fischer was trying to find his key for the elevator shaft but dropped them on the ground when Mr. Olsson darted past him and turned a corner in the hallway.

"Where are you going?" Iris called to him.

"That elevator only goes down to the main lobby. If we take the fire escape stairs, we can make it all the way down to the lower levels." He tried to slow himself before reaching the door, but wasn't ample enough and had to push himself back off it. Reaching back forward, he swung open the door and jumped down the first few steps leading down.

The staircase too was nearly black under the dark purple warning lights. Iris, followed by Mr. Fischer, stepped quickly down each level of the zigzagging staircase behind Mr. Olsson. They made it past the first door, and as they neared the second, it flew open. Two men dressed in navy blue jackets and matching hats entered the staircase shinning bright flashlights onto them.

"Biblioteket polis," one of the guards yelled. "Stanna dar!"

Guy threw his hands up and shouted something at them. Iris tried to hear what he was saying, but somehow her fear and adrenaline became audible and drowned out all of Guy's contention. The next thing she knew, both officers were lighting the way down in front of them.

After a few more turns in the staircase, they ended at a final door with LLD-1 stamped onto a placard next to it. The first guard grabbed the handle and shook, but nothing happened. "It's locked from inside," he said in Swedish. He reached for his set of keys, but before he got the chance to un-clip them from his belt, the second guard pushed him out of the way and planted a boot hard against the doors face.

The wood around the handle splintered and the door popped open but quickly sprang back closed.

"What the hell? Kick it again!" Olsson

shouted.

The big guard leaned back, let out a loud grunt, and kicked again. This time the door opened further, nearly a foot, before being pushed closed again. His blood pressure rose, and without being told, he braced a foot on the ground behind him and rammed his shoulder brutally into the broken door. Whatever was blocking it was pushed free, and the door opened quickly sending the man tumbling into the hallway beyond.

Something unusually soft and misshapen broke his fall. Clearly, he hadn't landed on the tile floor. Struggling, he rolled over and began picking himself up with aid from the other officer. Guy, Iris and Fischer flooded in behind them but stopped abruptly when one of the flashlights crossed over the floor in front of them.

Everyone froze.

The cold body on the ground lay on its side, dressed in the same navy-blue uniform as the two other men. Slowly, gravity took hold of one of its shoulders and rolled the corpse onto its back.

"Oh God!" Iris grabbed Fischer's coat sleeve and buried her face into it.

The blue hat fell off the man's head and exposed what was left of his face. Unlike the guard found murdered last week, the face of this man was not cut off. It was scratched off.

As if attacked by a wild bear, the man's face looked as though it had been clawed. Deep incisions ran vertical from hairline to chin as well as horizontally from ear to ear. Only the smallest traces of flesh remained hanging near the lifeless eyes—but they too had been punctured, and now sunk like deflated balloons into a pool of crimson tides.

Fischer didn't want to look at the body any more than the rest of them did, but had little choice. He held a hand against the back of Iris' head and cautiously guided her around it. "It's okay now," he said to her once they passed.

She hesitantly took her head from his sleeve and looked down the hall. The other three men hadn't waited for them, and now all she could see was the fading glow of the flashlights as they progressed further away.

"Wait!" she cried, and began running to catch up.

Olsson looked back over his shoulder and only slightly slowed his pace when suddenly a thought entered his mind. "Keep going," he yelled to the guards.

"What are you doing?" one of them asked.

"Don't worry. Just get to the depository." Olsson stopped and began running back the opposite direction. "Fischer," he yelled. "Give me that radio."

Just before reaching each other in the

center of the long dark hall, Fischer tossed the radio out to him. It was simply a matter of luck that he caught it, but regardless, he felt along the top edge of it and rotated the volume knob to switch it on.

As soon as it was powered on, Guy took Iris by the hand and began running back towards the two guards. "This is Guy Olsson," he yelled into the receiver. "Any available officers respond." He took his thumb off the side button.

A number of male voices answered his call, but the two-way radios couldn't handle the simultaneous communications and so each response was distorted.

He brought the radio back to his lips. "Position men at all lower level exits," he instructed. "Get someone up to security command and unlock all depository doors immediately! But make sure all exits are secure."

"Please repeat," a voice answered. "Did you say, *unlock* all doors?"

"Just do it!" He reached back and handed the radio back to Fischer. Ahead of them, one of the guards had waited for them to catch up. "What are you doing?" Guy yelled.

"You're right," the officer said. "He's locked us out from the inside."

"I've got someone unlocking it right now. Get over there."

"I came back because you'll need a

flashlight."

"What the hell for? There're no turns. Come on, we have to get over there."

The guard didn't answer, but turned and began running next to him. As they got closer to the metal door blocking entrance to the underground vault, the guard pointed his light to the ground. "We almost tripped over him."

Guy suddenly realized that in the middle of the hall lay the body of another security officer. "Oh, Jesus!" He turned around to see that Iris and Mr. Fischer were still behind them then jumped over the man's body.

"Nothing yet," the guard at the door said when the four of them approached. "You sure someone's on their way to open it?"

Before Guy had a chance to answer him, the loud bang of a steel beam slamming open shook the door. A revolving green light appeared over the polished metal and Olsson reached out for the large circular handle.

The door was heavy, but well balanced on a pair of large barrel hinges welded to the wall, and it swung open smoothly. Lead by one of the officers, the five of them entered the small room.

"We're in the wrong place," Iris cried. Truthfully, she was relieved to be in the wrong room.

"No," Fischer said. "This is the second security checkpoint people go through before entering."

One of the guards shinned his light onto a table to her right. On it sat a box of latex gloves and a metal detection wand. She then looked across the room at its opposite wall. Sure enough, there was a second steel door, identical to the one they had just passed through, and she felt her heart beat faster.

Olsson pushed his way past. "Come on." He reached out and grabbed the handle of the second door.

This time, the room beyond was much larger and a few degrees cooler. Diagonally across from them to the left sat the dark outline of the Codex Aureus of Canterbury, and directly in front of them was the ravaged remains of the Codex Gigas. And so far, under the dark purple lights, there was no sign of their intruder. And — there was virtually nowhere to hide. Aside from the two books, it appeared to be an empty room.

Suddenly Iris realized that she was standing in practically the exact same spot the creature had been standing when it looked up at her through the camera. She jumped quickly back and held herself tight to the wall.

Although their eyes were slowly adjusting to the dark reddish glow, the guard's flashlights provided a much better source of usable light. "Stay close to the perimeter," one of them said. His voice, even kept to a whisper, echoed throughout the room.

They all crouched down, one behind the

other, and began a perimeter sweep of the large depository. Completing half the rotation, one of the guards strayed from the group and crept over to the pedestal which held the Codex Gigas.

The others waited silently for him to pass a circle around the book. He returned into view and gave them a thumbs-up, then motioned for them to continue around the edge.

Iris held tight to the back of Mr. Olsson's jacket as they finished their survey of the room. But as they rounded the last corner, the guard leading them stopped.

"What is it?" Fischer asked.

He didn't answer right away. "Nothing... never-mind."

Finally, the stray guard stood up in the center of the room. "There's no one here," he said discouraged.

"He's got to be in here," Olsson challenged.

The officer pointed his light to the wall and made one last scan over the nearly empty room.

"Fuck!" Olsson shouted. "Where the hell is he?"

"I have no idea," said the other officer. "I thought maybe he might have gone through that door I felt against the side wall."

"What door?" Everyone turned to look at him—everyone except for Guy Olsson, who turned and looked at Fischer.

"But he couldn't have," the guard continued. "I pushed against it and it was locked."

Guy took a step forward. "It was locked? How could it be locked, Mr. Fischer?"

8

The three steeples rising above the Church of Sedlec were visible from the small bakery. Jake walked inside to look around before Cameron showed up, but quickly turned and walked back out. Inside the shop smelled strongly of podmasli, the Czech equivalent of buttermilk. But ever since he was a boy, he'd had an aversion to the stuff. Just the thought of making butter from the residue of sour milk was enough to make him gag.

He pulled his cell out of his pocket. Unfortunately there were no missed calls. *He's still got ten minutes,* he thought. Returning the phone to his pocket, he looked up towards the cathedral, but so far it didn't look like anyone was walking down.

Now he suddenly wished that he would have taken his time getting back here. All he had done for the past two hours was walk around town, but it's amazing how fast time fly's when you don't speak the local language. A buildings sign that he would have walked right past in England, now took him ten minutes to decipher the words "grocery store" from his pocket translator.

One building however, had had a sign out front which read *Phillip Morris CR – Muzeum Tabaku*. He didn't need his English-Czech dictionary for this sign. And although not a smoker himself, he wouldn't have minded taking a walk through the Marlboro Museum.

But it was too late now. At ten minutes to three, he had no choice but to sit and wait for Colonel Skull. He walked over to a small retaining wall in between two of the old buildings and leaned against it with his hands in his pockets. He began whistling the chorus to Journey's "Don't stop believin'" until a man wearing a thick beard shot him a dirty look.

"What?" Jake asked the question at barely over a whisper.

The man obviously didn't hear him and continued walking. But it made Jake feel good about himself and he pulled the phone back out of his pocket. He flipped open the cover and scrolled down to games. *Good ole Tetris*. The game took a second to load up, but shortly after and Jake was in the middle of a very energized competition against the fast falling blocks.

Suddenly the game paused. "Oh, what the bloody hell?"

Incoming call.

"Hey, Colonel Skull."

"Jake, I need you to..."

"Where are you?"

"JAKE! Shut up. Change of plans. Get back to the hotel right now and get our bags loaded into the car."

Jake looked back up the hill towards the church. "Okay. Where are we going?"

"Sweden," Skull answered. "There's a flight leaving from Prague in two hours. We need to be on it. General Kestner just contacted me, and there was a related break-in at the library in Stockholm about an hour ago."

"Why don't we just drive there?" Jake asked. "The Audi hauls ass!"

"Because it's almost 1500 kilometers. Listen, I've got to wrap some stuff up here at the ossuary, but I'll meet you back at the hotel as soon as I can. Just make sure the car's ready to go."

Before he could answer, Colonel Skull hung up. Jake pulled the phone away from his ear and looked down at the screen. The button in the center read *resume game,* and for a minute he thought about doing so.

Not a good idea and he knew it. So he flipped the phone closed and took one last look up the hill before turning towards the hotel.

Heading down the street, his adrenaline started pumping. This was the first real experience he'd had with Nightcorp and it made him more excited than nervous. He had only been introduced to James Kestner three weeks ago when his ex-sister in-law had visited London.

She had flown in to attend a multinational military conference at Central Hall in Westminster. Jake had been so intrigued by the event that he was persistent enough to convince her to take him with her. And although she couldn't stand his brother anymore, she always got along good with Jake, and agreed to let him tag along. So long as he promised to behave.

Jake had waited in the building's lobby until the conference was over, but was invited to join everyone when some of the members moved into the banquet hall afterward. James Kestner was the second man to approach them and had asked to buy Iris a drink. Not as a romantic gesture, but as a casual way to separate her from the crowd and speak with her privately.

To the rest of the attendees, Iris had introduced Jake as simply her guest, letting them form whatever opinion they wanted from that.

"They're gonna think I'm your date," Jake said.

She couldn't care less. "Let them think whatever they want." She scowled at him jokingly. "Just keep your hands to yourself. Got it?"

But when they made their way to the bar for a cocktail with General Kestner, Iris admitted to him that Jake was indeed her ex brother in-law. And after talking to Jake for a few minutes, Kestner agreed to let him help out with Nightcorp on a sort of internship, letting him handle some of their small errands—hand delivering letters, and things of that nature.

At the time, he never imagined that a few short weeks later, he would be rushing to load a car in the Czech Republic for a highly decorated Colonel.

Reaching the end of the street, he looked up and saw the street sign at the intersection — 28 Rijna. This was the correct street alright, but after walking all over town, he couldn't remember if he needed to go right or left to get back to the hotel.

Uh Oh!

He opted to head south, and so made a right onto the street. It all looked familiar, but that didn't mean it was the right way. Soon up ahead he could see another intersection, but the street he was on didn't continue through it, and the hotel was definitely on Rinja.

"Crap!"

He turned around and began jogging back. This was taking way too long, and he knew that Colonel Skull was going to be really pissed-off if he wasn't there and ready by the time he got back.

His feet began moving faster beneath him and soon he was in an all-out sprint. But as he stepped off the curb to cross a narrow alley, an older gray Mercedes G500 nearly ran him over. The heavy SUV tapped his side with its front bumper and pushed him out into the street.

"Eeyyy, watch it!" Jake yelled. He rubbed his left hand against his hip where the vehicle had struck him. "You're not even supposed to be driving on that road."

The rear doors of the Mercedes flew open and two very large men jumped out. They ran out into the street and grabbed Jake by the arms.

"What the f..." he began to yell.

The big man on his left released a hand from Jake's arm and used it to punch him in the face. Jake's head fell back, but he didn't lose consciousness.

"What are you doing?" Jake screamed as he tried to fight off the men. "Who are you?"

They quickly threw him into the back of the car, jumped in behind him, and slammed the doors. "I think you know who we are," one of the men said as the SUV sped away.

He was still trying to wrestle himself free. "I have no bloody idea who you are. Let go of me!"

"Sure you do," the other said in his thick Czech accent. "I'm sure that Mr. Skull must have told you about the Statni Bezpecnost."

9

"Which wall?" Guy demanded.

"Right there." The guard pointed to the wall left of the Codex Aureus.

"Give me that flashlight." Olsson snatched the light from the guard's hand and walked over to where the man pointed. All four walls of the room looked identical, especially under the dark purple tint of the facilities secondary infrared floodlights. "Why are our security lights so Goddamned dark?"

Fischer knew the answer to this. "We have no choice. To comply with NATO co-operation, we've adopted the English security classifications—Top Secret, Secret, Confidential and Restricted. Code 7 is Secret. And any alert above Confidential requires use of infrared." He pointed up to one of the small lights. It was positioned directly beneath a camera. "These lights may be difficult for us to see in, but the cameras see everything."

Guy pointed his flashlight to the camera. It adjusted its aim and slowly rotated a few degrees to catch a better image of the bright light being focused on it. He then dropped the beam of light to point it at Fischer's face. "How come I don't see anything against that wall?"

The guard stepped up next to them. "I didn't see anything either. I just felt it move a little when we passed by."

Guy didn't acknowledge the man. He kept the light shining on Mr. Fischer and waited for an answer.

Fischer took a step back and put his hands up next to his shoulders. "Okay, look... there is a passageway that goes from one depository to the other. But that's it. There's no other way out."

"Well why the hell didn't you say anything about it?" Guy asked, taking a step forward.

"The passageway is *Top* Secret. Aside from me, the only person who's supposed to know about it is Mr. Magnusson; the National Librarian."

Iris stepped in. "If it only leads from one depository to the other, then why would it be top secret?"

"You mean aside from the fact that it's extremely well hidden? Because..." he turned to her. "It's the only place in the Library that *is not* under surveillance." He looked back at Guy Olsson. "I didn't tell you about it because you said there were men at all lower level exits. So, either one of them has got our guy... or." He pointed around Mr. Olsson to the wall behind him. "He's still in there."

Olsson's eyebrows jumped up on his forehead. "Okay." He walked up to the other guard still holding his flashlight. "Go back out the same way we came in. Cancel the code seven so we can get some friggin light down here, then notify all security personnel of our situation." He held up two fingers in front of the man's face. "Two teams. One in each depository. Understand?"

The man nodded.

"Good. Then get going." He turned back to the others still standing in the room. "As for us, we do nothing until we're positive the second team in is position." He pointed the light at each person to make sure they were paying attention. "Oh, and Mr. Fischer. Do you think you'd be so kind as to tell us how we get that passageway open?"

Iris stood back quietly. For being a man in probably his late forties, Mr. Olsson certainly wasn't afraid to get involved. She had originally figured him as more the point-and-instruct kind. *Boy, did I get the wrong first impression of this guy.*

Fischer took a deep breath. Hopefully, considering the circumstances, he wouldn't lose his job over this. He sighed. "It's nothing special. Just kick the molding on the bottom of the wall. It'll release an internal lever. But the door's only about three feet tall and pivots outward on an upper hinge, so you have to pull out from the bottom and duck underneath."

The overhead florescent bulbs flickered twice then came on. "That was fast," Iris commented, looking up at the ceiling.

"Don't get to excited," Guy remarked. "We're still waiting for a team to get down here."

The radio in Fischer's hand spoke with static, followed by a man's voice. "Team two, in position."

You're kidding. Guy thought. *Damn, that guy is fast.* He turned to the sound of footsteps coming from the vault's door. A group of four men and one woman entered single file into the room. Two of them were carrying transparent plastic riot shields, and the woman, much to his surprise, was holding onto what appeared to be a long black metal tube. "What is that?" Guy asked her.

She held it up for him to get a better look. "RGS-50M grenade launcher."

"Grenade launcher?" Fischer shouted.

The woman turned to him. "Short range tear gas grenade. Team 2 is in position at the far end of the tunnel with gas masks. Once we introduce chemical agents into the tunnel, we re-seal this door. Then team 2 will enter from the other side and make the capture."

Now Iris was really impressed. Mr. Olsson had just lost control. And even though she didn't mind him leading the group, this woman was a serious *Bad Ass!*

"Let's move," the woman said. She obviously knew who Mr. Fischer was. She looked at him when she said it, waiting for him to make the first move. Although the first guard had informed them of the tunnel, only Iris, Guy and the other officer knew how to open the door. And Mr. Fischer of course.

"Come on!" she encouraged again.

"I'm going," Fischer snapped back. He knew this woman as well as she knew him. Sergeant Petra Johansson. Usually he liked her company, but he didn't appreciate the current position he found himself in.

Reaching the far wall, Fischer pulled his right foot back a couple inches and lightly released it against the molding along the floor. It made a faint click and he reached down for the bottom of the wall.

"I got it," another officer said, pushing him aside.

Acting quickly, it was hard to keep track of who was doing what. It only took a second for the man to raise the door. Johansson dropped to a knee under the man's arm as he held it up and fired a quick blast into the tunnel. Then, just as fast, the man dropped the door back down and pressed his back against it.

No one moved. Everything was silent — including inside the tunnel.

"What's going on?" Guy whispered.

Johansson held a finger to her lips. "Ssshhh."

They continued to wait until finally a voice came over the radios. "Area secure."

Sergeant Johansson picked her radio to her mouth. "Is the suspect in custody?"

"Negative. Area is clear. There's no one here."

"FUCK!" Guy shouted. He threw the flashlight across the room, nearly hitting the Codex Gigas with it. "This is ridiculous. Where else could he have gone?"

"That's it," Fischer assured him. "The only other option is that he made it out before we got down here."

"It did take us a few minutes to get here," Iris pointed out.

Guy rubbed both sides of his forehead with two fingers. They had come down the fire escape stairs. Maybe the guy was able to escape via the lower access elevator, and they literally crossed each other on the way. *Who tries to escape through an elevator?* Unfortunately, if the man had done that—it worked.

"Or he just went through the tunnel and took the stairs up from the other vault," one of the guards in the back offered.

"Fischer," Johansson called. "Where are the blueprints for the libraries floor-plan?"

"They're kept in the back of the archives."

He pointed up towards the ceiling. "Same floor as the security office."

"Alright," she said. "I guess that's where we're headed then."

Everyone began flooding towards the door leading out of the vault except for Iris. She had taken the first couple steps with everyone else, but stopped when she caught sight of the Devil's Bible resting still on its table. This was the first look she'd had at the giant book that wasn't distorted from a television monitor or dark purple lighting.

Suddenly she had a thought. "Mr. Olsson. Was that a picture of the Devil I saw on the open page of the Codex?"

He stopped and turned to her. "It's a pretty disturbing illustration, isn't it?"

"Yes, it is." She looked around the floor of the room. "That man ripped it out."

"I saw that. So what?"

"Well," she began. "He obviously wasn't just defacing the book."

"Why not," Guy asked, beginning to walk back towards her. "Probably some religious nut who wanted to destroy one of the oldest remaining pictures of Satan."

"Maybe," she admitted, "but, what religion?"

"What difference does it make? What are you getting at, Ms. Wilhelmsson?"

By now the rest of the group had also

stopped walking and was waiting for her answer. "Well, he didn't actually *destroy* the picture. He ripped it out. And look." She waved a finger across the open room. "He took it with him."

Everyone began looking around.

"He also took the next few pages that were behind it," she pointed out. "What was on those pages?"

For some reason everyone now looked to Fischer. He held his hands up again. "Why are all of you looking at me? I work security. I don't know what was on those pages."

Petra Johansson approached him. "No. But... you would know if the library retained any copies of manuscripts."

Of course! He snapped his fingers. "Right where we're going. In the archives. Research and knowledge development."

"Huh?"

"The coordinator of research and knowledge has been working with some of the other curators the past few years. They've been working on digitizing everything in the library to make it available online. It only makes sense that they would have started with the most important documents first. There's got to be a digital copy up there. Hell, there might even be one on-line already. The Codex Gigas is the most valuable manuscript we have."

"Okay then," Iris commented. "Let's go

see."

10

Colonel Skull tried to maintain a certain level of control as he backed away from the stone angel. On a similar expedition to Copacabana Bolivia in 1994, he had made a devastating mistake which almost took his life. A South American terrorist group known as the Comision de Nestor Paz Zamora took control of a religious megalith site, the Horca del Inca, overlooking Lake Titicaca.

After attacking a US Marine guardhouse, the rebel group set up operations around the megaliths as a base camp in a plot to take control of some of the country's gold mines. Skull had spent three weeks with a language specialist before going undercover as a deserter from the Bolivian Army.

During his second day with the group he had grown impatient. Just after sunrise he had affixed a small 1.3-megapixel camera to his collar and made a slow sweep through the camp. Regrettably, his actions were witnessed by one of the men who had woke early and gone outside his tent to urinate. With his cover blown, it was nothing less than a miracle that he was able to flee before being shot or captured.

It was a terrible mistake that he would certainly never repeat. So now, as he walked backwards away from the garden angel in the cemetery's churchyard, he made a very conscious effort not to forget that he was supposed to be a representative from the Vatican.

Father Matousek walked with him. He looked around and saw that Novaka was busy dealing with crowd control before speaking quietly with Cameron. "What do you think they were searching for?" he asked.

Cameron stopped then turned to look at the entrance to the cemetery. "I'm not sure." He turned again to look back at the angel. "Are there any lights on this cemetery at night?"

"No."

He smoothed out the short hair on his chin and tried to think. *When was the last full moon?* Thinking harder, he vaguely remembered it being a few weeks ago. "If I'm right," he said to Matousek. "Last night should have been close to a new moon." The Father looked at him but kept silent. "If that's the case, then this cemetery would have been almost pitch black a few nights ago."

Matousek squinted. "Yes, that sounds right."

Cameron looked again over his shoulder

at the archway leading into the cemetery. "If whoever did this entered through that gate, he would have probably never seen the angel. It's nearly black from dirt, and it's clear in the back." He turned to Matousek. "That could be why it wasn't vandalized. He might not have even seen it."

"That is possible," Matousek admitted. "You think there's something there?"

Cameron spoke louder. "Christ, I have no idea." He looked down at his watch. "Listen, Father. I have to get going. I'm catching a flight to Stockholm in a couple hours, but I should be back in a couple days. Can you do me a favor and find out everything you can about that angel?"

"I'll try," he agreed. "But I honestly don't know if there's any records on it."

"Anything you can come up with would be helpful." Cameron held up the strand of rosary beads. "Thank you, Father."

"Hang on to them. You'll need them again when you return. And perhaps they may help you in more ways than just a disguise," Matousek said, without much subtly in the hint.

Cameron was about to ask one final request, but Matousek smiled and beat him to it. "Don't worry Mr. Skull. I will keep this between you and I."

Cameron nodded, then turned and walked away from the priest. Passing by a pair of officers standing by the main entrance gate, he held up his hands in prayer and bowed his head to the men. They bowed slightly in return and let him pass without question.

He maintained a smooth pace for a hundred yards or so before looking over his shoulder at the church. It was beginning to fade in the distance and he quickened his steps to a jog. Soon he had passed the bakery where Jake was originally supposed to meet him, and then rounded the corner onto Rinja St.

"God damn it," he said to himself as he neared the hotel. "Where the hell is he?"

Gently slowing himself back down, he pulled the scarf off his shoulder and entered the hotel lobby. A few groups of people were scattered about, but there was no sign of Jake. Calmly he took his room key from his pocket and headed up the stairs.

Once reaching the room, he unlocked the door and swung it open. "Jake," he called into the empty room. "Jake, where the hell are you?"

He threw his key, along with the sash and rosary beads, onto one of the small beds and walked over to check the bathroom. It too was empty. He walked back over to the beds. Both his duffel bag and Jake's suitcase were lying unpacked on the floor.

"Damn it!" he repeated.

He moved over to the window and parted the blinds to look outside. They had re-parked the Audi just outside their room after checking in this morning. It was gone.

"Unbelievable."

He reached into his pocket and pulled out his phone. Finding Jake Evans under contacts, he hit send and held the device to his ear. It rang twice then went to voice-mail as if the call had been declined.

Shit!

The second call was to General Kestner. "Cameron, what's up? I'm on the other line with the Swedish-American embassy."

"James," Cameron answered. "Have you heard from Jake Evans? I'm here at the hotel and he's gone with the car."

"What do you mean he's gone? The two of you should be on your way to the airport right now."

"I know that. But he took off somewhere and he's not answering his cell. You haven't heard from him?"

"No, I haven't heard from him. Why isn't he with you? Try calling him again. You guys need to get moving."

"I know," Cameron said again. "But if he doesn't show up in the next few minutes, I'm gonna miss that goddamn flight. Where did you find this friggin guy?"

"Do you have a pen?" Kestner asked him.

Cameron held the phone against his ear with his shoulder and started opening drawers around the room. In the night stand between the two beds he found one and brought it quickly to the room's desk before answering. "Okay, yeah. What have you got?"

"Write down this number."

He jotted down the phone number as neatly as he could manage as Kestner read it off. "Who is this for?"

"Her name is Iris Wilhelmsson. She's Jake's ex-sister, or something like that. She's the one who introduced us. Right now she's in Stockholm working on the same case as you are. Call her and ask if she's heard anything from him. I have to go. I'll call you back later."

Cameron had heard the name Iris Wilhelmsson before. He tried to remember who she was as he took the phone away from his ear and hung up. But before calling her number, he tried again to reach Jake.

This time it only rang once and a man's voice answered. "Plukovnik Skull."

Cameron held the phone tighter to his ear. "Who is this?"

"My name is not important."

Give them nothing. The thought cemented itself to his mind and he remained silent. Quickly he turned and grabbed his bag from the floor and threw it onto the bed. With his free hand he began digging through his clothes. Under a pair of cargo pants he found the small pelican case that he was looking for. Thank God the airport had allowed it on the plane. He'd been able to convince security that it was just a backup battery pack for his computer.

"Why did you call, if you are not in mood for talk?" the man asked sarcastically through his heavy accent.

"Let me speak to Jake," Colonel Skull answered. Really, he was just trying to keep them on the line. Holding the phone again with his shoulder, he flipped open the lid of the case and started attaching cables from the small device to his laptop which still set open on the rooms desk. He had to be quick. The WorldTracker Enduro was a simple yet efficient device, but even combining it with AccuTracking.com's advanced technology was a process which took a few seconds.

"Ne," the man said. "You speak to me only."

"How did you find us?" Cameron asked. "What do you want?" There was no sense in pretending any longer that he didn't know who he was speaking to. The best way to keep the conversation going at this point was to ask legitimate questions.

"We know everything in Czech Republic," the man answered.

"I'm sure you do." Skull grabbed the wireless mouse next to the computer and quickly began his attempt to track Jake's phone. "What do you want me to do?" He knew that by letting the STB think they had control, he could keep them revealing valuable information.

"You don't belong in Prague." The voice became irritated and his accent even thicker. "Now you do *nothing* — American pig. This is your warning. Ve vill contact you." He hung up the phone.

So much for that. His plan hadn't exactly worked as he had hoped, but he dropped the phone onto the desk and leaned closer to the screen in front of him. The software was working, and as long as they kept Jake's phone powered on, the trace should still take effect.

Patiently he watched as the system located the phone. Moments later it appeared on a map in front of him as a small red dot traveling eastward on Rohacova. *They're close.* Rohacova was only a few blocks away.

With no mode of transportation however, Colonel Skull had little choice but to sit and watch as they drove away. Once they reached their destination, he could then decide how to approach the situation.

So much for catching a flight to Sweden.

Suddenly the phone he'd tossed onto the desk a moment ago rang. He picked it up and answered without checking the caller ID. "Colonel Skull," he said dryly.

"Good morning, Daddy," the little voice said.

"Hi baby, good morning," he answered

happily at the sweet sound of Kendall's voice. He glanced down at his watch. "What time is it there?"

"Hey Colonel," Frank said, from apparently another of the landline phones in the house. "Just after six. She just woke up and wanted to call and say hi."

"How are you, my little angel?"

"Fine. When are you coming home?"

"Soon baby. Just a few more days, okay. I miss you."

"Miss you too, Daddy."

"How's everything going over there?" Frank asked.

"Not that good, Frank. Listen, I've got to take care of some things, ASAP. Do me a favor though—keep your phone with you, alright? I might need your help."

11

The two teams had dispersed. Together, they took up most of the security personnel, and now they were needed to restore the rest of the library's composure. Fischer had gone back upstairs to security command, and officer Johansson had gone to the Catalog Room to access one of the few public computers and see if indeed there was an online version of the Codex.

That left only Guy Olsson and Iris to search the libraries archives for a digitized copy.

After Fischer remembered that he had dropped his keys by the elevator upstairs, Petra had taken hers off her key ring and handed it to them.

"Where do we start?" Iris asked when the door opened.

The lights in the room were already on, but did a poor job illuminating between the aisles. Not entirely dissimilar to a typical library layout, the archives were a collection of tall bookcases running the length of the room—the biggest difference being that here in the archives they were arranged much closer together. As well, their shelves did not contain a pattern of book bindings, but instead held hundreds of identical black plastic folders, each a few inches thick.

Guy took a moment to read the small tag printed on the bottom of the first of the folders in front of him. "First I think we should find out if their ordered alphabetically or chronologically."

"Good idea," she agreed, and began trying to figure out the organization tactics of the Swedish National Library. "It looks like maybe they're... oh never-mind, here we go."

"What did you find?" Guy turned to his right to see what she was looking at.

Above her head, mounted to the end of one of the shelves, was a sign that read DIGITAL LIBRARY, in very legible Swedish and English words. He walked over to her and started down the first of three aisles.

"They're alphabetized," he said. "Good. That's going to make this much easier."

"You know what I don't understand?" Iris asked as they began searching the shelves for documents beginning with C.

"What?"

Suddenly the door to the archives creaked open. Both of them froze solid and Guy held a finger to his lips. Slowly he slid himself against the bookcase to the front of the room and peeked around the corner. All he could see was the back of the man as he closed the door behind him, but Guy let out a small sigh of relief that the intruder wasn't dressed in a blue security uniform.

"Who are you?" Guy shouted.

The man nearly jumped out of his shoes. He dropped the papers he was holding and held up his hands. "I'm Dou... Douglas Taylor," he stuttered.

"It's okay," Guy told him. "You can put your hands down."

Douglas dropped his hands and skeptically turned around.

"Sorry," Guy apologized. "Didn't mean to scare you."

Douglas knelt down and started to pick up the mess of papers he just dropped. "That's alright. I'm sorry, am I not supposed to be in here?" he asked. "The door was unlocked."

Iris rounded the corner and began to help Mr. Taylor with his papers. "Who are you?" she asked. "I mean... do you work here at the library?"

"I'm new," he answered, not looking up at her. "I'm a history major working on my dissertation. I just took a job here for the summer." Now he looked up at her. "I've only been here a week."

Guy bent over and picked up the last packet for him. "The exchange student from England. That's right, I remember hearing about you." Douglas stood up and Guy handed him the papers. "Again, sorry about scaring you."

"I'll go," Taylor said, turning for the door.

"No no, its fine," Guy told him. "What is it you're looking for?"

"I wanted to access one of the archives computers. I'm trying to finish a paper on..."

"That's fine, Mr. Taylor. Go right ahead." Actually, Guy hadn't even known there were computers in the archives. It had been a long time since he'd been in there, and none were visible from the front of the room when they entered.

After Douglas thanked him, Mr. Olsson watched as he walked away and disappeared down the center aisle. "I wonder when they added computers up here?" he asked Iris.

"Don't know. Probably about the same time they began the digitization process."

"Yeah, probably huh." He turned to finish what they had started. "What were you saying earlier?" He turned back down the row they had just left. "Something you don't understand?"

Iris followed him and swallowed a hard gulp of air. Now she wasn't so sure that she wanted to talk about it, but made herself. "Well, he obviously stole the man's clothes so that he could wear them himself as a disguise."

"Which he did," Guy validated. Then he turned to face her. *"Twice!"*

She shivered slightly, remembering the terrifying image of the man as he glared at her through the camera. "But why did he... why did he cut off his hand and face?"

"I think I know why he cut off his hand." Guy found the thick folder belonging to the Codex Gigas and pulled it from the shelf. "My department, unfortunately, has recently advertised on our website that the libraries newest security feature includes biometric fingertip recognition on all restricted access wings of the facility."

"So, he needed the guard's hand to get past security."

Olsson flipped through some of the contents of the folder. "He might have thought he did. But no. We advertised that, but haven't got around to installing it. Ever since the world economy began collapsing a couple years ago, our government funds have decreased past the point of letting us do any upgrades." He pulled a thin CD case out of the folder and held it up. "I think this is what we're looking for."

"I suggest you bring the entire folder," she said, sounding a bit vain.

He felt a little dumb for a moment but didn't want to admit it, so he stuck the CD's back into the packet and started walking towards the back of the room. At the end of the aisle the room opened up a bit. The back corner was free of black plastic folders and contained a six-foot rectangular table. Two desktop PC's sat at opposite ends, and Douglas Taylor was using the one farthest from them.

"Do you need me to leave?" Douglas asked.

"Not at all," Iris answered. "We'll use this one." She pulled a chair from the side of the table around to the end, letting Mr. Olsson take the one in front of the computer. "Why do you think he cut their faces?" she asked before sitting next to him.

He shook his head disgustingly and curled his upper lip. "I have no idea. I don't even want to think about it." He removed one of the CD's and stuck it into the computer. "You don't need a log-in code for these, huh?"

Douglas looked over the top of his screen. "Only first thing in the morning, when administration first turns them on."

Guy picked up his eyes to look at him.

Sheepishly, Douglas returned to his business.

"I don't want to think about it either," Iris continued. "But it's something we're going to have to figure out. He did it to all the guards. At least to two of them." She looked down at her feet. "I, uh... didn't look at the last one."

"I didn't either," Guy admitted to ease her embarrassment. "But you're right. I'd be willing to bet that if we had, his face would have been..." He stopped, knowing there was no reason to finish that sentence.

A box popped up on the screen in front of

them. NEW SOFTWARE FOUND. REMOVABLE STORAGE: DRIVE (E:). He clicked on the button below to run or install program. Below the desk, the soft whine of the computers cooling fan sped up, and moments later the screen filled with a file directory.

In all, the CD contained 13 separate folders. Scrolling down the list, both of them read silently — *Alphabets, Old Testament, Iosephus Flavius, Isidorus*, and so on. "These must be listed in order of how they appear in the book," Iris commented.

"It looks that way, doesn't it?" Guy squinted and leaned closer to read the small print on the screen.

"Right there." She touched a finger to the screen. File number nine was titled *The Devil*.

Guy maneuvered the mouse over and double clicked on it. A new page opened, and on it was the same hand drawn portrayal she had seen earlier. Nearly the full height of the page, a medieval portrait of Satan appeared in front of them. His face was a faded shade of green and his skin reptilian. He rose from the bottom of the page, crouched on bent knees, with hands, feet and head spoiled by red claws and a pair of curved horns.

"That's definitely it," Iris whispered. "That's the picture he tore out."

Guy had seen the drawing before but was still awed by it. Many theologians had studied the picture over the years—each coming to different conclusions. A few things were certain however. This was not only the largest, but also the only representation anywhere in the world where the devil appeared alone. Also, the devil was dressed in a small white loin cloth— something usually reserved for royalty.

"Go back," she said. He had not responded to her last comment. "See what the next folder is. That should have the other pages that he tore out."

Olsson clicked back a page. The file that followed was perhaps more disheartening than the one titled "The Devil." The next file was titled—*Conjurations.*

"Conjuration?" she whispered even softer than before. "Open it."

He clicked the next file. Seven pages appeared before them. He clicked on the first to enlarge it. Luckily when he did, two things came up, a picture of the actual document and an English translation next to it.

"It's like an incantation," he told her. "Or a spell to invoke the supernatural."

One page at a time they read through the spells.

"Most of these seem to be good," Iris said surprised. "They all start the same way, "I conjure... then they seem to be magic spells to fight off illness."

"This one's an exorcism," Guy pointed

out.

"Yes, but…, if you read further, it's an exorcism to expel evil from humans and objects." She leaned back in her chair. "I guess I imagined that it would be something, well… opposite."

"Yeah, I suppose that's what I was expecting too."

She leaned forward again. "I guess we might as well look through all of them though. They were important enough for him to steal."

Guy looked at her. "Maybe that's what he wanted. Maybe he wanted spells to rid things of evil."

She kept her gaze at the computer, waiting for him to open the next one. He did, and she sat quietly reading it. "Wait a minute," she finally said. "This one's not like the rest." She read further. "This one's about someone named Dino." She shrugged her shoulders. "Pull up the next one after this."

He pulled up the following spell. This one too spoke of someone named Dino. It described him as being bloodthirsty and having 150 talons. The way it was written made it somewhat confusing to read, but seemed to speak of theft and a virgin medium to the underworld.

"Who's Dino?" Guy asked.

Across from them, Douglas spoke up just loud enough for them to hear. "It's pronounced *Die*-no," he said from behind the computer.

"Like, *dino*-saur. Not Dee-no."

Iris and Guy waited for more information. "And?" Guy finally questioned from across the table.

Douglas stuck his head up over his screen. "Sorry. I'm a history major, remember."

"Of course," Iris shouted.

Guy turned to her quickly. "Of course what?"

"Dinosaur." She looked at him and smiled. "And I'm a language specialist— remember. It's Greek. It means "terrible-lizard." The passage isn't referring to someone by name. It's just referring to them as *Terrible*."

"Those must be the spells he was looking for," Guy said.

"But... wait a sec." She leaned back. "Why didn't he take those pages the first time he broke in? Why did he have to come back for them? He obviously knew where they were in the book."

"Maybe not," he told her. "The video shows him flipping through the book the first time around. Like he was looking for something. Maybe he couldn't find them. If this is available online, then he could have had to come back later after researching it."

Iris scratched the top of her head. "No. That doesn't make sense. He knew about the fingerprint scanners. Why would he have been so careless about this? Did he do anything else the first time?" Now she wished that things would have worked out differently earlier, and that she would have been able to watch the videos for herself.

Guy had to think about it. At first, the intruder seemed to just skim through the Codex. But re-playing the video in his mind, he realized that he had indeed done something unusual. "Now that you mention it, he did stop at a certain point in the book and run a finger down the inside of its spine."

She looked at him confused. "Run his finger down the spine?"

"Yeah... but in a really strange fashion. He pried the pages apart and bent down almost close enough to touch his nose to the book. Then he just slowly ran his finger down the middle." Guy paused and purposely shivered his upper body. "It was weird. It was almost like he was caressing it. Kind of sexual."

"That is weird." She thought about it. "I don't know what it could mean though." *Sexual?*

Her phone began buzzing through the leather case of her portfolio. She turned and fished it out. It wasn't a number that she recognized, definitely international, and it looked like an American number. "Hello?"

"Iris Wilhelmsson?"

She pressed a finger in one ear and held the phone tightly to the other. "Yes. This is Iris. Who is this?"

"Mrs. Wilhelmsson. My name is Cameron

Skull. I'm a Colonel with..."

She stopped him. "Colonel Skull. I know who you are. My brother in-law is with you. Jake Evans. How's he doing?"

"Well actually, that's what I called to talk to you about."

12

Cameron kept his eyes on the red dot slowing down on the map in front of him. "Missus Wilhelmsson, first thing I need to know..."

"Miss."

"Pardon me?"

"It's Miss. Wilhelmsson. Not missus. It used to be Missus Stephan Evans, but not anymore."

"Sorry." Skull switched to speakerphone and set it next to him on the desk. "Miss. Wilhelmsson, can you still hear me?"

"Yes."

"Okay. Hang on a second." He drew a line under Iris's phone number on the notepad. Then, turn by turn, he began mapping each move Jake's phone made on the screen. *Left on Sokolska. Right onto Na Nameti.* "First thing," he continued. "Does Jake have any medical conditions? Is he on any medication?"

"Not that I know of." Her voice became frightened. "Why? What's going on?"

Continue east. "How 'bout his personal fears or dislikes?"

"What do you mean?"

"Is he afraid of anything in particular? Heights? Spiders? Anything that you know of?"

"I... I, don't know."

Colonel Skull was well familiar with methods of interrogation. In 1991, he graduated secretly from the School of the Americas in Fort Benning, Georgia. He was one of the few men who studied both the US Army and CIA approaches. The program taught elite candidates everything from counterintelligence and combat intelligence, to interrogation and a class titled, Revolutionary War and Communist Ideology.

Then in 1996, due to the Freedom of Information Act, the Pentagon declassified many of the training manuals, one of which contained a section on how to discover what your prisoner's loves and hates are. The idea being, don't shut off the lights if your prisoner isn't afraid of the dark. Instead, find what they are afraid of, and manipulate their environment to intolerable levels in order to extract information.

"Ms. Wilhelmsson, I need you to stay calm, okay." *Route 28. They're backtracking! Where the hell are they going?* "How about family members? Does he have any children or close relatives?"

Her voice grew shakier by the minute. "No children. His brother lives in Liverpool."

"Parents?"

"His mother died when he was young.

And I don't think he's spoken to his father in many years."

Skull could overhear a man in the background speaking to her. It sounded as though she had taken the phone away from her ear and was trying to talk to him. Cameron reached over and picked up his phone. "Ms. Wilhelmsson," he shouted into the receiver.

She didn't answer him, but it sounded like she had just told the man that she had to leave.

"Ms. Wilhelmsson," he cried again. "Stay focused. I only have a few more questions."

She came back on the line. "Colonel Skull, I'm coming over there."

"That's not a good idea. You're better off staying in Stockholm."

Now she sounded more demanding than afraid. "What's going on with Jake? Why won't you tell me what's happened?"

He hesitated then took a deep breath. "Your brother's been apprehended by the Czech secret police."

"Secret police? What did he do wrong?"

"He didn't do anything wrong. They're called the Statni Bezpecnost, or... the STB. Not the most reputable group of people. Don't worry. I'm going to..."

"You're going to what?" she asked angrily. "I got him into this mess. It's my fault. There's an airport forty-five minutes from where

I am. See you in a few hours, Mr. Skull." She clicked off the phone.

"Damn it!" Skull said. He clicked off his phone and concentrated harder on the current location of Jake. "Where are you taking him?" he asked softly to the computer screen.

He checked the time on his watch again. Just about 4:00 pm. Much too late to catch the flight over to Sweden. He looked at the screen. The red dot seemed to be keeping a steady course for the moment, so he left the desk briefly and took another look out the room's window. Not expecting to see the Audi returned to its original parking spot, but just in case, he felt the need to confirm it visually.

His mind began racing as he turned from the window and sat back down. This mission to the Czech Republic was supposed to be a simple intelligence gathering operation. Kestner's instructions had been to thoroughly evaluate the desecration of the Church of Sedlec, then relay all nonpartisan Intel to Swedish National Guard. And only if things went bad, he was to isolate himself and commission emergency defense code red.

Things weren't quite that bad yet. Or were they? Kestner's newest recruit had been kidnapped, he was without transportation, and some impulse driven woman was boarding a flight from Stockholm. He took another deep breath, trying to slow down his thoughts.

On the screen in front of him, the little red dot changed its heading. It merged westbound onto toll-road D11/E67. He picked up the pen and jotted it down.

They're heading to Prague.

He picked the phone up from the table again. Instead of calling back his home number, he dialed the long international sequence of area codes that would connect him directly with Frank's cell. Not that he didn't want to talk again with Kendall, but that would have to be later. Right now he needed to establish a secure contact near Kutna Hora.

Frank answered quickly. "Yes, Colonel. What do you need?"

"Frank," he held the phone with one hand and began pulling everything out of his duffel bag with the other. "Who do we have over here?"

"Our closest guy is in Bratislava."

Cameron found his black jacket and threw it over the back of the chair by the desk. "How far is that from here?"

"Far. It's in Slovakia."

"Crap. Alright, forget it." Again, he pinched the phone between his ear and shoulder and dug quickly through his bag looking for the small multi-tool he usually carried. It wasn't there. Quickly improvising, he pulled one of the framed pictures off the wall. "Here's what I need you do. Find out everything you can about

Prague and surrounding areas. Look for STB influence around the city. I need to know where they would operate out of."

"Sure thing, Colonel."

Skull tried pulling the nail from the wall with one hand but was unsuccessful. "Thanks. Get back to me as soon as you've got something." He threw the phone down on the bed and squeezed the head of the nail with both hands. One last hard tug and it pulled free.

Quickly he brought it to the front door. Opening the door slightly, he held the nail against the metal plate surrounding the lock and slammed the door onto it. The impact was enough to smash the tip of it flat.

This should work.

He turned immediately back towards the desk and flipped over the laptop. The flattened tip of the nail slid easily into the screw holes on the back of the computer. Thank God they weren't in there to tight. Using the nail as a tiny screwdriver he removed the back-plate of the laptop and began disassembling the hard-drive. As soon as it was loose, he stuck it into one of the pockets of his coat, then reassembled the back of the computer and set in upright again on the desk.

Making one final sweep of the room, Colonel Skull threw the WorldTracker Enduro back into its case and checked his pockets for wallet, phone and room key. Everything was accounted for. Lastly, he threw the jacket over his arm, picked up Father Matousek's sash and rosary beads, and headed out the door.

Making it quickly to the front desk at the bottom of the stairs, he handed the room key and 100 korunas to the young man working the front counter. "I'm gonna be gone for the night," he whispered to the young guy. The kid looked down at the cash and the room key confused. "Oh. This key doesn't seem to be working," he told him. "Could you have the locks changed and a new key ready for me when I get back tomorrow?"

"Yes, Sir," the young man answered.

In fact, the key worked just fine, and Colonel Skull had no intentions of returning. But the STB had Jake. Which also meant they had Jake's other room key. This would at least stall them and acuse attention if they tried to get into the room.

Not that they would find much though.

"Thanks." He winked at the kid then walked calmly out the front door of the building. A block up the street, Skull took a quick look behind him, then casually tossed the black pelican case into a trash bin.

13

His footsteps were louder than hers as he chased her down the hall. "Ms. Wilhelmsson," he shouted. "IRIS." She stopped at the door to the security office and banged loudly against the door. "Where are you going?" he yelled again.

"Mr. Fischer." She pounded the back of her fist against the door again. "Mr. Fischer. It's Iris. Can you open the door please?"

Guy caught up to her the same time Fischer opened the door. He bent over briefly to catch his breath as she scrambled inside to retrieve her laptop.

"Where is it?"

It had been lying in the middle of the floor when Fischer got back, and he had moved it against the wall behind the door. "Oh, I put it over here," he said. Reaching around her he pushed the door closed with his fingers.

"Ms. Wilhelmsson," Guy repeated out of breath. He stood up straight, just in time to see the security door being closed in his face. He put his hands on his hips and shook his head. "Open the door, Fischer." Now his voice was irritated.

The knob turned and once again the door opened. Fischer stood staring at him nervously behind his thick glasses. "Sorry, Mr. Olsson."

Guy ignored him and walked into the room next to Iris. "Where do you think you're going?" He looked down at his watch. "You can't leave. The Czech ambassador is going to be here in..." He looked at his watch again and squinted at the numbers on it. "A couple hours."

"I'm sorry, Mr. Olsson. But I can't stay."

"But you can't leave."

"It's called, *a conference call*, Mr. Olsson." She motioned with her eyes for him to step aside and let her out of the room. "If I came so highly recommended, and he won't accept any other translator, then he can get me on the phone. But *I am* leaving."

He held his hands up in defeat. "OK, OK. But slow down. You don't even know when the next flight leaves. It might not be for hours. Hell, it might not be till tomorrow."

She hated him for having a point. But she guessed it was probably close to five o'clock already. *What if there are no more flights to Prague tonight?* She pulled her blackberry out of her jacket pocket. The number to Stockholm-Arlanda Airport was still in her phone. As it began to ring, she kept her eyes fixed on Mr. Olsson. Finally a woman picked up and greeted her. "Jag maste kolla avgangstider," Iris said. "Prague."

"PRAGUE?" Guy yelled. Iris kept talking

over him to the woman on the phone. "You're going to Prague?" He took a step forward. "No, no. You don't want to go there."

She hung up the phone. "There's a flight leaving at seven and I just bought the last ticket."

"Why in the world are you going to Prague?"

"That's where my brother is. Mr. Olsson, please. I don't have time to explain."

Again, he looked at his watch. "At least let me drive you to the airport then?"

—

Evidently, being head of International Cooperation for the National Library paid well. Mr. Olsson drove a supercharged black Jaguar XKR.

"You want to tell me again why you're going to Prague? He asked as they sped down interstate E4.

No. She didn't want to tell him—but she did. "My ex-brother in-law is there. I think he's in some trouble."

"Ms. Wilhelmsson, I have to tell you that that's probably not the best place to be right now." The car's engine quieted as he released some pressure from the gas pedal. "The legend of the Codex Gigas begins in the Czech Republic. And, as you already know, our troubles seem to revolve around that book." He turned to look at her. "That's the whole reason the ambassador is flying in. There've been some disturbances there as well."

"I'm aware," she said. "My brother being arrested is a pretty big disturbance to me."

"That's not what I meant."

"I know that's not what you meant. You're referring to the books. But for some reason, you still haven't told me anything about them."

He inhaled a long breath of air. "It doesn't matter. But if you must know..., there were three books stolen from the library last week. One of them is called *Kostince*. It's a history on the Sedlec Ossuary. Another's a biography on King Rudolph II. The point is, that all of them tie in somehow with the Devil's Bible."

She looked out the window. This time of year in Sweden, the sun wasn't scheduled to set until late into the night. "What about the third book?"

"The third book," he answered, "is about the Codex itself. It's origins and legends."

"The legend of the possessed monk."

"Right. The monk in Bohemia who scribed the book."

"But I'm not going to Bohemia."

He spoke without facing her. "Bohemia is now the Czech Republic. And the day after the books were stolen, someone destroyed the cemetery outside the Sedlec Ossuary." He paused. "It's no coincidence."

That must be why Jake was there with Colonel Skull. She hadn't actually known what her ex-brother was doing there. She was just happy for him to be included in something. Maybe that's why she always liked him. Maybe she felt bad for him. Jake was never the kind to have many friends.

She looked out the front window of the Jaguar. Up ahead in the horizon she could start to make out the airports control towers lining the runway. In less than an hour, she would be on one of those planes lifting off—headed for Prague.

14

Cameron stuck both arms through the sleeves of his jacket and flipped up the collar. He didn't want to make a phone call while walking around in public, but he needed to get in touch with General Kestner, or anybody that could help him identify members of the Czech STB.

Damn it, I need a car! He thought. Although it wasn't too far, all but the last part of it could be driven, and Colonel Skull was definitely getting tired of walking it. He made the final right hand turn onto Cechova and glanced quickly over his shoulder. Turning around once again, he could see the church about a quarter kilometer up the road.

It appeared to be less crowed than it was earlier, but that only made him even more paranoid. In about an hour the sun would start going down, and he knew the streets would soon likely fill with misfits and inebriates. Without lodging or transportation, he was not looking forward to walking the streets among Kutna Hora's less than illustrious residents.

Once he got within a few hundred feet, he unfolded the white scarf and threw it back over his shoulder. One of the same officers who was monitoring the cemetery gates earlier was still there, and so far, he hadn't noticed Skull walking up to him. But it really didn't matter if he did.

"Hello," Cameron said as he approached the man.

The officer was leaning back against a wall with his left foot propped up behind him. At the sound of Cameron's voice he quickly stood up straight and covered his mouth as he coughed out gray puffs of smoke. Skull had obviously startled him and he tossed the cigarette off to his side.

"Father Cameron. Ahoj."

Cameron sniffed the air. No, it wasn't a cigarette after-all—at least not a tobacco one.

Again, Colonel Skull was cautious not to break character. "Did I frighten you, my son?" The more he thought about it now, the better it seemed to him that he didn't have a car. For some reason, at least in his mind, he never pictured clergymen driving.

"I was just..." The man stepped to his left to block Cameron's view of the butt on the ground, thankful that it wasn't Novaka who had walked up and caught him. "A little," he finally admitted. "What are you doing back so late?"

"I promised Father Matousek I would help with preparations for tomorrow's sermon." Cameron lied.

The officer leaned over and looked towards the front door of the cathedral. "The chapel is closed already. I'm not sure he's still here."

"Oh." Cameron too looked around to the

front of the building. "I hope I haven't missed him. Are the doors locked for the night?"

"I believe they are. The ossuary closes at six. That was near an hour ago. But I didn't see him leave, so perhaps he is still in there."

"Bless you," Cameron said. "I'll go have a look."

The man, anxious to retrieve his smoke and light up again, smiled and bowed his head as Colonel Skull walked to the front doors of the church. Coming to the large wooden doors once again, he reached out and pulled on one of the handles. As the officer had said it would be, it was locked. But before walking away he tried the second door. This one opened with ease.

Walking in and pulling the door closed behind him, he quickly realized that psychologically he had not entered the same building that he had earlier. The view now inside the ossuary triggered a list of new sensations.

The air around him felt stale, and the only sounds came from his own joints cracking and his heart beating. Down the steps in front of him, the main chamber that had hosted an array of visitors this afternoon, now sat stagnant and dry. And the florescent lights were now replaced by the setting sun.

The soft stream of light found its way in through the narrow window behind the statue of Christ down below. Eerily, it tunneled through the chamber and reflected off the bottom of the white staircase—cast back up into the air to illuminate the hollow eyes of the human skulls hung over the archway.

Without moving his body, Cameron swept his eyes from left to right across the entryway.

Holy crap!

He moved silently through the first room towards the stairs leading up to the chapel. Matousek had to be in here somewhere or he wouldn't have left the door unlocked. But still, with the place being so quiet, he felt as though he too had to remain silent.

This notion however, faded as soon as he reached the first step. Each one that his foot landed on creaked louder than the last until he finally gave up trying.

"Father Matousek," he called out. His words echoed through the building. Not loudly, but consistently. His single cry must have resonated into half a dozen more. No one answered.

"Father," he said again, not so loud this time.

Again, there was no answer.

He dragged his right hand against the wall as he neared the top step. Peeking around the corner he could see again the eternal flame burning steadily next to the altar. Everything seemed just as it was earlier—except one thing.

Father Matousek's bible sat open on the pulpit.

He looked around the rest of the empty room. There was no one in there. Slowly he made his way over to the right side of the altar and stepped onto it. *Why did he leave his bible sitting here?* Knowing that the pulpit in a catholic church was reserved for clergy, he walked up to it anyways. Father Matousek's bible laid open to the gospel according to Paul.

It had been in his chambers earlier. That Cameron was sure of.

Suddenly something felt strange. A bad feeling came over him, and he had learned long ago not to turn his back on such emotions. Slowly he backed away from the Holy book and slipped into the shadows against the wall. One wary step at a time he inched his way closer to Matousek's chamber door.

What the hell is that?

He leaned his ear closer to the door. What was that sound? It sounded like something was being squished. Like someone squeezing the juice out of an orange, over and over again.

He reached over slowly and quietly opened the door just a few inches. Sneaking a look into the chamber, he saw Father Matousek bending over behind his desk. It eased his nerves enough to open the door the rest of the way.

"Father, what are you doing? Did you drop something?"

Matousek didn't answer him. All Cameron could see was his hunched over back as he bent behind the desk. His shoulders were moving around like he was dancing a slow tango.

"What are you doing?" Cameron asked again, almost laughing. "I hate to tell you this, but you look ridiculous."

Matousek stuck his head up from behind the desk.

But it wasn't Father Matousek.

The back of the head that rose from behind the desk was hairless and pale. Cameron jerked back quickly. Suddenly a hand appeared and ghoulishly gripped the edge of the table. It smeared streaks of fresh blood over the polished wood as it picked up the creature attached to it.

"My God," Cameron said terrified.

A silhouette of the beasts' head came into full view behind the desk. But cloaked in the darkness of the room's shadows, Colonel Skull wasn't able to make out its features.

With the initial shock now gone, Cameron reached out to his left and grabbed a tall candelabrum that stood next to the door, dumping the burning candles to the floor. Like a lion tamer, he held the iron bar out in front of him defensively and pivoted slightly clockwise on his left foot.

Then, like the lion stalking its prey, the man shrewdly maneuvered himself around the edge of the desk and into the flickering light of another candle.

Cameron didn't care who this person was. There was a much more troublesome question in his mind. "What are you?" he asked softly, unsure if he was looking at man or beast. Its face was horribly scared and its teeth were filed to sharp spears.

It lunged at him.

Skull braced himself and tried to counter the attack with the metal candelabra. It hit him with enough force that he lost his footing and fell hard to his back — his left shoulder landing in a small flame that was now beginning to grow out of the carpet.

Squirming beneath the creature, Cameron looked up at it. It was hideous. Even more grotesque now than it had appeared only seconds ago. Its tongue, like that of a serpent, was forked and its breath smelled like it had been feeding on rotten flesh.

Skull's eyes grew wide, and although he found himself panic-stricken, his survival instincts immediately took control. He pressed the back of his head firmly against the ground beneath him, then shot forward and slammed his forehead into the face of the creature. It groaned angrily and Cameron pushed up hard on the candelabra and sent the beast tumbling off of him.

Quickly Colonel Skull rolled over and

stood himself up. The creature took one final look at him then ran for the door. And even in the soft light of the priest's chamber, Cameron could see a small stream of blood beginning to flow down the man's face where he had struck him.

So, you are a man after-all! Skull's uncertainty quickly changed to confidence. "Fuck you!" He ran after the man into the chapel and dropped the candelabra as he rebounded himself off the side wall of the staircase.

Two steps from the bottom, Cameron thrust himself into the air with his arms outstretched in front of him. He caught the man around the throat and tackled him to the ground. But the momentum quickly turned against him and he bounced off the floor and crashed hard into a column in the center of the room.

The column was one of four that occupied the main cavity of the ossuary, made from a stack of human skulls. It exploded under the force and sent a shower of heads flying about the room.

Again, he tried to quickly pick himself back up. Rising to his feet, he turned and saw the back of the man as he ran up the steps leading out of the cathedral. Cameron bolted after him up the stairs and out the front door.

He wasn't fast enough. The man began disappearing down the street and Skull turned to look for the officer who had been standing post. "Shoot him," Cameron yelled. He turned again. The man was quickly escaping.

"Fuck!"

The officer finally appeared from behind a bush, pulling up the zipper of his pants. "What happened?"

It was too late and Cameron knew it. The man had gotten away. Quickly he turned and ran back into the ossuary. Jumping over the fallen bones, he ran fast back up the stairs and into Father Matousek's chamber.

"Father," he called out. The room was filling with thick smoke, and flames were beginning to devour the curtains over the small window. Cameron held the inside of his left elbow over his mouth and ran around the priest's desk.

"OH God!"

Father Matousek was sprawled out on his back, his right leg twisted up behind him.

Cameron had to shut his eyes for a moment. Matousek was still alive, but his face had been torn to pieces, nearly off. He looked up at Cameron and took a painful breath.

"Father," Cameron cried. The squishing sound he had heard earlier replayed in his mind and he had to choke back a reflex that almost caused him to vomit.

There was nothing left of his lips to cover his teeth, but Matousek tried to speak.

"Uuuuhhhh..."

"I've got to get you out of here." Skull bent down to try and hoist him off the ground, but stopped when he felt Matousek put a hand on his shoulder. "Don't worry. I've gotcha." He knew there was nothing he could do for the priest, but still he couldn't leave him there.

"Jjjooo..."

The smoke was getting to thick and Cameron began to feel light headed. "Father, I've got to get you outside."

"Jooohhn."

Cameron kept a hand under the back of his neck and looked down at him.

"Joohhnnnsss."

"What is it, Father?"

"Johhnnsss eightteeenn."

There were no eyelids to close, but Cameron knew that that was the end. Father Matousek's body went limp.

John's eighteen? Who the hell is John?

Suddenly the centuries old church cracked and Cameron felt the floor beneath him drop. He gently rested Matousek's head back onto the floor and turned to run from the building. Dogging the flames, he ran out through the church and again down the steps.

The smoke was thinner in the main chamber but the cracks were getting louder and he knew the centuries old roof was about to cave in. Making it less than ten feet from the short steps leading out, the ceiling buckled and the massive chandelier in the center of the room swung and broke loose.

Thousands of human bones began falling and shattering off the floor. He kept one hand over his mouth and tried shielding the top of his head with the other as he kept running.

The front door opened before he got to it and the officer outside came in with his gun drawn. "What's going on?"

"GET THE HELL OUTTA HERE!" Cameron yelled. He bent over and shouldered the man out of the way as medieval ossuary collapsed around them.

15

Vatican Necropolis — 2 stories below the Papal Altar of Saint Peter's Basilica.

The city streets and sand colored brick walls of ancient Rome still stood strong. Standing in the corner of mausoleum S, Archpriest Andrea Canale looked through an opening in the wall into Field P—the original spot where St. Peter was buried on Vatican Hill.

It wasn't often that he came down this far anymore, but tonight he wanted to walk alone. At this hour the Necropolis was empty, unlike the persistently congested streets of Vatican City up above.

He had taken his time getting here. Nearly two millennia old, the long walk through the underground alleys was calming to him. He would stop at each mausoleum and sarcophagus long enough to reminisce and whisper a prayer for the forgotten dead.

"Through length of time are forgotten, by their friends and by all. Spare them, O Lord, and remember Thine own mercy, when others forget to appeal to it."

One sarcophagus in particular, that of an unknown child, always earned his special attention. But even the depiction of Lucifer hidden behind the 16th century foundations in mausoleum U was never rejected from his thoughts either.

But standing now beside the tomb of St. Peter, Archpriest Canale let his mind sink deep into meditation. He studied the scripture of Peter the Apostle and envisioned the world he must have lived in. What would it have been like for a simple fisherman to have witnessed the transfiguration of Jesus upon Mount Tabor?

The thoughts astounded him, but were adversely interrupted by footsteps coming down the staircase to his left. Calmly he let his reflection turn to worship and finished with a final prayer of serenity.

The man stood next to him patiently, not wanting to impose any further upon the archpriest. He had come down the steps from the Constantinian Basilica and entered through the Clivus. It was Henry De Luca, the younger of the two Sacristans who interacted with the archpriest. Dressed similarly in a traditional black Rabat and Roman collar, Henry waited quietly for him to finish.

"Che cosa ti porta a me?" the archpriest asked him.

"La tua santita," Henry answered. "There's something I think you should know."

"The hour is late," Andrea said softly. "What troubles you so badly that it brings you to find me here in the necropolis?"

"I was near. I just finished preparing the altar for tomorrow's celebration of the liturgy." His eyes lowered to the floor in shame. "I was listening to radio vaticana, but I changed to another channel and was..." His voice trailed off.

Archpriest Canale smiled at the boy. Sacristan De Luca was just 19 years old, making him the youngest member of the Vatican to hold such an important role. So far he was doing well as a fellow in the church, but his youthfulness sometimes distracted him.

It was no great sin to listen to modern music, so to ease the boy's guilt, Archpriest Canale put a hand on his shoulder and spoke to him more like a friend than an elder. "Don't worry about it, Henry. You're a growing boy. I don't blame you for wanting to explore the world around you."

Thankful he was not being reprimanded, Henry picked his head back up and looked at Father Andrea. "I was listening to Guardia Costiera, the news station for sea travelers, and I heard them mention Golgotha."

Again, Andrea smiled at him. "Ah! The Golgotha. You want to know more about it?"

"I already know of the Golgotha," Henry

said. "But the men on the radio were talking about a cemetery near Prague. They referred to the cemetery as Golgotha."

Not everyone knew of the sacred cemetery. Even some members of the Iscariot— the secret wing of the Vatican that outsiders are not permitted to know about—were unaware of the church in Sedlec.

Archpriest Canale knew of it well though. "Yes. The ossuary in Kutna Hora does indeed contain earth from the Golgotha," he told the boy. "What did they say about it?"

Henry wasn't at all surprised that Father Canale knew of it. The archpriest seemed to have knowledge of everything. That was one of the reasons Henry had requested a place in St. Peter's Basilica. So that he could work directly with him. "They said it was desecrated. They said that someone had gone there and dug up all the graves."

Andrea's eyebrows dropped on his forehead. "The cemetery has been vandalized? When did this happen?"

"A few nights ago," Henry answered. "They said at first it was thought to be just a robbery, but now they think someone might have been searching for something."

The archpriest stood silent. He hadn't heard of these happenings, and the thought disturbed him.

Henry shuddered at the thought of

continuing, but knew he had to tell him the rest. "They also said that..." He had to pause and look away.

Andrea looked down at him. "It's alright. What else did they say?"

Finally he looked back up. "They said that the priest, Father Matousek was killed."

Andrea felt as though the wind had been kicked out of him. A hard thumping beat against the inside of his chest and he found it difficult to breath. "A priest was murdered?" he whispered mostly to himself.

"But not the same night," Henry continued. "This was breaking news on the radio. It just happened."

"What? Tonight?"

Sacristan De luca nodded his head slowly up and down. "They also said... they said that his face had been torn off."

No! It can't be. "Come with me, my son," the archpriest instructed. "Tell me the rest as we walk." He took the first step past Henry and started up the stairs leading out from the Clivus.

Henry turned and followed him. His words were growing more and more terrified by the minute. In his few years at the Vatican he had never seen the archpriest react this way. "They said that the church is nearly destroyed," he continued. "That it caught fire and they're trying to put it out right now."

Andrea kept moving up the flight of

stairs. He was listening to Henry but his own thoughts were intruding.

The archpriest started walking faster and Henry had to hurry to keep up. "The only other thing they've said so far is that there's already someone there from the Vatican."

Canale stopped and looked down at Henry on the steps behind him. "An official from the Vatican is there already?"

Again, Henry nodded his head. "They said his name is Father Cameron. He was inside the church when everything happened."

The archpriest remained perched on the steps above him. "I'm afraid something is unfitting." He turned and finished the few steps to the door of the Constantinian Basilica. "I'm going to my rectory."

"What should I do?" Henry asked.

"Call Da Vinci-Fiumicino airport and arrange a plane for me in one hour. Its short notice, so civilian passengers on board is fine.

16

The Czech police were clearly very unhappy about having to return to the ossuary. Had everything happened an hour later, most of the men would have finished their shift and gone home to their families. But instead, they found themselves stuck working overtime back at the cemetery.

Colonel Skull stood in the middle of the street out front of the ossuary with a wet towel held against his forehead, looking up at the fire still raging out from the top floor of the building. Against the night sky, the flames burned bright and attracted onlookers from all over town.

Slowly he pulled the towel away from his head. The worst of his injuries came from the lump that was quickly forming where he had head-butted the man—at least, that's what hurt the most. His arms were pretty scratched up and his shoulder took a bad beating when he'd crashed through the column, but nothing compared to a self-inflicted blow to the thinker. However, he took a great deal of satisfaction knowing that that filthy beast he hit was hurting worse.

Without warning, a loud crash suddenly erupted from inside the church and a swarm of officers and firefighters flooded out screaming. "The whole place is coming down!" One of the men yelled.

The outer stone walls of the cathedral were strong and held firm, but the weak and fragile bone sculptures and wooden beams inside disintegrated under the heat and pressure. A second loud crash exploded inside the building and a massive plume of dust and debris burst out the front doors, engulfing the last of the men in a cadaver filled cloud of gray smoke.

The bystanders around him jumped back in panic but Skull dropped the towel and ran towards the men. He grabbed the first officer he came to by the arm and pulled him towards a nearby ambulance. As he was about to turn and run back to aid another of the men, a large hand squeezed tightly around his bicep.

With his adrenaline still on the rise, Cameron turned quickly, preparing to lay a fist into whoever was grabbing him, but stopped when he saw the dark purple ring around the man's right eye.

"Who are you?" Novaka asked him angrily.

Cameron shook his arm loose from the detective's powerful grip. "It's me," Cameron answered. "Father Cameron. I met you earlier with..." He thought about the horrific end to Father Matousek. And now the poor man's body lay abandoned to be consumed by the very same inferno that he himself had caused.

Novaka spoke in a quiet but stern voice. "You are not priest. Tell me who are you?"

To hell with this! Skull stepped closer to him and scowled his eyebrows. "That's right detective. You caught me. I'm not a priest." He pointed a finger up under Novaka's chin, unthreatened by the man's large physique. "But how 'bout you go try and help your men, and stop worrying about who *I* am."

"Or." Novaka smiled. "I have you arrested."

Skull's jaw locked in anger before he could speak. He stood up straight as a board, lifting him close enough to Novaka's own eye level to change the detective's demeanor. "U.S. private military commander, Colonel Cameron Skull. And I'm advising you that you are now interfering with a top-secret multinational investigation. So, unless you want to continue this conversation in the office of the President of the Republic, I recommend you stand down, detective."

Novaka's eyes grimaced then gradually opened in curiosity. He spoke slowly, his accent prohibiting the proper pronunciation of Cameron's title. "Colonel Skull?" He thought hard. "I heard rumor of American secret army."

Cameron held a hand up in front of his face. "Well now you know it's not just a rumor, and I suggest you to keep this between you and I." Cameron nodded his head coachingly, waiting for Novaka to mimic the motion. "Understand?"

As planned, the detective did indeed nod in agreement.

"Good," Cameron whispered. "Then go finish getting your guys out of there." He picked up a clean towel from the back of the ambulance before turning to walk away.

Novaka stopped him again, but this time his attitude was more like an excited child asking his dad for his first BB gun. "Colonel. What do...? Can I help?"

Skull stopped and wiped some of the ash off his checks. "Matter of fact." He turned back around. "Why don't you see about getting me a bottle of water?"

The detective shunned. "I meant..."

"THEEEN," Cameron continued. "You can have some of your men seal off the cemetery. I don't want anyone allowed in there except for me and you."

"Anything else?" the detective asked.

"Two more things." He pointed down the street. "Get these guys moving. I'm sure he's long gone by now, but the man that attacked me ran off down that way."

Novaka looked down Cechova then back up at the flames still burning in the church.

"That's the fire departments job," Cameron said when he saw his expression. "And I didn't say to move *all* your men." Again he turned and was about to walk away when he thought of something else. "Oh, detective. Last thing. Find me a shovel."

Colonel Skull didn't give him another chance to speak. He walked away and disappeared into the black expanse of the cemetery.

I need to know what they were searching for. All his instincts told him that whatever it was, it had been mistakenly overlooked beneath the garden angel. If the man had found whatever it was when he dug up the cemetery a few nights ago, then why had he returned tonight?

Just as Cameron expected, the stone angel nestled in the back of the cemetery was almost impossible to see in the darkness. Careful not to trip, he stepped his way over and through the ruined cemetery until he finally reached the iron gate.

As he had earlier, Cameron again grabbed hold of one of the rusted metal bars. But this time he wasn't gentle with it. He straightened his arm, shifted his weight onto his back leg, and pulled hard. The entire front section of the fence broke loose from its corner supports, and he had to jump back quickly to avoid being struck by the gate as it crashed onto the dirt by his feet.

Then, just as he was about to step over the bars and into the small plot of earth guarded by the mysterious cemetery angel, the iPhone in his hip pocket vibrated. He pulled it out expecting an incoming call. NEW TEXT MESSAGE. FRANSESCO FERRARI. He opened it. CALL ME FROM A SECURE LINE. "Can't right now, Frank," he said to the screen on his phone. He powered it off to save the remaining few percentages of battery life and returned it to his side pocket.

Pulling out a matchbook that he'd pocketed from his hotel room earlier, he tore one off, struck it against the back cover, and then stepped carefully into its glow and over the downed metal fence. Once crossing over the last rusted bar he started kicking through the vines and dead-fall to uncover the ground beneath. It was useless. The entanglement of the evergreen vines was too tight to simply kick aside.

Where's Novaka with that shovel? He turned to look but saw no one approaching. Giving his attention back to the stone angel, he walked a few steps closer to it and tried to figure out its purpose. *Is it just for decoration? Why is it gated in then?*

The tips of the angel's wings were only a few inches from the wall behind it, making it impossible to walk a full circle around it. He looked over one side then moved around to the other, confirming what Father Matousek had told him earlier. There were no markings or inscriptions anywhere on it—at least no visible ones. *God only knows what's under all that dirt and vegetation.*

He took one more look at the front of the cemetery then shook out the spent match and lit a fresh one. He held the light back to the ground and started walking away from the angel. But as he took his second step, it felt like Kendall was next to him, tugging like she often did on the side of his jacket.

"What the...?"

He turned around quick. It was the angel. The right arm of the statue was reaching out, holding a small wreath in its hand. But it was also holding onto the pocket of Cameron's coat.

Colonel Skull raised an eyebrow at it. *That was weird.* With his left hand he freed the pocket of his jacket.

Suddenly, still looking at the face of the stone angel, he began to feel dizzy. As if a sudden spell of vertigo had come over him, everything around him began wobbling. He dropped the match and brought both hands up to the sides of his head. *What the hell?*

He took another peek at the angel from the corner of his eye. It was coming at him! Forcing his body to cooperate, he jumped a step backwards. It wasn't vertigo after-all. The angel was actually coming at him. *Oh shit!* The pull on it from his coat pocket must have yanked it over, and now it was falling towards him. It landed hard on the ground in front of him.

"Are you kidding me?" The statue must have weighed a few hundred pounds. There's no way a small tug from Cameron's coat should have knocked it over.

He leaned to his left and looked at the ground where the angel had just stood. From this distance nothing was visible with the dim light from another match, so he walked over and knelt next to the angel's feet.

There was a small hole in the dirt. It couldn't have been more than a foot deep and looked like it had been dug with someone's bare hand. And whatever had been hidden there, if anything, was gone now.

"Damn it." He scooped up a small handful of dirt, tossed it around in his hand, and threw it back down. *Why did they go through the trouble of covering it back up?* He wondered.

None of this made any sense and it was starting to give him a headache. Everything else in the cemetery had been destroyed without any concern of secrecy. So why was the hole dug under the angel covered up? And did they find what they were looking for under there?

These were both questions that Colonel Skull knew weren't going to be answered quickly. Especially while trying to study the evidence while also keeping a flame from burning the tips of his fingers.

He stood back up and dusted off the front of his pants, then took a final look at the small hole and turned to walk away.

Thankfully the Czech fire department was a pretty efficient group. They had gotten the fire under control a while ago, and by the time Cameron made it back to the cemetery gates it was completely out. Still no sign of Novaka and a shovel though. But it didn't matter anymore. Finding the hole hidden under the stone angel was enough.

He exited the cemetery and rounded the front of the building to see if he could offer assistance to any of the officers who had reentered the church. Just before he reached the doors something caught his attention out in the street to his left.

He turned to see a woman stepping out of a silver minivan with a yellow taxi light on its roof. The driver of the cab ran around the front of the van and helped her unload her bag. Cameron then watched as she handed the man some money, then took the handle of her bag and turned towards him.

Where have I seen her before?

The woman looked very out of place. She was wearing high heels, a black business skirt, and her long blonde hair was draped over the front of her jacket. As she approached him, he could almost swear he'd just heard her call out —
"Mr. Skull."

17

Archpriest Canale's rectory sat in the Suburbicarian See of Albano, about ten miles outside the Diocese of Rome. He walked off the stone covered path of the Appian Way and unlocked his front door.

The inside of his small house was decorated in simple Christian fashion. The walls were a soft shade of white, graced by framed pictures of Mother Theresa and Pope John Paul II. Furniture was scarce, but his favorite sofa filled the center of the living room, surrounded on three sides by lavish bookcases.

He hung his keys on a hook next to the front door and walked past his small kitchen down the hall and into his bedroom. Like the rest of the home, his bedroom too was antiquated and modest. A cross hung from the back wall above his twin bed, and a square window looked out the far wall into his backyard.

He opened the sliding door to his closet and quickly took out his suitcase and threw it onto the bed. Before leaving Vatican City, he'd rethought his departure time and asked Sacristan De Luca to make it two hours instead of one. But that still didn't leave him with much time to pack and get to the airport.

Unfortunately, the timing wasn't right. Had it been later in the year, he would have already had a bag packed and ready to go. Beginning in late summer and lasting throughout most of the winter, Archpriest Canale also worked as a chaplain at many Roman jails. Sometimes he would travel from one to another directly, speaking with inmates and prison staff about the Word of God.

During those months of travel, he always kept his suitcase packed. But not today. He quickly pulled out his civvies and a black suit jacket and stuffed them into the bag. Then grabbed a few other items from his nightstand, added them to his suitcase, and pulled it behind him towards the front door.

Taking a final inspection of his home, he took his keys from the wall and flipped off the lights before reaching for the door. But as the front door opened into the black of night outside, Archpriest Canale froze solid. There was a man standing on his front porch staring at him, and two other men positioned down by the street.

He had only seen pictures and heard rumors of the man who stood looking at him. "Praepositus Generalis," Andrea whispered.

The man was known by many names — Padre Generale, Master General. But no matter what part of the world you were in, all names meant the same. He was the Superior General of the Jesuits — the Black Pope.

Contrary to popular misconception, the hierarchy of the Catholic Church worldwide is actually quite simple. It starts with the Pope then falls to one of the nearly 3000 Bishops, then lastly to priests. Even serving as the Superior General, the Black Pope was not above an Archpriest, who too was considered a Bishop. However, the secrecy and coalitions behind the man made him intimidating — even to Father Canale. And although the man's diocese was in Rome, his physical address could not be located on any map. And it was often rumored that he spent much of his time inside the walls of Vatican City working unseen with satanic sects.

The man took a step forward, forcing Andrea back into his home. Like Andrea, the Black Pope was dressed in the traditional Rabat and Roman collar. His gray hair, round glasses and deep wrinkles made him look aged beyond his years. And the somber expression on his face made Father Canale nervous.

"Where are you going at such a late hour?" the Father General asked him.

Andrea continued to back up further into his home. *What is he doing here?* He tried to remember the last time he'd even heard mention of the Black Pope. It had been a long time and it took him a moment to remember that his name was actually Giovanni Santalla.

"I have received news from Prague," the Archpriest admitted. "Troubling information about one of our churches in Sedlec." He waited for the Pope to respond, but instead, Generale Santalla remained silent. "Considering the circumstances," he continued. "I thought I would travel there myself and check into it. Perhaps offer my assistance."

"But as you know, Father Canale, we have special departments who are assigned to just such tasks. Have you notified them of your discovery?"

Andrea wished he hadn't shut off the lights. Now a few steps into his living room, all he could see was the silhouetted outline of the Popes head as he stood inside the doorway. "No, Padre Generale, I have not yet. I have asked Sacristan De Luca to inform both the Pontifical Council as well as the Office of Bishops."

"So, you are to just abandon your duties at the Basilica and travel to Prague?"

"My duties," Father Canale corrected, "are to God and the Holy See. I shall only be gone a few days."

The Superior General walked a step closer to him. "But is it really you who can provide the light in such times?" He paused. "More so than the council?"

The Archpriest studied the calm movements of the Pope and his eyes grew wide. "You already know of the desecration?" It was as much a statement as it was a question.

The Black Popes building anger began to reflect in his voice. "I have knowledge beyond that which you can understand, Father Canale. Things that you don't see, I see. Things that you don't hear, I hear."

"Then reveal them to me, so that I too shall have the understanding."

General Santalla ignored his request. "Do not make your journey, Padre. The happenings in the Czech Republic are not my doing. But unless you infer the true essence of life *and* death, you will never have my understandings."

Andrea stood silent. What could he do? A visit from the Superior General did not command him, but at the same time, if he chose to act independently of the church, he might later face oppression.

"Return to your bed," General Santalla told him. "And tomorrow, return to Saint Peter's with the comfort of knowing your parish is safe." The Pope put a hand on his shoulder. "I have always liked you, Archpriest Canale. From the time you joined the clergy as a boy. It would be a shame to see you abandon your responsibilities. Remember... sometimes there is more than one catalyst that feeds the fire. You must accept them and know how to isolate them. Let's just say — if the fire's electric, there can be *harsh consequences* by throwing water at it."

Santalla smiled an unnerving smile, then turned and walked out, leaving the front door open behind him. Andrea stood in confusion, watching as the mysterious Black Pope reached the sidewalk and turned back to look at him one last time. He grinned again at Father Canale, then his eyes narrowed and his grin dissolved to a scowl. "Abbiamo finito qui," he spoke to his men. Together they walked away down the street.

Andrea looked at his suitcase standing upright near the door. *Why does the Father General know about this, yet do nothing?* Soon it would be well known throughout the Vatican, but yet he had made it sound as though it should be kept secret. *Sacristan De Luca has surely gotten word out by now.*

He looked again at his suitcase, unsure of what he should do. Face the inevitable criticism, or return to his Basilica? He closed his eyes and asked the Lord for guidance. Suddenly, the front door creaked and he reopened them. A gentle breeze had blown it open ever so slightly. *Thank you, my Lord.*

Grabbing the handle once again, he pulled the suitcase and closed the door behind him.

18

The woman dragging her bags behind her and walking up to him was very attractive. Even in the midst of tonight's chaos, the biochemistry of the male sex hormone $C_{19}H_{28}O_2$, was truly the behind-the-scenes controller of every man— Colonel Skull being no exception. He quickly combed his fingers through his hair and tried wiping off some of the dirt he could feel clinging to his face.

"Excuse me," Cameron said, trying to sound official, and perhaps even a little smooth. "This area's..." *Wait a minute. Where have I seen her before?*

The blonde woman maneuvered herself around the back of a police car and called out to him again. This time it was very clear what she was saying. "Mr. Skull."

Cameron watched in curiosity as she made her way closer. The flashing lights on top of the police car were now behind her, leaving only the scattered flashlights of the officers around him to light up her features. He turned his eyes slightly to his right and saw detective

Novaka standing a few feet away. "Detective," Cameron called out.

Novaka turned to him with a look of awkwardness on his face. He was holding neither a shovel nor a bottle of water.

Colonel Skull waved his right hand across his body. "Forget it. See if you can find a couple tripods and set up some halogens around here. We need to light this place up." He turned back to the woman. She was now standing directly in front of him on the sidewalk.

"Mr. Skull." She let go of her bag and held out her hand. "I'm Iris."

Cameron didn't speak. He looked down at her outstretched hand and slowly reached out to shake it.

"Have you found anything out about my brother?" she questioned bitterly.

He looked back up at her and lightly shook his head. "Not yet. As you can see, I've sort of had my hands full around here."

"It's been over five hours since I last spoke to you," she said, irritated. "And you've got nothing?"

He wasn't liking her attitude. "Well *exccuuuse* me, lady! Take a look around." He held one hand on his hip and pointed up with the other at the destroyed building behind him. "I'm sorry that I haven't been able to track down your brother — *on foot* — while I was busy being attacked by some scarred up freak inside a collapsing building."

"Oy vey!" She looked briefly at the building then back at Colonel Skull. "It's always..."

"OH, now I remember you." Cameron pointed a finger at her. "I met you a couple years ago at the DSEi exhibition. You're that translator Kestner was trying to recruit."

"That's right, Mr. Skull. Iris Wilhelmsson. And I guess I'm going to have to..."

Again he cut her off. But this time he was more shocked than hateful. "Wait a minute. Jake's your brother?"

"He's my ex-brother in-law. Not that it's any of your business."

He went back to being angry. "Actually, it is my business. And it'll be much easier for me to find him without you tagging along and getting in the way."

"Ha! Yeah, it looks like you've done a great job so far. Thanks, but no thanks, Colonel. I'm starting to get the feeling I might be better off on my own too." She looked over his shoulder at the destroyed church. "Don't want you accidentally blowing me up next."

Cameron's head jerked back to try and dodge the verbal slap she had just thrown at him. "What are you even doing here?"

Iris laughed again. "You have a hard time keeping up with things, don't you?"

"Ah..." He found himself speechless for a

second. "I mean, why the hell didn't you stay in Stockholm? Despite what you might think of me, Ms. Wilhelmsson. This isn't my first barbeque." *Maybe barbeque wasn't the best word.* She rolled her eyes at him. "And I've got a guy right now back in the states working on finding your..." *Frank's text message,* he remembered. Skull looked at the pocket of her jacket. "Let me see your phone."

"What for?"

"God damn it — just let me see it!"

Iris pulled the blackberry from her pocket and handed it to him. As much as she wanted to hate him, she couldn't help but find it cute the way he acted when he was angry. And she also liked the thought of knowing that she could get away with it. If she wasn't a woman, she knew that Colonel Skull probably would have hit her by now.

Cameron dialed Frank's number and held the phone to his ear. As it was ringing, he looked up at Iris. She smiled at him and he raised an eyebrow in confusion. *What is she smiling at?*

"Ferrari," Frank said when he answered the phone.

"Frank, it's Cameron."

"Colonel. I've got some interesting news for you."

Cameron kept his eyes on Iris. "Were you able to find the STB?"

"Cazzo! No. They're dug in deeper than a

fat woman's face in a pool of butter. But I did check out some stuff on that ossuary you're at."

Damn. He thought. *She's not Kaitlyn, but it's too bad this woman's such a...* "What about it?"

"Well," Frank began. "I looked further into the missing books from the Swedish Library. It's more than just the timing of their disappearance that connects them to the church."

"I had a feeling it might be. What else is there?"

"One of the books is a history on that place. It's called Kostince. I started cross referencing dates and subject matters and found that it links to another book called the Codex Gigas."

"The Codex Gigas?" Skull repeated.

Suddenly Iris' eyes lit up. "What about it?" she asked loudly to interrupt him.

Cameron frowned at her and held up a finger in front of his lips. "Shut up," he whispered. "Keep going Frank. What else?"

"The Codex Gigas is also known as the Devil's Bible. It's kept at the Swedish library, but it wasn't brought there until 1877. Before that, it seems the book had quite a history. And wherever it goes, it seems disaster follows."

"Oh great," Cameron said sarcastically.

"At some point during the fourteenth century," Frank continued. "Just before the Bubonic Plague struck, it was sold to the white monks who inhabited the monastery there in Sedlec."

Colonel Skull thought about it for a second. "But if the book is now kept in the Swedish library, what were they looking for in the cemetery here?"

"That I don't know yet," Frank admitted. "But I'm working on it. One thing I am sure about though is that the Devil's Bible is definitely the source. All three of the other missing books tie to it. That ossuary you're at was once home to it."

"Well yeah, that does explain why there've been instances here and in Sweden. What about the other two books?"

Iris was growing very impatient. She took a step closer to Cameron as he continued his conversation with Frank. She wanted to know exactly what they were talking about. But standing so close to him now, she became distracted by the rugged smell of sweat and Stetson Black cologne seeping off of him.

Colonel Skull took a step back and again looked up at her confused. "Okay, thanks Frank. See what else you can dig up for me, and I'll call you back in a couple hours." He hung up Iris' phone. "What are you doing?" he asked her.

She refocused herself. "Nothing. I, uh, was just trying to hear what he was saying."

"Uh huh." He handed the phone back to her. "He hasn't found where the STB might have taken your brother yet. But he's working on it."

"What did he say about the Codex Gigas?"

"I thought you were here to help your brother. Why do you care what he said about that book?"

She became instantly outraged. "I AM here for my brother. But don't forget, I just left Stockholm and I can probably tell you a few things about that book myself. Like what just happened over there, for example." Her voice softened. "If you even care what I have to say."

Cameron sighed. "Frank said that one of the other books was some sort of biography about King Rudolph." He put one hand in his pocket and spun the other around in the air in front of him. "I guess he owned the Bible at some point as well."

"So, someone's trying to trace the history of it?" She thought a moment. "What for?"

"Who knows? Frank's gonna try and find out more about this *King Rudolph* right now."

"Then while he's doing that, we need to go find my brother."

Cameron threw both hands out to his sides. "Oh! Now it's WE, huh? What happened to, "I don't want you blowing *me* up next?""

"God, men are jerks," she whispered. "Will you stop with the ego and start making yourself useful? Geez."

Men are jerks? I hope she's not a lesbian. He

studied her appearance closer. *No. She can't be.*
"And where do you propose we start Ms.
Wilhelmsson? If you hadn't noticed, we're sort of
stranded here for the moment. My car's missing
and you came in a stinkin taxi." He pointed to
the empty spot in the street where the cab had
dropped her off a few minutes ago.

"If finding a vehicle is our biggest
problem, then I'd say we're doing pretty good."

She was right—he hated that she was
right. "And where would we go, exactly?"

Her temper weakened. "You really don't
know anything?" she pleaded softly.

He rubbed his forehead. "Look, all I know
is that they were headed in the direction of
Prague. But I wasn't able to stick around long
enough to see where they stopped."

"Well it takes like an hour to get to
Prague. So, if we can find a car, at least we can
start heading in that direction."

Cameron looked over both shoulders at
the scene surrounding him. Truthfully, there
wasn't much more he could do here. At least not
right at the moment. He had to keep himself
focused. Right now his two biggest priorities
had to be finding Jake and figuring out what
was dug from under the stone angel.

Fine. Where can we get a car? He looked
around some more.

Iris began searching around for a vehicle
as well, when suddenly she realized something.

"Wait a second," she yelled.

Skull turned to her. "What now?"

She looked at him. "When you were talking earlier... about what happened. Did I hear you say that the guy who attacked you was scarred?"

Skull cringed at the memory of the creature's hideous face. "More than just scarred. It was terrible looking."

Terrible. "The man who broke into the library," Iris continued. "I only saw him through a security monitor, but it looked like he was terribly scarred as well."

Cameron's initial reaction was to emphasize the intense magnitude of the man's disfigurement, but something told him that whatever Iris had seen was just as frightening. He stood back and folded an arm over his chest, then rested his other elbow on it and rubbed the bridge of his nose. Two thoughts afflicted him. *It can't be the same person. There wasn't enough time.* And the second thought — much less relevant but equally exasperating — *God she's cute.*

Iris began to speak when she saw Cameron's look of contemplation. "It must've been the same guy."

"No," he told her. "There's no way he could have made it here from Stockholm in that amount of time."

"So, we're dealing with more than one nutcase? Great! That makes me feel better."

Skull conceded with a lift of his shoulders. "It looks like there's at least two of them."

"So now what?"

He looked over his right shoulder. "We get back to finding a vehicle."

—

Detective Novaka was quickly growing anxious. It was getting really late into the night, and he was just as ready to go home as the rest of the officers were. However, he knew it was still going to be a while.

After adjusting the aim of the final halogen light he turned to walk back over to the front entrance of the church.

"Jste jasne zadaní," One of the firefighters told him as he neared.

Novaka nodded to the man. "díky." He then took another few steps towards the door before seeing Colonel Skull and a blonde-haired woman approaching him.

"Detective," Cameron called out.

Novaka stopped. At first he had been intrigued by the presence of Nightcorp. But now that the initial shock had passed, he was getting tired of being the Colonel's errand-boy. "Your lights are in place," he told Cameron. "I have to get back to my men."

"This'll just take a minute," Skull assured

him. "I'm without a vehicle right now. Where can I find a car?"

The detective shrugged. "At this hour, there will be nothing. But Hostel Procafe is just down Zamecka if you need lodging."

"We don't need a place to stay," Iris cut in. "We need to get to Prague."

Novaka turned and smiled at her. "Yes, Praha is too far to walk." He looked back at Colonel Skull. "I'm afraid you have to wait for morning to rent car. Tonight, only taxis."

Cameron looked over at Iris.

"Oh no." She stepped back and held up her hands. "I'm not getting in another cab right now. Maybe we can borrow a car or something." She looked back at Novaka. "Is there any way..."

"Ne," he answered quickly.

She waited for him to give an explanation of why he wouldn't let them borrow a vehicle, but he did not. The word *No*, was all that came out of his mouth.

"Forget it," Cameron said. "Come on. Let's go." He took her by the wrist and began leading her across the street.

"Wait a second," she screamed.

Skull stopped for a moment as she reached out for the handle of her suitcase, then continued to walk away from the ossuary.

"Where are we going?"

"We're going to borrow a car," he explained. "That wasn't a bad idea."

"Yeah but..."

"Shit," Cameron whispered. Not far down the street was restaurant U Balanu. He remembered wanting to eat there earlier when he and Jake had made the walk that afternoon. Unfortunately, the restaurant, *and* its small parking lot, were now empty.

"You were thinking about stealing a car, weren't you?" Iris asked angrily.

"Borrowing," he corrected. "I was thinking about *borrowing* a car." He kept his eyes searching around the dark parking lot. "But it doesn't look like that's going to be an option."

"I should hope not."

Cameron turned to her and smiled a wickedly satisfied smile. "We're taking a motorcycle."

"Ha!" Iris laughed. "A motorcycle? You are an idiot, aren't you?"

His smile grew even bigger and he let his expression do the talking. He loved the position he was able to hold her hostage in for the moment.

Her voice changed quickly from the look on his face. "Are you crazy? We ARE NOT taking a motorcycle."

"Hey, at least it's a BMW." He almost couldn't contain his urge to laugh.

"Mister Skull. This isn't funny. And if you hadn't noticed, I have two bags with me. AND! I'm wearing a skirt. So we are not taking a motorcycle."

Oh, I noticed alright. "Look Ms. Wilhelmsson. It's either we take the bike, or sit here and wait for another taxi to show up. And I know how much you love the cab rides here."

She didn't know what to say, but was able to shake her head from side to side.

"Do you want to go find your brother or not?" Cameron finally demanded.

Her head shake slowly turned to a nod.

"Then stop complaining and cram as much of your shit into the saddlebags as you can. Sorry, but everything else stays behind."

Infuriated, she walked towards the bike, bumping her shoulder into him as she passed. "You're an ass," she whispered.

Again, he smiled.

"And what are we going to do about this?" she asked, holding up a helmet. "There's only one."

Skull stepped passed her and threw a leg over the seat of the motorcycle. "Well as much as I hate for you to ruin your hair, it's probably best if you wear it." He held both hands on the handlebars and looked at her over his shoulder. "You know. Just in case I blow this thing up."

19

Guy Olsson parked his Jaguar back outside the library just before midnight. After dropping Iris off at the airport, he had gone home to try and get a few hours' sleep, but it was to no avail.

The library had long since closed and the coroners gone, but with all the recent troubles, much of the staff, as well as a small handful of police officers, remained on site throughout the night. As a result, the single eight car parking lot at the back of the facility was full, forcing him to park along Humlegarden and make the walk up the gravel road. Fortunately, at night the Royal Library was illuminated by decorative street lamps to highlight the buildings romantic style architecture in contrast to the rolling green terrace surrounding it.

As he approached the main entrance, he took a last look behind him at the quiet streets of Stockholm. Surprisingly, there was a young couple walking along holding hands, and another woman across the street with a tiny white poodle who was dragging her along at an uncomfortably fast pace.

It soothed him knowing that he wasn't the only person awake right now.

Turning back towards the building, he reached out and pulled on the front door, and it concerned him to find it unlocked. But no more than three feet inside the main entrance, two officers came to attention as he stepped inside.

The guard to his left was the first to speak and began objecting to his intrusion. "Kungliga Biblioteket ar stangd."

The guard opposite him reached across the foyer and put a hand on the man's chest. "Det ar regissoren," he whispered. Then he looked at Guy. "Please excuse him, Mr. Olsson. How are you tonight?"

"Tired," Guy answered. "Do you know if Mr. Fischer's still here?"

"I think he's with Sergeant Johansson in the systems development department. Want me to send someone to get him?"

"No, that's alright." Guy stepped passed the two guards and turned around before continuing. "Johansson's still here? Christ. Doesn't that woman ever go home?"

The man laughed and shook his head. "I don't think so, sir."

Olsson grinned. "Thanks guys." Then he turned away and began walking down the same hall that he had lead Iris down earlier that afternoon. And just as before, once reaching its end he inserted his key into the elevator control and waited for the door to open.

He wanted to review the tape from the live feed they had watched that afternoon. An unwelcome side-effect of responding quickly to catch the man was that they had not been able to determine his route of escape. But with the urgency subsided, he could now review the tape and see exactly how the man was able to slip past them.

As the elevator gently came to a stop at the upper floor of the library, Guy stepped off and walked slowly to the security office. It was only out of politeness that he had knocked on the door earlier, but if Fischer was in the IT department, this time Guy would have to let himself in. He took his keys back out of his pocket and unlocked the door.

Immediately upon entering the small room he walked over to the live feed monitor they had watched earlier. *That's strange.* He hadn't paid enough attention this afternoon, but now realized that this particular monitor seemed out of place. All other live surveillance videos played on a bank of monitors supported along the opposite wall in front of Fischer's desk. Why was this one staged by itself next to the playback desk?

The answer to that didn't matter as long as it kept a recording. Guy leaned behind the screen and looked for the audio-video cables coming in and out of the screen. Strangely, there were none. Only a power supply cable ran from the back of it.

"How the hell does it receive a signal?" he questioned to himself.

Feeling along its edge, Guy's fingers stopped when they came in contact with a small feature protruding from the lower right side of the monitor. He leaned over to inspect. It was a USB flash drive.

"What the hell is this?"

He pulled the small memory stick out and brought it over to the room's central computer. And as soon as the computer recognized the new device, Mr. Olsson opened the control panel and clicked his way through the commands that would allow him to retrieve the one file that had been stored on it. As expected, it was a video file of the man breaking into the depository. For the second time today, Guy watched as the man turned and looked up at the camera.

"Oh shit!" He suddenly realized that if he was watching this from a recorded video playback, and there were no AV cables coming into the back of the monitor, then it couldn't have been a live feed they had watched earlier.

He closed the video and right clicked the mouse on the file titled ZWEITEOPERATION.asf. Scrolling to the bottom of the list that popped up, he opened the files general properties. Just below the files location and size were three dates. Date created, date modified, and date accessed.

Quickly processing the time-line in his head, it didn't take long for Olsson to realize that the footage they had seen was actually recorded the same day as the original break-in.

"Oh my God!" He began to grow frightened, and felt a sense of stupidity at having been fooled earlier by a piece of white tape that someone had scribbled the words LIVE FEED onto.

Fischer!

Quickly pushing with his feet, he rolled the computer chair to his left across the tile floor and looked up at the row of screens hung from the wall. As the guard downstairs had said, Olsson could now see Sgt. Johansson standing with Mr. Fischer in the systems development department.

He pulled his phone out of his jacket pocket and called Petra's phone number. "Come on. Answer your phone," he encouraged her image on the screen. A couple seconds later, he watched as she held a finger up to Fischer and checked the caller ID on her cell.

"Hello. This is Sergeant Johansson."

"Petra. It's Guy. Listen to me. Keep calm. I'm up in security command, and I just found a USB drive with a video file on it. The footage we watched earlier was pre-recorded. I think Fischer set us up."

Still staring at the screen, Guy watched

the black and white image of Sgt. Johansson as she looked up at Mr. Fischer.

"I'm not sure I understand," she admitted.

Guy leaned closer to the screen and kept his voice low. "Nobody broke into the vault today. What we thought we were watching as live feed was actually a recording from a few days ago. We were tricked. That's why we weren't able to catch him. There was no one there *to* catch."

Petra didn't respond, but Guy could see her slowly reaching for her handcuffs on the back of her belt.

"Sergeant, don't. Wait till I get backup for you. Just don't let him leave."

It was too late. Fischer must have sensed something from the look on her face and turned and ran from the room.

"Damn it." Guy quickly reached over for the security phone and hit the intercom button. "All officers respond to IT," he yelled into the phone. "Suspect is Alex Fischer. Detain him by any means necessary."

Olsson threw down the phone and brought his cell back up. "PETRA!"

She was running after Fischer but still had her phone in her hand. Fortunately, Guy's scream was loud enough for her to hear and she brought it back up to her ear. "Where did he go?"

Olsson quickly scanned each of the monitors in front of him. "There he is." He pointed a finger uselessly at one of the screens. "I've got him. He's running east, towards the periodicals reading room."

"Got it." Johansson spun to her left and sped down the hall.

On the screens in front of him, Olsson could see security personnel flooding towards them. One officer was nearly there already, and if Guy's calculations were correct, the man should be intercepting Mr. Fischer within a matter of seconds.

Petra rounded one of the corners in the hall. "I see him," she said to Mr. Olsson, obviously forgetting that he was watching everything as it happened.

Suddenly a door at the end of the hall opened, and just as predicted, the officer appeared a few feet in front of Fischer. "STOP," the man shouted with his arms outstretched.

Fischer weaved to his right and shouldered his way through an unlocked emergency exit door and into another stairwell. Oddly, he chose to run up instead of down, and Guy quickly began searching the screens to determine where the steps led to. "That's roof access," he yelled to Sergeant Johansson.

Grabbing the libraries intercom once again, he picked it up and gave security their new orders. "All men near an exit, head outside.

Suspect is heading for the roof. Set up a perimeter around the building."

The officer and Sgt. Johansson chased after Mr. Fischer into the stairwell. Running for his life, Alex Fischer was much faster than them, and scaled up the steps two or three at a time. Once reaching the top, Fischer broke through the final door and ran out onto the roof.

Unfortunately, there was only one rooftop security camera, and it was located near the stairwell. As Fischer continued to run, his image became smaller and smaller as he gained distance from it.

Sgt. Johansson was yelling to the officer running next to her, but Guy could hear her through the phone that she still held open in her hand. "We'll have him cornered. You head that way and block him from circling around."

Fischer must have reached the end of the rooftop. He was still close enough for Guy to vaguely make out his movements. Olsson leaned forward in his chair. Suddenly it looked as though Fischer had stopped abruptly and held his arms out for balance. He then turned his head and looked back over his shoulder at Sgt. Johansson who was quickly running up on him, and then turned back around.

"What the fuck?" Guy yelled. "No!"

Spreading his arms back out to his sides, Alex Fischer stepped up onto a ledge and leaned forward—his feet somersaulting over his head.

He plummeted to the ground below. And although Guy could neither hear nor see his body land, it sent a tremor of panic and shock surging through him.

20

"Why are we stopping?" Iris tried asking.

Without a helmet, the wind blowing over Cameron's ears at 50 mph was almost deafening. He didn't hear a word that Iris had just said.

The bike continued to slow as Colonel Skull guided it down off-ramp 35, Vrbova Lhota. He leaned it gracefully around the long sweeping turn and came to a gentle stop on the side of the road. To their left and right were empty fields, mirrored by two more on the opposite side of the highway.

Skull shut off the motor on the bike which also turned off its headlight, leaving the two of them now sitting in total darkness.

"What are we doing?" Iris asked again as she struggled to free herself from the helmet. "Why did you stop?"

"I've gotta see a man about a horse." Cameron answered. He turned around to look at her. "Do you need help with that?"

Finally she managed to pull the helmet off her head. A few strands of hair had clung to it and she shook her head to straighten it out before answering him. "Thanks. I got it." She swung a leg over the seat and stood up. "So, what are we doing here? You have to do what?"

"I've gotta..." He looked down and pointed at his crotch. "You know."

She was standing with her weight on one leg and holding the helmet under her right arm. "You're joking?"

"No, I'm not joking," he said as he got off the bike next to her. "I gotta go. What do you want me to do? Piss myself?"

"Ugh!" She turned her back to him and crossed her arms. "Hurry up."

Cameron, cautious not to trip on anything, stepped off the street and behind one of the bushes lining the side of the road. *Jesus. Always something to complain about.* "Hey, since you're just standing around," he called out. "Why don't you dig through some of your crap and see how much money you have?"

She shook her head but refused to turn around. "Why would I tell you how much money I have?"

Even though he could hardly see anything in the dark, he didn't trust taking his eyes off the ground in front of him, so he spoke up a little louder to compensate for not facing her. "Because it's best to pool our resources. I've got a few hundred on me. But in situations like this, you don't want anything coming as a surprise. So... what have you got?"

She rolled her eyes. "Fine. I think I've got maybe seventy or eighty kronas."

Skull shook himself off and zipped up.

"Did you hear me? I said, I think I've got..."

"I heard'ya," he said, walking back out to the street. "Why do you have Czech currency?"

"Not, *Korunas*, Mr. Skull. Seventy or eighty *Kronas*. Swedish currency."

"Oh." He stopped walking. "You got any change?"

"I'm not giving you my money."

"No—*change*. Coins." He pointed a finger to the highway. "This is a toll-road. We haven't hit one yet, but sooner or later we're going to have to pay. And I don't have any change."

She rolled her eyes again so he could see it this time then walked over to the saddlebags on the motorcycle.

Cameron's eyes had now adjusted to the dark and he did indeed see her roll her eyes at him. But he also saw how the back of her skirt had not settled properly from the ride, and now crept slightly up the back of her thighs as she walked away from him.

She must have realized it too. Just before bending over to reach into the bag, she straightened it out.

Oh well.

"I don't have very much," she said, just before closing the top of the saddlebag.

"Wait a second," Cameron said before she latched it shut. "Is your phone in there?" He walked up next to her and held out his hand. "Let me use it again before we go."

"What's wrong with yours?" she asked. "Why do you have to keep using mine?"

"Why do *you* ask so many questions?" He looked up at her. "My battery's almost dead and my line's not secure. Yours might not be either, but there's less of a risk that it's been tampered with."

She didn't hand over the phone right away. Earlier she hadn't noticed, but something about the way the little bit of moonlight was hitting his facial hair caused a few strange sparkles. *He's got gray hairs in his beard. I wonder how old he is?*

"Ms. Wilhelmsson." Cameron snapped his fingers. "Your phone?"

"Sorry. I was thinking about... my brother. Here." She handed him the blackberry. "You're paying the bill later though."

He took the phone and looked up at her. "This isn't a GSM phone?"

"A what? No, it's just a phone."

"A global... oh forget it." He dialed Frank's number again and held up the phone.

"Colonel, I'm glad you called back," Frank said after the first ring. "I've got a lot of new information for you. What do you want first? The good or the bad?"

"Jesus Frank, I don't care. Give me the bad I guess."

"Well, the bad news," Frank started. "I spoke with General Kestner about the STB, and he confirmed exactly what I was afraid of. There's absolutely no way to pick them out of a crowd. So keep that in mind when you meet new people."

Skull held the phone tighter to his ear and peeked out the corner of his eye at Iris.

She held an open hand behind her ear. "What's he saying?"

Cameron put a finger to his lips and shook his head. "Okay. I kind of already expected that. What's the good news?"

"Well the good news is that there've been rumors floating around Prague lately about an increase in STB activity."

"And that's good news?"

"That's very good news," Frank corrected. "I spoke with someone from the Czech Armada and tried to pinpoint specific areas where the rumors originated. I also checked further into that King Rudolph, and coincidentally, they're geographically similar."

"King Rudolph ties to Prague also?"

"Not just Prague," Frank said boastfully, "Castle Prague."

"*Castle* Prague?"

"That's right. And it seems the STB has taken special interest in it lately."

Skull began pacing back and forth next to the motorcycle. "What do I need to know about Rudolph?"

"I haven't got it all figured out yet," Frank admitted. "But here's what I know so far. King Rudolph II, born 1552. Eldest son of Maximilian II and ruler of Bohemia from 1575 to 1611. He came in possession of the Codex Gigas in 1594, and brought it to his castle in Prague."

"Is that it?"

"Like I said, I haven't got all the details yet. But apparently this King Rudolph was a strange dago. He was an alchemist. He believed in astrology and immortality. Crap like that. But as he got older, he started getting paranoid about everything. He became a loner, and eventually his own family banished him from the throne."

Cameron looked again over at Iris. She was standing with her arms wrapped around her. It was a fairly warm night, but she was probably chilled a bit from the ride. "Not that that's not fascinating or anything Frank, but I don't really care about his weird fetishes."

"Well that's all I've got for you right now."

"That's plenty," Skull assured him. "At least now I know where I'm headed." Cameron was about to say goodbye to Frank but stopped himself short. "Hey Frank? How's Kendall doing? Is she okay?"

"She keeps asking about you," Frank admitted. "But I took a break earlier and let her beat me at a game of hide-and-seek. It tired her right out."

Cameron smiled. "Thanks buddy." Again he was about to end the conversation but one last thing came to mind. "Hey Frank, one more thing."

"What do you need?"

Cameron turned to Iris and softly apologized to her for the long call. "I almost forgot," he told Frank. "Before Father Matousek was killed, he tried telling me something."

"A priest was killed?" Frank asked surprised.

Oh shit, that's right. I haven't told him about that. "Yeah. Anyways... I'll explain more later on. But before that happened, he tried to tell me something. It sounded like he said, John's eighteen. Can you try and research that for me too? Find out who John is, or what it could mean?"

"John the Apostle."

"Huh? What?"

"John the Apostle," Frank repeated. "You said he was a priest, so he was probably referring to John the Apostle."

Cameron's head fell back in self-disappointment. *Yep, that would make sense.* "Right. Well, look up John 18 for me then. Let me know what it says."

"If you want to hang on a minute," Frank encouraged. "I'll look it up for you right now. Do you have a bible around here?"

"Sure. I'll hang on a sec. There should be one on the bookshelf in the den." Cameron lowered the phone and covered the mouthpiece with one hand. "Sorry, Iris. I'm almost finished," he promised. "At least we know where to go now."

"Castle Prague. Sounds exciting." Her voice had just a touch of sarcasm in it. "We could have been there by now." She didn't give Colonel Skull a chance to retaliate. "And talk as long as you want. I wasn't joking about you paying the bill later."

Cameron smiled at her and held the phone back to his ear, but he could still hear the pages being flipped as Frank searched through his bible. He lowered the phone again.

"So...?" Iris began. "Who's Kendall?"

Cameron's eyes melted. "She's my little girl." His smile remained, but pacified. "She just turned five last week."

Iris smiled back at him.

"Colonel? Colonel, are you there?" Franks muffled voice called from under Cameron's hand.

He raised the phone back up. "I'm here. Did you find it?"

"Yeah I found it alright. The First Letter of John. Chapter 2:18."

"Well," Cameron squawked. "What does it say?"

"This is from the New American Bible," Frank stated. "It says—'Children, it is the last hour; and just as you heard that the antichrist was coming, so now many antichrists have appeared. Thus we know this is the last hour.'"

21

Archpriest Canale hadn't driven himself to the airport. Instead he had picked up the Leonardo Express Train from Termini Station in Rome. The half hour journey along the Italian railways was nearly over and he began preparing his bag for an easy departure from the train.

Unfortunately, before he left Rome, he had tried to contact Henry but was unsuccessful. Which meant that now he was left unsure of what airline he should be looking for.

"Hello, Father."

Andrea looked up from his bag. The man sitting across from him was smiling. "Ciao," Canale said back. He waited for the man to reply, but all he did was keep his smile. Usually when people approached the priest, they were looking for guidance or forgiveness, but this man seemed genuine in just trying to be friendly. Andrea smiled back at him as the train began to slow.

Once its speed dropped to a rate that was comfortable to stand many of the passengers rose from their seats and headed for the exits.

Andrea stood as well, but remained poised by his chair with one hand holding his bag and the other gripping the back of the seat in front of him. This was not his first trip on the Leonardo Express, and he knew that at any moment the train's brakes would squeal and everyone left freestanding would be nearly toppled by the sudden halt.

At last the doors opened and Archpriest Canale followed patiently behind the man who had just greeted him. He stepped off the train and began looking around. Now *he* was the one who needed guidance.

The train had dropped him off inside an indoor station. Andrea buttoned the bottom button of his black suit jacket, leaving the white collar exposed around his neck, as he took a moment to look around. Normally he would have headed straight for British Airways which flew out of terminal 3, since the majority of his travels took him to London. But Prague was unfamiliar territory to him, and he had no idea where Czech Airlines departed from.

Luckily, after a minute of searching through the crowd, he spotted a member of the Guardia di Finanza — the Italian Customs Police. And although the man looked to be on break, perhaps he would be kind enough to offer directions.

"Ciao signore," Andrea said as he approached the man.

"Hello Father," the officer answered. "Is there something I can do for you?"

"Please. I am trying to get to the Czech Republic. Can you tell me what airline I need?"

"Si." The officer quickly pointed behind him. "Either Czech or Smart Wings Airlines. Both fly out of terminal three."

"Ah. Terminale tre. I am familiar. Grazie."

"Di niente."

Andrea bowed his head to the man and walked off. Terminal 3 wasn't too far from the train station, so it should only take him a matter of minutes to reach the ticket counter. But as he finessed his way through the crowd, his mind continued to ponder the alarming description Sacristan De Luca had given about the church in Sedlec.

Why does the Superior General object to me going? It doesn't make sense. And why hasn't the Vatican called for an emergency summit?

Andrea stopped and turned. Someone had accidentally kicked his suitcase as they were walking past. Whoever it was though had quickly disappeared into the crowd. He checked the time on a digital clock above one of the airports flight time display systems. It was a little before 1:00 in the morning, but judging by the amount of people walking around one would have expected it to be 1:00 in the afternoon.

Again, he turned and continued towards

terminal 3, rubbing his forehead with his free hand. The murder of a catholic priest was not something to be overlooked, and it gave him a headache. Actually, it was never overlooked. Just last year, 37 priests, seminarians and missionaries were slain around the world, and the Vatican had sent an archbishop to investigate and console immediately following each.

The Black Pope rarely exposes himself, yet he appears at my door tonight already knowing of the desecration – and my intentions.

Up ahead Andrea could see a familiar face. The young woman had worked at terminal 3's ticket counter for quite a few years. Andrea smiled at her as he approached.

The priests face was torn off. What kind of... Lord I pray to you. Let my fears and suspicions be misguided.

"Padre Canale," the young girl said as he walked up. "I didn't receive any notice of you flying out tonight."

He rested his bag against the front of the counter and shook his head. "I had to book my flight last minute. There was no time for me to arrange a private plane." He glanced at the paperwork that sat open on the desktop in front of her. "I should have a commercial ticket to Prague waiting for me."

"I don't..." She paused. "Let me double check."

Andrea waited calmly as the girl looked

through the pages of her register.

"I'm sorry Father. I don't have anything for you. What time did you call?"

Archpriest Canale stood confused. "Actually, young Sacristan De Luca was supposed to arrange it for me."

The girl looked at him sympathetically. "I can put you on standby for the next flight. It boards in about an hour." She glanced quickly down at the documents in front of her again. "Unfortunately, there are no seats available, so I can't guarantee you a ticket. But you will have first priority of course."

What more could he do? "Grazie. I suppose I will wait then."

She smiled apologetically at him as he leaned over to grab the handle of his bag. "Check back with me in about a half hour," she said.

He returned her smile. "I will do that."

Pulling the suitcase behind him again, Archpriest Canale walked away from the ticket counter and began looking for a place to sit for a while. Much of the room around him was populated by numerous twisting lines of people waiting to check their bags, so he leisurely made his way towards the front entrance. Without passing through security first, he couldn't wander the shops and food court, so he found a small bench in front of a glass wall and took a seat.

Taking in a long relaxing breath, Andrea reached into his coat pocket and pulled out a small silver medallion — Christopher, the Patron Saint for safe travel. He carried it with him whenever he left Rome. Slowly he brushed his thumb over the medal.

Saint Christopher, watch over me.

His thoughts were interrupted by the Airports intercom announcing a flight preparing to board, and the man sitting next to him groaned as he heaved his heavy frame off the bench. Andrea only briefly looked up at him, and then turned his attention back to Saint Christopher.

Then, unexpectedly, two other men sat on either side of him at an uncomfortably close distance. Andrea picked his head up again and looked first at the man to his left. *What?* He turned to the other on his right. *Why?* They were the same two men who had accompanied the Black Pope to his rectory that night.

Simultaneously, each of the men held Andrea by his wrists. "Come with us, Padre."

Although Father Canale couldn't see the man behind him, Generale Santalla stood just outside the glass wall — watching as his two henchmen lifted the Father from his seat.

22

Antichrist

Cameron wasn't sure what to make of it?

"Colonel Skull? Are you still there?" Frank asked.

Still Cameron said nothing.

Iris stood off to his side trying to evaluate the look on his face. She couldn't tell if he was angry or confused, but she could tell that something had just roused him.

"Colonel?"

God damn it! Frank's interruption made Cameron lose his train of thought. "Frank, I'll call you back in a little while." He ended the call without waiting for Frank's response and handed Iris back her phone.

"What did he say?" Iris asked.

Skull held up a finger. "Give me a minute." He took a long breath. *Am I supposed to believe that I'm dealing with..., the antichrist? Matousek obviously thought so.* Strangely enough, it didn't seem too illogical, but not for the obvious reasons. Although the man who killed Father Matousek looked like an abomination, he was still just a man. But then again, truth of the antichrist reveals that he is in fact Satan's human emissary on earth, the arch-deceiver, the lawless-one, sent by Lucifer to act as the central figure during the apocalypse.

Colonel Skull rubbed the top of his head. Something still wasn't playing out. Ever since Kaitlyn had passed, his insomnia had spawned a new-found gratification in the History channel. But everything he had learned from the countless documentaries suggested that the antichrist would take on the role of someone attractive and charismatic. Certainly not a repulsive creature.

He bit his bottom lip and tried to recall everything he knew about the prophesies in the Book of Revelations and the coming of the antichrist. Unfortunately, his midnight rendezvous with the television were often accompanied by a stiff Kentucky brewed nightcap.

"Cameron," Iris interrupted.

He huffed out his breath. "What?"

"What do you mean *what*?" She threw out her hands then rested them on her hips. "What did he say? Why are you acting all weird now?"

Instead of answering her, Cameron took a step closer and changed the subject. "What happened in Stockholm? All *I* know is that there was a break-in, but you said earlier that you could give me more details. What did you see?"

She backed off a little. Skulls attitude wasn't necessarily forceful, but she still felt like she was being subdued. "Well," she began. "I already told you about the man I saw. I think it was the same...,"

"And I already told you that it can't be the same person. There's no way he could have made it from Sweden to Kutna Hora in... what was that?"

She looked down at the phone in her hand. "I got a text message."

"What does it say?" Cameron asked impatiently.

She brought the phone up to her face, causing a yellowish glow to enhance her already angelic eyes. "Oh my God. It's from Guy Olsson at the Swedish Library. It says that Fischer is dead." She held a hand against her upper chest. "I... I don't understand."

"Who's Fischer?" Cameron asked quickly.

She looked up at him. "He's the libraries head of security."

Cameron's eyes narrowed. "What else does it say?"

She glanced back at her phone and paraphrased the long text for him. "It says that it was a suicide, and that the video we watched was a trick."

"Is that all? What video?"

She brought the phone away from her face. "It ends with him telling me that he'll call after the National Guard leaves. And that I should be careful."

"What video?" he asked again.

"I don't know," she said defensively. "I didn't get a chance to watch any of the tapes. All I saw was the live video of him breaking in this afternoon."

"THEN THAT'S WHAT HE'S TALKING ABOUT!" Cameron cried, stating what he found to be the obvious. "He's telling you that what you saw was a trick." He held up his right hand and fanned his fingers towards his chest. "Describe the video to me."

Iris had to give herself a minute to catch up. "All I saw was the guy come into the vault and tear a bunch of pages out of the Codex."

Colonel Skull was much quicker at processing the information then she was, and it took him no time at all to realize what was going on. "Then it didn't happen," he said quietly, thinking out loud.

She was offended. "What the hell are you talking about? I watched it happen."

"You watched *something* happen." He pointed at her phone. "That's what he's trying to tell you. Whatever it was that you watched, it was a trick." Suddenly he realized something else and began rambling, mostly to himself. "Wait. If what you saw was fake, then... days later... scars... maybe..."

Iris reached out and grabbed his hand.

"What are you talking about? You're not making any sense."

He stopped and looked at his hand in hers before turning his attention to her face. "Maybe you were right. Maybe it was the same person. That changes everything. What else happened over there?"

She shivered but did her best to describe how the three murdered guards had had their faces cut off.

Colonel Skull hadn't known about that, but now there was no doubt. Whoever had broken into the library a few days ago was indeed the same fucked up person who had killed Father Matousek earlier. Even the two guards at the library that were killed today didn't disprove his theory. Iris had pointed out that their faces were not cut the same way as the guard a few days ago. Fischer must have killed the last two men as a distraction then killed himself when he got caught.

"I don't know if I should be happy, upset, or worried about this," Cameron admitted. "Is there anything else you can tell me? Let's get it all out in the open right now."

Iris thought a moment about the video, but nothing helpful came to mind. "Like I told you, he tore out a bunch of pages." She held up a hand. "Before you ask, I already checked with Mr. Olsson. The pages contained a list of medieval spells." Her outstretched hand now rubbed the back of her neck. "What where they called? Oh yeah, conjurations."

Conjurations? Antichrist? What the hell is going on? "I've never heard of there being magic spells in a bible?" Cameron commented. *But this isn't your typical Holy Bible.* He said silently to himself. *This is, the Devil's Bible.*

"Me neither." Iris shrugged. "But there are, um... were, in this one." Suddenly she snapped her fingers. "Wait a second. I didn't see it happen, but Guy told me that on the first video the man had acted strange. He said that the man had spread the pages apart and slowly caressed the inside of the binding. He even described it as, "sexual." In my opinion he..."

Iris kept speaking but her words became clouded. Cameron's mind drifted uncontrollably into an early chapter of his subconscious autobiography.

> — *"Cameron, you little son-of-a-bitch," his father yelled out. "Where the hell's my flask?"*

Joseph Skull had grown up in an area of Chicago known as "The Patch." Just two buildings down from the childhood home of the infamous 1930's mobster, George "Babyface" Nelson. Maybe it was just that neighborhood, or maybe Joseph Skull had simply picked his role model for all the wrong reasons, but either way, Cameron's father took to violence and drug abuse at an early age.

"I didn't touch it," the now 15-year-old

Cameron yelled back. "You're drunk. You probably drank it all this morning."

Joseph's face shook from anger. He pulled back his right arm and struck Cameron hard across the face. "Don't you talk back to me, you little son-of-a-bitch."

For the first time in his life, Cameron became so enraged that he lunged forward and attacked his father. Both men tumbled to the ground before the sober, and much stronger Cameron was able to pin his father to his back.

"Cam, don't!" his mother cried out, afraid that the young boy was about to kill his own father.

Cameron looked up at his mother standing next to them with tears running from her eyes. He looked quickly back down at the sad excuse for a man pinned beneath him, then pushed himself up and started to walk away.

Still furious however, Cameron slammed a hand down onto the open pages of a book sitting on the coffee table as he walked from the room. Turning his open hand into a fist, he then grabbed and ripped out the pages beneath it and threw them to the ground behind him.

His mother, unable to restrain herself, hiccupped a small cry of heartbreak and Cameron looked back over his shoulder at her. She held both hands to her mouth, but was not looking down at Joseph. Instead she was looking at the crumpled pages lying on the floor behind him.

Cameron's eyes shifted. It was then that he realized that the book he had just destroyed was his *great grandmother's diary. He stood silent with a heavy heart as he watched his mother bend over and slowly pick up the pages. She gently smoothed them out and then set them back onto the table and picked up what remained of the book.*

Holding the diary up in her left hand, she gently brushed a finger down the length of the book. Caressing the inner binding where the pages had just been.

"Colonel." Iris lightly shook him by the shoulder. "You okay?"

"Missing pages," he whispered.

Iris pulled her head back slightly. "Huh? Yeah, they're missing. He took them with him."

"No." Skull turned himself a few degrees clockwise in order to face her directly. "That's what he was doing when he ran his finger down the inside of the book. He was feeling for missing pages."

"Oh, I get what you're saying. If the video I watched was a fake, then maybe what Mr. Olsson saw happened later. Maybe he was feeling along the book *after* he had already torn out the pages."

Cameron didn't respond to her observation.

"Right?" she asked.

"I don't think so," Skull answered, beginning to pace around her. "You were just there. If Mr. Olsson actually saw what he says he did then there wasn't time for a second video to be recorded."

"I'm not sure I follow what you're saying," Iris admitted.

"What I'm saying, is that either Mr. Olsson lied to you about the first video, or there were already pages missing from that book before he..."

"Before he tore out the spells," she finished.

Cameron tilted his head down to silently applaud her. "Right. I wonder..." He interrupted his own sentence and stuffed a hand into his pocket. Pulling out and powering on his iPhone, he held the device above his head to try and get a clear signal. "Damn."

"What?" Iris asked.

Colonel Skull looked down at her. "You get a signal out here. See if you can access the internet."

"Okay." She gave it a couple tries, but with each attempt the phone closed the application before she could log on. "It's no use," she finally told him. "Stupid things not going to cooperate."

Skull blew out a frustrated breath of air, placed his hands on his hips, and looked down the street. "Well I guess there's not much we can do about it." He looked over at Iris and dropped his phone back into his pocket. It struck against the hard plastic of another object as it fell, and quickly he reached back in to feel what it was.

"Oh shit."

"Now what?" Iris asked.

He pulled his hand out and showed her a small black and silver item, not much larger than a credit card and definitely smaller than his phone.

She strained to see it clearly but it was too dark outside. "What is that?"

He smiled. "It's the hard drive from my laptop. I pulled it out before leaving the hotel this morning."

"So?"

"It's got the tracking software I used to follow your brother on it. If we can find a computer to reinstall it on, I should be able to continue the trace of his phone."

Her eyes grew big and she sounded much more enthusiastic then she had only minutes ago. "And you'll be able to get on the internet. Let's get going." She took a step around him and began putting the motorcycle helmet back on.

He didn't see a problem with her suggestion, so he turned around and threw a leg over the seat of the bike. "I remember seeing a town not too far outside of Prague when we drove in this morning." *Holy crap! Was that this morning?* "We'll stop there."

"Sounds good to me." She mounted the bike behind him, set her feet up onto the rear pegs, and put her arms around his waist. "Let's go."

23

The taller of the two men followed close behind him while the shorter bald-headed man led the way through the busy airport. Outside his home earlier, the two men had been dressed in long black robes which made them nearly invisible against the night sky. But here in the airport both men wore black slacks with a white button-up shirt and black necktie. And around each of their necks hung a silver chain with a badge that read, CORPO DELLA GENDARMERIA - CITTA DEL VATICANO.

To the unsuspecting eye they would have appeared to be Vatican State Security, but Archpriest Canale knew better. Although he was not sure what position, if any, the two men served at the Vatican, he was certain that they were definitely not members of the Gendarmerie. But unfortunately, to the rest of the airports travelers their presence wouldn't have appeared unusual—a high priest being escorted by private security.

"Where are you taking me?" Andrea asked.

"Keep walking," the man behind him answered.

"But I don't understand. Have I done something wrong?"

The bald man in front of him turned around just slightly, revealing a small scar above his right ear. He continued to walk, ignoring Andrea's question but asking another. "Is there anything in your bag that will cause security to search it?"

Andrea knew that sometimes people would pose as priests in a never-successful attempt to bypass airport security. "Why are we going through security?" he asked.

The man repeated his question in a much more aggravated tone.

"No," Andrea answered this time, "only some clothes and toiletries."

The short bald man turned his head forward again. "Good. Then when we get to security, let go of your bag and stay directly behind me."

"Let go of my bag?"

"Marco will take it through the metal detectors."

Andrea turned his head and looked up at the big man standing behind him. The man didn't speak but gave a confirming nod of his head.

"Stay to the left," the bald man finished.

Why are we going through security?

Suddenly Father Canale became hopeful. "Where are we going? Are you going to help me get to the Czech Republic?"

Neither man answered him this time. Up ahead, the steady flow of passengers came to a halt as the lines to pass through security stretched back nearly fifty feet. Marco reached out and put a hand on Andrea's shoulder, gently guiding him to their left and around the back of the lines.

It was not unusual. The two men were leading him around to the security booth used for disabled passengers, members of clergy and foreign dignitaries. Although not empty, there was only one woman in a wheelchair, along with what appeared to be her private nurse, trying to pass through the gate in front of them.

As asked, Andrea let go of the handle on his bag and looked back at Marco. The big man leaned over and took it, then pointed a finger forward. "Keep walking," he instructed.

Before Andrea could ask any more questions, the man in front of him spoke again. "Do not say anything or ask any questions. Do not make eye contact or hand signals. Stay behind me and walk through quickly."

By now it was becoming clear that these men were not here to help him. Andrea stopped walking and spoke calmly. "Where do you intend to take me?"

Marco put a hand on his back and

pushed. "Passeggiata!"

Andrea kept himself composed and turned around to face him. "I want to know where we are going first."

Marco stepped closer to him. And at the same time, Andrea could also feel the presence of the bald man walking up behind him.

"Father Canale," the bald man said quietly from behind him. "Don't act surprised that we are here. You foolishly chose to ignore the request of Generale Santalla. And for that, you're now going to accompany us without any further argument." He paused for a moment. "I wasn't surprised when young Henry showed contention. But I thought a man of your maturity would understand when to remain cooperative."

Andrea sucked in a quick breath. *What did they do with Henry?* Slowly he turned back around. "What..."

"Don't worry about Mr. De Luca," the bald man advised. "I trust however, that you do understand the severity of our situation now."

Andrea nodded.

"Good. Then do as I said. And I promise that soon you will have your answers." He turned and continued to walk towards the security gate.

By now the young woman and her nurse had long since passed and disappeared into the terminals. Without hesitation, the bald man emptied his pockets into a tray and set it onto the conveyor, then walked quickly through the arch-shaped metal detector. It beeped loudly as he exited. "Knee replacement surgery," he told the officer standing on the far end.

The security guard looked at him skeptically despite the Gendarmeria badge around his neck. "Hold out your arms please."

The short bald man smiled. "Take a look." He bent over and pulled his right pant leg above his knee. "The whole thing's titanium."

The guard looked down then waved his wand over the man's knee. As promised, the wand beeped loudly as it passed over it. "Sorry about that. Thank you." He waved the bald man aside and signaled for Andrea to step through next.

Again, the machine beeped and Andrea looked down at himself confused.

"Do you have anything in your pockets Father?" the guard asked.

Andrea shook his head, but then he quickly realized he'd forgotten to remove the Saint Christopher medallion from his jacket. "Oh, si. I'm sorry, I forgot." He pointed at his pocket.

The guard walked up and pulled out the small medallion. As he inspected it the bald man stood back, staring angrily.

"No problem, Father." The guard dropped the medal back into his pocket before signaling Marco to pass through next.

"You don't listen very well, do you Father?"

"I forgot," Andrea told him.

"Somehow I doubt that." The bald man looked over his shoulder and waved to Marco. "Let's go."

Marco grabbed Andrea's bag off the far end of the conveyor and followed behind them. He quickly caught up with Andrea and the other man and followed them down the escalator to the lower level and into terminal B.

Andrea, disappointed, began looking for signs of what airlines flew out of terminal B. Unfortunately, he didn't get a long opportunity to search. The bald man leading them stopped quickly at gate B1 and began looking for an acceptable place to sit and wait.

Where are they taking me?

He knew that whatever flight it was that they were waiting for was not scheduled to board for quite some time. The rest of the people standing around had no luggage with them, which clearly meant that they were waiting to greet a passenger, not become one.

"Would you object to me using the restroom?" Andrea asked.

The question was directed at Marco, but the big man looked to his companion for the answer.

"Not by yourself. Marco, go with him." He looked down at the empty seat behind him.

"No, wait. I'll go. Marco, you stay here."

Pleased that he didn't have to do any more walking around, Marco plopped his big frame down onto the nearest seat.

"Grazie," Andrea said sincerely.

"Whatever. Let's go."

The restrooms in terminal B were just across from the gate at the base of the escalators. Both men walked in together and Andrea was relieved when the bald man stepped into one of the stalls and closed the door.

"You don't leave this room until I'm done," the man ordered from behind the partition.

Truthfully, it hadn't occurred to Andrea to leave while the man was using the toilet. But now he began to think about it. *How would he stop me?*

"Did you hear what I said?" the bald man called out again.

I can go right now. Andrea looked at the closed door of the bathroom stall, then at the door leading out into the terminals. He knew that if he did want to risk it, now was the time. "Si. I won't leave," he lied, then turned for the door.

His answer hadn't come fast enough and now it was too late. The stall door flung open behind him and the short bald-headed man came bursting out. Andrea's heart raced and he quickly ran for the door. But as he reached out for the handle, a tremendous pain bit into his side and he fell to his knees.

"I told you not to..."

"Hey? What's going on?" another man in the restroom yelled over his shoulder.

Andrea tried looking up to find the voice. Instead, he found the reflection of the back of a bald head coming off the mirror above the sink. He picked himself up a little more. Enough so that now he could see the blade that the short man held in his hand.

"Wait!" Andrea cried. "What are you... No! DON'T!"

It was too late. Father Canale watched through a smudged mirror as the bald man stuck the knife deep into the other man's back as he stood at the urinal.

"No," Andrea whispered. The pain of having to witness this innocent man stabbed for trying to help was worse than the pain from his own injury. And even though he found it difficult to breath, Andrea forced himself to his feet.

Ruthlessly, the bald man continued to plunge the knife into the man's body until it fell hard into a pool of blood on the tile floor. Then he turned and wiped some sweat from his eyes and looked down at the floor for Father Canale. "Che cazzo!" He was gone. The man tried pointlessly to quickly clean some of the blood splatter off his white shirt before running back out into the terminal. "MARCO!" he yelled out.

The big man was reclined back in his seat with his hands behind his head and his right leg crossed over his left knee.

"MARCO!" he yelled again.

This time Marco heard him and sprang up from the chair.

The bald man didn't say another word. Instead, he pointed a finger repeatedly at the escalator.

Marco nodded and ran towards the steps, while the short bald-headed man ran off in the other direction — deeper into terminal B.

—

Andrea could feel the warmth of the blood as it began seeping through his shirt and onto his fingers. He held his hand tight against the wound as he ducked around a corner at the top of the escalator, but he was quickly becoming lightheaded.

He was back on the upper level of the airport. And somewhere up here, buried among the retail shops and fast food eateries, he would find terminal 3 and the young woman he had spoken to earlier. But by now he knew there was little time. The girl had said that the flight to the Czech Republic was to depart in one hour.

He took a few more deep breaths and pulled the back of his head off the wall behind him. Slowly he looked down at his blood covered fingers and then at the congested shopping mall to his left.

Suddenly Marco's large frame appeared at the top step of the escalator. Andrea pulled his head quickly back against the wall and held himself still for a few seconds.

Please help me Lord. He prayed. *Assist us, O Lord our God; and defend us evermore by the might of Thy holy Cross.*

"Are you alright?" someone asked.

Andrea opened his eyes and looked at the face speaking to him. It was a middle-aged woman and her young son who she held close to her side. The young boy looked frightened and Andrea realized that he had seen the blood on his hand.

"Don't worry yourself young man. I'll be just fine." He tried smiling at the boy's mother, but the pain was beginning to worsen. "Thank you. I must go now."

He pushed himself off the wall again and limped towards the flight gates. Marco was nowhere to be seen, but at this point it didn't matter much. If Marco found him now, he would have little choice but to cry out for help.

Finally the airport became familiar territory to him and the strong smell of Lavazza gently wafting out of a coffee shop assured him that he was getting very close to terminal 3.

Soon he was able to see the face of the

young girl who had helped him earlier. He kept his arm held to his side and waved at her as he neared.

"Father Canale." She waved back at him. "Hurry. I got you a seat but we've already called final boarding and they're about to close the doors."

He struggled to speed himself up.

"Father? What's wrong?"

"Nothing, my dear. Everything's alright." He waved again, this time at the man standing next to the air bridge door leading out to the plane. "Uno di piu," he called to the man.

"Father," the girl pleaded again. "What happened? Where's your bag?"

The archpriest ignored her this time. He didn't want to, but he couldn't lie to her, and telling her the truth would only frighten her. Not to mention gather the attention of the real Corpo della Gendarmeria, and almost certainly stop the flight from leaving.

"Thank you for waiting, signore," Andrea said.

The man smiled and held open the door. "You're welcome, Father. Have a nice flight."

24

Highway E67 was pretty dark in the middle of
the night and Cameron didn't see the sign fast
enough. The small town of Jirny was where he
had intended to stop, but with Iris riding on the
back of the motorcycle he wasn't comfortable
weaving the bike at the last minute to catch the
off-ramp.

Shit!

His eyes left the road when his head
turned and followed the exit as they drove past.
Maybe I can turn around. He looked at the road
ahead of them again but saw nothing but a long
stretch of empty highway.

Inadvertently, he rolled his hand down
on the throttle and the bike quickly responded. It
lifted up on the front suspension and Iris had to
grip tighter around his waist to keep herself
from falling backwards. She thought about
yelling at him to slow down, but even she knew
that there was little chance of him hearing her.

There's got to be another... Suddenly the
road ahead began to brighten on the horizon.
Leaning the bike, he merged into the right lane

and guided it down the next ramp. It was a Shell gas station and truck stop with another sign that read, TVRZ HUMMER/FORT HUMMER.

Although he wasn't sure what that meant, he didn't care. A truck stop was a good place to stop. Along with food and sometimes showers and lodging, most truck stops offered wireless internet access. But unfortunately, the off-ramp dropped them off north of the freeway, which only housed a few gas pumps. The main building and small hotel were south.

He circled the bike around in the parking lot and crossed over a bridge leading to the other side of the highway. Pulling into another parking lot, it quickly became very clear to both of them what the sign had said. FORT HUMMER was in fact the English translation. It actually was a Fort.

Completely surrounded by a tall wooden fence and several lookout towers, Fort Hummer looked like it was straight out of an old John Wayne movie. Had he been here for any other reason he would have loved to stop and check it out. *Kendall would get a kick out of this.* He thought. But right now there were more important things to worry about.

He continued past the forts main entrance gate and ticket counter and parked the bike next to the trailer of a large semi-truck.

Iris wasted no time pulling off her helmet and looking around. "Do you know where we are?"

"Just some truck stop," he answered honestly. "We're only a few kilometers from Prague. This'll be a good place to convene so we don't go storming into a castle like a couple'a idiots."

Her foot accidentally caught Cameron in the back as she swung her leg over the seat. "Oops, sorry about that."

"It's fine." He got off the bike behind her and reached his hands above his head to stretch out his muscles that were beginning to cramp from the ride. "Let's head inside. I could use something to eat anyhow."

"What? We can't sit and eat. We've got to keep moving."

Skull turned around. Iris was still standing next to the motorcycle so he took a few steps back. "Don't eat then. I don't care. But I'm grabbing something while we're here. Now let's go." He turned around again and walked away from her.

What a jerk. She straightened out the bottom of her skirt again and tried jogging to catch up. "Will you at least wait for me?" she called out.

Cameron did wait for her and together they walked through the automatic doors of the truck stop. Upon entering, each of them took a minute to look around. It was much larger than it appeared from the outside. Turns out, the building actually was devoted to the General Motors "Hummer" off-road vehicles. There was a large gift shop along with a full automotive center that specialized in everything from military H1's to the recently popular civilian H3 models.

"What a weird place," Iris commented.

Cameron finished looking around. *What's the deal? Is there nowhere to eat?* He turned to look at her. "Well, not really. Of course, I don't understand what that fort outside is all about."

A man standing behind one of the cash registers in the gift shop overheard Cameron's comment. "It's just for fun," he told them. "Festivaly. Sort of like your American renaissance fairs."

"Oh, you speak English. Good."

Iris followed Cameron over to the man.

"I don't suppose you sell computers here?" Skull leaned an elbow onto the counter. "Do you?"

"Computers? No, I'm sorry. You want to buy t-shirt? Maybe coffee mug? Yes?"

"No, thanks," Cameron answered, and turned back towards Iris.

He pulled the iPhone out of his pocket again and went into its settings. Just as he suspected, the building had a strong Wi-Fi connection. That was good. He switched the phone back off and returned it to his pocket. "Come on," he called to her.

"Where are we going?" She followed Cameron back outside where he checked the signal on his phone one more time. "What are you doing?"

Colonel Skull looked up at the building behind him and then out at the parking lot. "This place sends out a signal that's strong enough to reach all the way out here. It must be so that truckers can use their laptops while still in their trucks."

"So what?"

"So," he answered. "We need to find an empty truck?" He saw the expression on her face and continued before she got to upset. "The truck we parked next to looked empty. If the driver left his laptop in there, we can use it to reinstall my hard-drive."

"You're going to break into someone's truck?" she cried.

It was too late. Cameron was already a few steps away from her, heading for the truck. Once reaching the side of the cab he reached up for the door handle. "Damn."

Iris caught up to him. "What's the matter? You're surprised they didn't leave the door unlocked for you?"

He scowled at her, not appreciating the sarcasm. But instead of arguing back, he walked a few steps to a toolbox mounted just below the trailer. After a quick look around him, he pulled on the latch and the metal box popped open.

"Come on, Cameron. What are you doing?"

"Just keep an eye out," he instructed. "Whistle at me if someone starts walking up."

He pulled a metal bar out of the toolbox, probably something the driver used to tighten down loads, and walked back up to the passenger door. After taking one last look around him, he reached up and firmly tapped the end of the bar against the window. It shattered into the cab and Cameron quickly reached in and unlocked the door.

"Get in," he said, pointing up into the truck.

"I'm *not* getting in there," she said sternly.

"Fine." Skull grabbed the handle and pulled himself up into the cab. "Stay by the bike and let me know if someone's coming."

She nodded at him in agreement, but then a man coughing from the other side of the trailer startled her and she jumped up into the cab behind him.

He shook his head as she climbed over his lap and into the rear sleeper section of the truck. Then he reached out and pulled the door shut. The trucker's laptop sat closed on the driver's seat next to him, plugged into a 12-volt AC power inverter.

"How did you know for sure that he'd have a laptop in here," Iris asked.

Cameron smiled and pointed to the foot

of the small bed that she was sitting on. There was a DVD case titled "Kinky Asian Teens" and an open bottle of lubricant next to her.

"Ohh... my... God! You have got to be kidding me." She slid herself carefully down the bed and away from the half-empty bottle of lube.

Skull chuckled as he opened the slightly outdated HP laptop and hit the power button. It took a moment, but finally the screen brightened and he clicked immediately on the Internet Explorer icon.

"What are you doing now?" Iris asked impatiently. "I thought you were going to try and hook up your hard-drive?"

"I am," he assured her. "But there's a few other things I need to check first." He ran a search — *missing pages of the codex gigas*. The list of related websites was limited to only a few. Most of which were conspiracy theories. However, the pages that did identify with his search parameters confirmed one important thing — there were indeed pages missing from the infamous Devil's Bible.

Skull clicked on a few of the sites and found that most believed there to be 7 total pages missing, while a few others claimed it was 8. After a bit more reading, it appeared that the common belief was that the missing pages once held the written Rule of St. Benedict.

"That would make sense," he whispered

to himself.

"What would make sense?"

He tried to remember everything he knew about the book so far. Everything that Iris, Frank and Father Matousek had told him. "Well." He turned to her. "If I'm remembering right, the Codex was scribed by a Benedictine black monk."

"That's the theory anyways," she corrected.

"Right. But the monks who ruled the monastery in Sedlec were a white clothed sect. Not under the governance of St. Benedict."

"So?"

"Sooo... when the book was transferred from one group to the other, it would have made sense that the white monks would have ripped out the pages that didn't pertain to them."

"And you..."

"That must be what he was searching for in the cemetery!" Cameron interrupted. "He must have found the missing pages buried under the stone angel."

"What stone angel?"

"It doesn't matter. I'm sure..." Cameron scratched on his facial hair, which was beginning to feel longer than just his typical stubble, and started talking to himself. "But why go to that much trouble to recover something so superficial? That's got to be it though." He turned around to look at her. "But what value would the Rule of St. Benedict have? What's the significance?"

She shrugged her shoulders. "Why are you asking me?"

"I'm just thinking out loud." He looked back at the computer. "I guess that's going to be another project for Frank."

He cleared the search bar on the screen. This time he typed in the words, CASTLE PRAGUE, and of course, the first website to show up was his arch-nemesis — the dreaded *Wikipedia*. He hated that site more than any other. Being in his line of work, specifically Nightcorp, research often played a critical role in the success of his missions, and he couldn't count how many times he had received bad information because of the publicly controlled cybernated encyclopedia.

He continued to scroll down the list until he came to an official Czech website for the castle. And fortunately for him, at the top of the page there was a button to automatically translate it to English.

"What are you looking for?" Iris asked softly from behind him.

"This." He pointed at the screen and clicked on the available link. CASTLE GUARD ORGANIZATIONAL STRUCTURE. His finger brushed across the screen as he read the article to himself. *Prague Castle is guarded 24 hours a day by elite units... military brigade of 660 persons... armaments... model 61 Skorpion submachine guns.*

Suddenly the sound of men talking outside the truck interrupted him.

"Cameron," Iris whispered.

"I heard it," he said back.

"We have to get out of here."

"Not yet. I need to find a map of the castle first."

The voices outside were getting louder. "There's no time." Iris reached over him and shut the cover of the computer. "Don't give me that look. You want to go to jail for breaking into someone's truck?"

He peered out the front windshield. So far he couldn't see anybody, but the voices were still resonating louder through the parking lot along the driver's side of the truck. He unplugged the computer from the dashboard and tucked it under his arm.

"Come on," he whispered.

Iris pulled herself forward by the headrest of the driver's seat and ducked out of the truck behind Colonel Skull.

"Kde je dalsi zastavka?" one of the voices asked.

"Ostrava," the other answered.

Cameron held Iris' hand as she took the last step down from the truck. He then shut the door behind her as quietly as he could and jumped the few steps over to the motorcycle. "Hurry up and get your helmet on," he encouraged.

While Iris fumbled with the strap under her chin, Cameron opened the saddlebag of the bike and tried cramming the laptop into it. It was no use. Iris had packed the bags full. He started looking around the bike for another way to carry the computer when suddenly one of the voices called out from next to him.

"Hej! Co to delas s mou laptop?"

Son-of-a-bitch! Cameron held the thin computer to his chest and zipped his jacket up around it. He jumped onto the bike and frantically struck the two bare wires together under the ignition switch. Bright sparks of electricity flared out from the exposed copper. Then, at the fourth contact between wires, the motorcycle fired. "LET'S GO!" he yelled to Iris.

She took one quick look at the truck driver running towards them then hurled herself onto the back seat behind him. Cameron wrenched down on the throttle and the rear tire of the bike broke loose. The man running after them was quickly closing the distance, but a heavy cloud of smoke from the rear tire engulfed him and the BMW fishtailed out of the parking lot.

25

Skull residence, Benton County, Oregon.

Frank looked over his shoulder at the clock above the microwave — 4:26 P.M. "Hey Kendall, let me know when you start getting hungry, okay."

His computer sat open on the coffee table in front of him with a slide-show of pictures from last year's fishing trip scrolling across the screen. He was sitting on the edge of the sofa with his nose still buried in Colonel Skull's bible.

He was trying to figure out why the priest in the Czech Republic had tried to warn Cameron of the antichrist. But as he dug deeper, Frank found it difficult to properly decipher the bible's true definition of who the antichrist actually was. The Apostle John was the only one who actually referred to someone as "antichrist." And even he declared that the world would see many antichrists.

In the second Epistle to the Thessalonians he is described as the "son of perdition," the "man of sin," while the Book of Revelations refers to him as "the beast." And although much of the bible seemed to agree that the world would see many antichrists between the first and second coming of Christ, the books also seemed to agree that there will be one great antichrist who will rise to power during the end of times.

The final hour.

Frank looked up from the book and searched around the room for Kendall. She hadn't answered his call a minute ago. "Kendall," he called again.

The Skull's living room remained silent. Frank turned and looked at the staircase behind him, thinking maybe she went upstairs to her room.

He closed the book and set it down on the table next to his computer. Pushing up on his knees, Frank got up from the couch and walked over to the base of the steps. "Keeenndaaall. Are you hiding from me?" He grabbed the banister and walked up the first few steps. "Not fair," he said jokingly. "It's my turn to hide."

He stretched his neck out to try and get a premature look at the open loft at the top of the stairs, but so far all he could see was the rustic décor of Cameron's office. A solid oak desk overlooked the downstairs living room, while a hand painted sign that read, *Angler's welcome*, ornamented the far wall—humorously hung above Cameron's 28-gallon freshwater aquarium against the wall beneath it.

Then, as he was about to take the next step, he heard a giggle from what sounded like outside. He turned back around and walked through the living room to the front door. It was a nice day outside, so Frank had left only the screen door closed earlier.

As he approached, he could see Kendall out front in the grass. He hadn't worried about her being alone outside, considering Colonel Skull's closest neighbors were almost a half mile away. She was busy chasing a fat little squirrel through the lawn under one of the tall pines and it made him smile.

He rested his right forearm against the door-frame and watched her play for a minute. Although not his child, he had literally watched her grow up, and loved her like she was his own. "Is that little squirrel being mean to you?"

She stopped running after it and looked up at the house quickly. "No Uncle Frank. We're playing."

Frank opened the screen and walked out shaking his finger. "Cause I'll beat him up if he is."

"NO! We were playing." She ran over and let Frank pick her up by the arms.

He held her out in front of him. "Nobody messes with *my* niece." He set her back down. "Isn't that right?"

Kendall just laughed and ran past him

and into the house.

Frank spun on his heel and followed after her. "Hey, are you getting hungry yet?" he yelled. "I'm gonna make tacos tonight. Does that sound good?"

"Yeah, but I'm not hungry yet."

"Okay," he said, walking back into the living room. "Just let me know when you do start getting hungry."

She plopped herself down in her dad's big leather recliner next to the couch. "When's daddy coming home, Uncle Frank?" She didn't give him a chance to answer. "Can we call him?"

Frank looked down at his watch and mumbled to himself. "Four thirty, plus nine hours... No honey, I think it's a little late right now to call him. Why don't you watch some TV?" He picked up the remote and handed it to her. "Just not to loud, okay. Uncle Frank's got a little work to do."

"Kay." She clicked on the television and was under a Spongebob Squarepants hypnosis in no time.

Frank left the bible where it was on the table. He was no expert on religion and the past couple hours of bible study made him feel like he was back in high school. *I don't know who wrote that thing,* he thought, looking down at the front cover of the bible. *But if you can understand that, you probably love reading Shakespeare.*

He picked up his computer and set in on

his lap. Generally, when conducting R and D for Nightcorp, Frank would go immediately to one of his connections at Trident Technology Research or DARPA. But unfortunately, his resources for investigating Catholicism were a bit scarce, if not completely nonexistent.

He went back to looking up King Rudolph instead. The man had intrigued him earlier, especially because very few accounts of him mentioned his possession of the Codex Gigas. All of them however remarked on his favor of the occult sciences and how he had been prone to melancholy since childhood.

It seemed that Rudolph had devoted his life to the mystical arts, and to strange devices which he believed to hold magical properties. One such item was an alchemical substance known as the philosopher's stone. Many believed it to hold the secret of changing worthless metal into gold. But Rudolph took it a step further. He believed that the legendary substance held the key to creating an elixir for immortality.

His fixation with such things nearly drove him to madness. So, it was no surprise that in 1594, when Rudolph first heard the words — *Devil's Bible* — he did everything in his power to obtain it.

As Frank continued to read further, things only got stranger. Finally, he had to take a sip from his bottle of water to wake himself up and remember what he was supposed to be doing. *Stay focused Frank.*

He scanned quickly over the rest of the page. But as his eyes came to an obscure astrological chart, he couldn't help but stop and look it over. "What is that?" he whispered.

"What is what, Uncle Frank?"

He'd forgotten that Kendall was sitting in the chair next to him. "Oh, nothing, honey. Are you starting to get hungry yet?"

She looked back at the television. "No."

"Okay. You just let me know." He leaned in closer to try and figure out the chart, but it was written in a language that he didn't understand. He searched around for a description but wasn't able to find one right away. *It's like some kind of horoscope.*

He continued to look around the screen for an explanation but still had no luck finding one. Finally he gave up and was about to close the web-page when something else caught his eye. In the top of the center square in the diagram was the word, *Rudolphus*, surrounded by roman numerals. It was beginning to look like a time-line of his life. The roman numerals appeared to be dates.

Then he looked at the bottom of the square. The chart had been signed by its creator.

A very recognizable signature—Per *Michael Nostradam.*

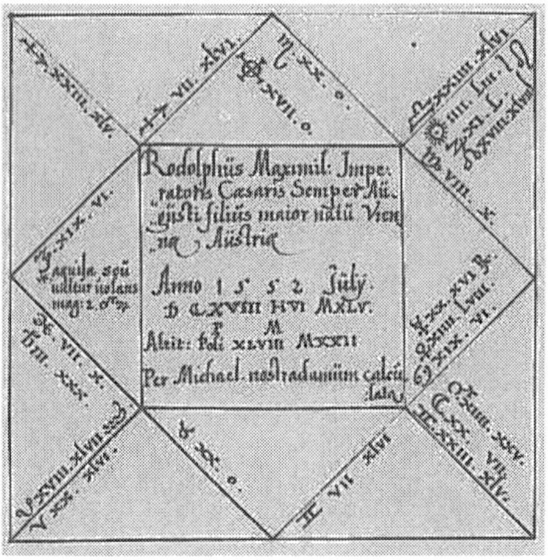
Rodolphus Maximil: Impe-
ratoris Cæsaris Semper Au-
gusti filius maior natu Vien-
na Austriæ
Anno 1 5 5 2 July
D C XVIII H VI M XLV
Altit: Poli XLVIII M XXII
Per Michael. nostradamum calcu-
lata

26

Cameron killed the engine on the motorcycle. Castle Prague sat just across the river from them. And from the eastern bank of Charles Bridge, it was an extraordinary sight. The cloudless horizon provided a picturesque backdrop for the soaring towers of Saint Vitus Cathedral. And the illuminated gardens and castle walls reflected brilliantly off the calm waters of Vltava River.

Cameron balanced the bike upright with both feet but neither of them got off. The view was captivating, and despite all the urgency, it deserved a moment of appreciation.

There's not going to be anywhere for me to access the internet out here. Colonel Skull held a hand against the laptop in his jacket. Amazingly, zipping it up in the front of his coat was a pretty convenient way of carrying it. Maybe once or twice it had shifted during the ride, but never enough to concern him that it was going to fall out.

"How are we going to get in there?" Iris asked softly.

Cameron looked down at her petite

hands, still wrapped around his waist, before straining his neck to turn around and look at her. "I'm not sure we have to get in there." He looked again at the massive fortified castle in front of them. *Do we?*

"What are you talking about?" she leaned forward and asked. "Isn't that the whole reason we came here?"

He turned again, but not so far this time—just enough so that he could see her from the corner of his left eye. "According to Frank, the STB is probably holding your brother somewhere in the vicinity. But he didn't say anything about them actually being inside the castle."

"Yeah, but without accessing your hard-drive we have no idea where to start looking for him. But we do know that whatever is going on with the Codex is directly tied to that castle."

Colonel Skull looked again at the view across the river. Prague Castle was no longer isolated from the threat of enemy civilizations as it had been hundreds of years ago. Today, the bustling capital city of Praha swallowed up the surrounding land right up to the castle walls. *She's right. The city's way to big.*

"One of the books stolen from the library was a link between the Codex and this castle," she said. "I don't know what it is, but there's something in there that's important."

Holy shit, she's right. He was disappointed

in himself. How could he have forgotten already? *God, I must be getting old.* Another one of the books had been about the ossuary in Sedlec. And now that place was ruined, if not totally destroyed. Thinking about everything in that perspective, Colonel Skull started to realize that they might be too late. Or — were they right on time?

"The man that attacked me..." he realized. "This is where he must have headed after fleeing the ossuary. Christ, he might be in there right now."

"That's what I'm saying." Iris returned. "But *why* would he be here?"

"Why would he be here?" Cameron asked himself. "If he found the missing Rules of St. Benedict under the stone angel, then what reason would he have for coming here?"

Iris didn't say anything. She was out of ideas and knew that Colonel Skull wasn't actually asking her. He was simply thinking out loud.

"And what is he planning on doing?" Cameron continued. "I still don't get why he would want those missing pages in the first place. But he's obviously willing to kill for them."

"So, what should we do?"

He looked again at the incredible size of both the castle and the surrounding city. "We've got to find a map." He turned again slightly and raised an eyebrow at her. "*I tried* getting one before we left the truck stop."

"Yeah, you sure did. And you should be thanking me that you're not sitting in jail right now."

His eyebrow lifted even higher. "Thanks."

She wasn't fooled by his sarcasm and let her chin rest slightly on his shoulder. "So where do you think we're going to find a map? It's got to be after midnight."

"After midnight my ass." *It's got to be almost two in the morning.* He reached down and grabbed the wires and the motorcycle fired back up. The headlight came on and he gave the motor a quick rev. "You ready?"

"Yep." She squeezed tighter around his waist.

"Okay then." He picked his feet up from the ground and steered them onto the bridge. It was only about a quarter kilometer long, but even in the middle of the night there were a few other cars crossing the river — and Cameron was impatient. He pulled harder on the accelerator and weaved the bike around a slow-moving European smart-car. He shook his head at the vehicle. *That thing would look bigger on my television than it does in real life.*

Reaching the opposite bank of the river the road veered to the right. It led them around the open courtyard of towns square and into the heart of downtown historic Prague. But before going too far into the city, Cameron circled the bike into another parking lot and again killed the motor.

Fittingly, the name of the building they had just stopped at was HOTEL PRAGUE CASTLE. And at such an early morning hour, it was the only building in sight with interior lights on.

"This is perfect," Cameron said, looking through the front doors of the hotel.

Iris was skeptical. Although she didn't know what plan Colonel Skull had in mind, something inside her was telling her that this was a waste of time.

"We'll get a room," Cameron told her, as once again she fought with the straps of the helmet. "That'll give me some time to reconnect my hard-drive." He stepped off the bike and waited for her before walking towards the lobby. "And we'll kill two birds with one stone. They've probably got tourist guides with maps in there."

Again, she didn't say anything. Although she wasn't as excited about their new plan as Cameron was, she didn't have a better idea.

But Colonel Skull could sense that something was bothering her. "What's wrong?"

She shook her head. "Nothing. I was just thinking... never-mind. Let me just get a few things first." She opened the passenger side saddlebag and pulled out a handful of crumpled up clothes and what looked like a makeup bag. "Okay, I'm ready."

"Good." Cameron walked in front of her through the front door of the hotel where a very young and very attractive woman greeted them at the front desk. "Well hello," he said, leaning an elbow on the counter. "I need a room for tonight."

The young brunette looked him in the eyes, and then looked at Iris standing behind him in her black skirt. "Um... I don't know that I have one available." She had an uncomfortable look on her face as she glanced down at the sign-in sheet on the desk in front of her.

"Oh for God's sake!" Iris pushed Cameron out of the way and set her clothes on the counter. "Look, I know what you're thinking," she said to the young concierge, "but let me tell you right now that you're wrong. We got into town late and we just need a room for a night—maybe two. Alright?"

Before the receptionist could answer, Cameron jumped in. "What? What is she thinking? What are you talking about?"

Iris turned to him and frowned. "It's two o'clock in the morning. You look like some business exec who's told his wife he had to work late, I'm standing here in a wrinkled up black skirt, and we're trying to rent a hotel room. Get it?"

"Oh, she thinks you're a... and I'm trying to..." He turned back to the girl behind the counter. "No, no. You've got this all wrong."

The girl held up a hand and lightly shook her head. "It's not my business. I'm sorry."

"Yeah, but that's not what's..."

She interrupted him. "I've got a standard room with a queen size bed, or one of our executive suits."

He rolled his eyes at the girl then looked at Iris and waved a hand at her. "Oh, for Christ's sake. Whatever."

"The standard room is fine," Iris said to the girl. "You need a credit card?"

"Here." Skull reached quickly for his back pocket. "Use this one." He handed the young woman a specific credit card from the inner pocket of his wallet.

"Thanks, um..." She looked at the name on his card. "Mr. Walker."

"You bet," Cameron answered quickly. "Hey, does the hotel have any maps of the city?"

"There's a brochure catalog next to the elevators." She motioned with her eyes.

"Thanks again."

Iris waited until they were a few steps away before saying anything. "Walker, huh?"

He smiled at her. "Derek Walker actually."

"Uh huh. Okay Derek." She walked next to him until they reached the elevators. Their room was on the third floor, and as they waited for the doors to open, both of them began flipping through the selection of free handouts.

Finally the elevator door chimed open but Cameron didn't move. He was still busy searching through the brochures until Iris offered him a suggestion. "You know these things are free, right?" She began grabbing one after another. "Just take one of each. We can sort through them upstairs."

"Yeah, that's what I was about to do," he lied. He grabbed one of the last few fliers that she hadn't got to yet then stepped into the elevator. The doors slid closed and he began thumbing through some of the pamphlets. "Hey, here we go." He pulled one of the brochures out from the stack. "Check it out. It's a visitor's guide to Prague Castle."

Iris nodded at him but didn't speak until the doors reopened on the third floor. "I got it," she said, stepping off the elevator, "a tourist's map of downtown Prague." She read the title as if she were an official Czech tour-guide. "Everything you need to know about the heart of historic Prague."

"Perfect. Let me see that." He tried to grab it out of her hands, but she was quick to pull away.

"Relax... Jesus. We'll get to it." She pointed at the closed door that they were now standing in front of. "You want to open it, or just stand out here in the hall?"

He swiped his room key through the card reader on the door and flicked on a light switch as he entered. The room was pleasant. Not much larger, but most definitely nicer than any Motel 6. Soft tan colored walls, a mini-fridge built into the desk, and a small television. But nothing caught his attention as much as the swirled abstract pattern laid out on the floor. The carpet was a mixture of bronze and a shade of olive drab green that looked like it was borrowed from the US Armies jungle fatigues.

Iris saw him scrutinizing it. "Yeah, that's some interesting carpet."

He looked up at her with a perplexed look on his face but quickly shook it off. "It's definitely..." he couldn't come up with the right word, so instead he walked over to her and held out his hand. "Let me take a look at that brochure."

She handed it over and Cameron quickly unfolded it across the desk. But immediately stood back up, rubbed his forehead and handed it back to Iris. "What the hell are we supposed to do with that?" he whispered.

She was confused. *What's wrong with it?* But as she looked down at the unfolded pamphlet in front of her she quickly realized that the map inside looked like it was hand drawn by Walt Disney himself. The buildings and streets were all obnoxiously bright colors and extremely off-scale and cartoonish. "Oh... right." She looked back up at him. "Okay, I'll look for a different one. Why don't you start setting up that computer and see if you can find my brother."

Skull was fine with that idea. He set the stolen laptop upside down onto the desk. "Hey, wait a Goddamn minute." He turned around with a very irritated look on his face. "Didn't I see you pulling a laptop case when you got out of the cab? You have a computer. Where is it?"

"It's in the other bag on the motorcycle."

Cameron took an aggressive step towards her. "Then why the fuck did I go through all that shit to steal this one? What kind of crap are you pulling with me?"

She backed away from him until the back of her knees caught the edge of the bed and forced her to take a seat. "Calm down. It's not a *personal* computer. It's protected by not only U.S. advanced encryption standards, but also by DISA."

Colonel Skull couldn't calm himself down right away. But rather than yell back at her, he took a minute to process what she was telling him. *She does work for the government.* And he was very familiar with DISA — the Defense Information Systems Agency. Most of his electronic equipment issued by Nightcorp was monitored by the same group.

"If you so much as *think* about tampering with it," she continued. "We'll have government officials from two different countries up our asses in less than an hour."

He backed up a step.

"Damn it," she said frustrated. "Take a deep breath. You okay now?"

—

"This is a nightmare!"

"It's still not working?"

"No." Cameron somewhat forcefully hit the side of the computer screen with his hand. "Nothing's working. Call the front desk and ask for the wireless password again."

Iris was in the bathroom finally changing out of her clothes. If someone would have asked her yesterday if it was even possible to ride on the back of a motorcycle in a business skirt, her answer would have been, *absolutely not.* But ask her that same question today and she would defy anyone who said otherwise. "I've already called twice," she yelled from behind the bathroom door.

"Well I can't..." It was no use. The damn thing just wasn't going to work. And without internet access, Skull was virtually at a standstill. "My tracking software is useless off-line."

The bathroom door opened. "What? Sorry, I couldn't hear you."

Cameron turned from the computer. *Holy crap!* His jaw dropped.

Her long blonde hair was brushed flat against the side of her face. She wore a dark brown Abercrombie top that clung tight to her breasts over a pair of designer jeans that were frayed and ripped down the front of her legs. "I didn't exactly pack for... well, whatever this is that we're doing."

Wow, she kind of looks like Jessica Simpson. "You look great," he said sincerely.

She brushed the last knot out of her hair then smiled as she walked over to him. "So now what do we do?"

Oh man, she even smells good. One compliment was enough for right now though. He was still having a hard time getting over her attitude towards him earlier. "Looks like we're doing this the old-fashioned way." He opened the visitors map one more time and spread it across the bed. "I took a look at this while you were rinsing off." He touched a finger to the map at the position of their hotel. "I think our best bet is going to be to head north and try and enter the castle through the back."

"Oh look," she said, making a joke out of it. "We're gonna go right by a McDonald's. Can we stop and get an ice-cream?"

He swatted her hand away from the paper. "Hey, this is the only map they've got alright." He shook his head, but inside, he too was secretly laughing at how ridiculous it was. "ANYWAYS, It looks like if we head north on Pod Bruskou we'll be able to cut across to the castle just before this fork in the road."

She leaned over and looked at what he

was pointing at. "What makes you think that's the best way in?"

"We've got another one of these stupid maps somewhere that shows the castle in a little more detail. There's an area to the east called, "The Golden Lane," that looks like it might not be too heavily guarded."

Her voice softened a bit. "Cameron. What if that guy's not even in there? This could all be a waste of time."

He put his other hand on the bed and leaned forward. "I don't think so. Even if *he's* not there, *something* is." Still leaning on his arms, he turned his head towards her. "There's something about Prague Castle that ties it to the Codex."

"Yeah, King Rudolph."

"There's more to it than that. I'm sure of it. If it was that simple, why steal the book from the Swedish library? Something must have happened while the Codex was there. Or maybe Rudolph discovered something." He inhaled a quick breath. "I don't know. But either way, whatever's in there... it might help us figure out why he's killing people."

27

Kendall sat next to her uncle Frank on the sofa as they ate chicken tacos in front of the TV. She pouted a bit when he turned off her cartoons for the evening news, but quickly got distracted when a spray of ketchup shot out the back of her taco and onto the floor.

Immediately she looked up at her uncle. His attention was still on the television so she slid her butt to the edge of the sofa and tried to covertly wipe up the mess with the bottom of her shoe. Unfortunately, her cleanup tactics were much less concealed then she had hoped.

"What are you doing?" Frank wiped a napkin across his mouth and turned to her. "Ohh, Kendall. What happened?" He pushed his tray table away from his lap and started to get up from his seat.

"I'm sorry, uncle Frank."

"Ugh! I told you to be careful." He walked into the kitchen to grab a towel. "Damn it," he mumbled, "ketchup of all things. Who puts ketchup on chicken tacos?" He pulled a dish towel off the handle of the oven and was about to head back into the living room when he stopped walking and listened carefully to the voices coming out of the TV.

"So far the Vatican has denied all accusations about the boy's death," one of the reporters announced. "But we've just been informed that they plan to give an official statement once the family has been properly notified."

"I'm sorry Uncle Frank," Kendall said again when she saw him standing in the kitchen.

He went back into the living room and started mopping up her mess. "It's okay, honey." He winked at her. "We won't tell your dad about this."

She smiled.

The news story that followed was much less interesting. Another group of students at the University of Oregon were protesting the new controversial immigration law in Arizona. "Let's go live to Alex King for an update."

"Oy vey!" *If they'd just come here legally, they wouldn't have to worry about it,* Frank thought as he finished wiping up the last of the ketchup.

"Students and faculty are gathering here tonight in preparation of..."

"Sorry Alex. We have to interrupt you." The television cameras switched views back to the news anchor behind his desk. "More breaking news from the Vatican. It seems that the archpriest of St. Peter's Basilica has also gone missing. So far Vatican City police have been unwilling to comment about the possibility of a second homicide. However, we've been able to determine that the body found earlier of Sacristan Henry De Luca is also connected to the Basilica."

Again, Frank stood motionless for a moment in front of the television as he listened to the evening news team.

"Uncle Frank."

He turned to Kendall and held a finger to his lips. "Hang on a second. Uncle Frank wants to hear what they're saying."

"Father Canale was last seen entering the necropolis earlier tonight, but sources tell us that he..."

"But I can't see the TV," she whined.

"KENDALL. Be quiet for a moment."

"Stay tuned to channel 5 for all the latest updates in what's now being referred to as, *Sin in the Holy land.*"

"Cristo. What's going on with this world?" he muttered, as he sat back on the couch and looked at his plate of half eaten tacos. Now that his stomach had taken a break to digest his food, he found himself not very hungry anymore. "Are you done eating?" he asked Kendall.

She didn't speak but shook her head up and down.

"There's more if you're still hungry," he

assured her.

"I'm full."

"Okay." He got back up and took her plate, along with his, into the kitchen and dropped them in the sink. As he turned on the water to rinse them off, he called to her in the other room. "Why don't you go put your PJ's on. Then you can come down and watch a movie before bedtime."

"Can we watch Toy Story?"

"Sure, if that's what you want." He finished up the dishes and dried his hands on another towel. "I'll get it all set up for you down here, okay. But I've got some work to do upstairs in your dad's office."

She was disappointed that her uncle wasn't going to watch the movie with her, but ran up to her room to get changed anyhow. Frank threw the towel onto the counter and grabbed his laptop and the bible off the coffee table before following her up the steps.

Along with a comfortable work station, Colonel Skull also kept a relatively extensive library in two redwood bookshelves on opposite sides of the aquarium. And most importantly, from behind Cameron's desk upstairs, Frank could still look down over the railing and keep an eye on Kendall as he worked.

He set down his computer and plugged it into a nearby wall outlet before getting himself situated in the leather chair. The laptop quickly restored his last browsing session and he scrolled back to the chart of King Rudolph that he had begun to study earlier. Again, he looked at the signature on the bottom of the horoscope—Nostradamus.

That's interesting.

He opened a new window and began a separate search for the predictions of the famed French prophet. Specifically any that could relate him to Rudolph or the Czech Republic. Unfortunately, ten minutes or so of research only produced information regarding the horoscope that he had already looked at.

Quickly growing discouraged, he backtracked through the web pages and was about to exit the program when something else caught his eye. A single compound word listed under the category of "prophesies fulfilled."

Anti-Christs.

"It's plural," he whispered to himself.

Kendall came scampering out of her room in her light purple pajamas holding a Buzz Lightyear doll. "Kay. I'm ready to watch the movie, Uncle Frank."

He inhaled quickly, leaned back in the chair, and spun around to face her. "Come give your uncle a kiss first."

She giggled, then ran up to him and kissed him on the cheek.

"Okay, *now* you can go watch your movie. It's all ready to go. Just hit the play button."

She took off down the stairs and Frank turned back to the computer. *Why is it plural?* He scrolled through the list of websites and began selecting them in no particular order. And this time it was much easier to determine their implications.

Michel Nostradame predicted that the world would see three antichrists — not one. And today's modern world agreed that according to his predictions the first antichrist was the French military leader Napoleon Bonaparte. The second, also accepted as truth, was Adolf Hitler.

Yeah, there's a surprise!

But it was the third and final antichrist warned of in the prophesies that was slightly more disturbing and difficult to decipher. After reading through multiple interpretations of the predictions Frank decided to abandon contemporary research for nostalgic.

He rolled the leather chair over to the wall and leaned his elbows on his knees as he began to rifle through the selection of books in Cameron's library. There was everything from a 1930 print of F. Scott Fitzgerald's "The Great Gatsby," to a field manual titled, "Special operations warrior: SAS survival techniques for hostile environment." After a few more minutes of searching he came to another book titled, "Les Propheties."

"Here we go."

He pulled the book from the shelf then looked back at the computer screen to remind himself what exactly he was looking for. "Century II and Century VI." He began flipping through pages. "Quatrain...?" He looked back over at the computer screen.

Fairly quickly he was able to find the correct passages that many believed described the coming of the third antichrist. Unfortunately however, they made absolutely no sense to him. "Fuck me. You'd have to be a fucking *savant* to understand any of this."

He put a hand over his mouth. Fortunately, Kendall had the downstairs TV up loud enough that she couldn't hear her uncle swear.

He glanced again briefly at the English translation of the French prophesies. No use. He didn't understand any of it. But he did find it chilling that there were now *two* sources pointing to an antichrist—father Matousek, and of all people, Nostradamus.

"UNCLE FRANK," Kendall yelled from downstairs.

He rolled himself back over to the desk and leaned forward to look over the edge of the loft. "What is it honey? You okay?"

She leaned the back of her head against the cushion of the couch and looked up at him. "Your phone is beeping."

"Oh. okay, thank you." He felt the outside

of his pocket. Sure enough, he had mistakenly left his cell sitting on the coffee table downstairs. "Kendall," he called again. "Do you want to bring it up to me?"

Her answer was too quiet for him to hear but she hopped off the couch, grabbed his phone and hurried up the steps. "Here you go," she said happily. "Is it my dad? Can I talk to him?"

He looked at the display on the phone. "Sorry, honey. It's a text message."

Her smile drooped. "Oh."

Frank felt terrible for her disappointment. "We'll call him in a little bit, alright," he promised. "Why don't you go finish up your movie?"

"Okay." She slowly turned and walked back downstairs.

Although still feeling guilty, Frank looked again at his cell. Maybe it wasn't a phone call, but *it was* her father who sent the text—and now he sort of felt like he had just lied to her.

He took another deep breath before reading the message—NEED CONFIRMATION: # MISSING PAGES. 8? RULES OF ST BENEDICT?

28

A small bistro sat on the bottom floor of a four-story building. Architecturally the restaurant was nearly identical to the rest of downtown Prague — sharp 90-degree angles on sand colored walls, topped by a red tile roof. But Colonel Skull had noted its location and rather convenient attributes before leaving their hotel.

Just before Pod Bruskou made a sharp left-hand turn he pulled the motorcycle into the buildings small parking lot and shut down the motor. Iris quickly undid the strap on her helmet again and swung a leg over the seat to get off the bike. "You think it's a good idea to leave it parked here?" she asked him quietly.

"It should be fine." He kept his voice to a whisper as well. "I just wish there was a way to get it closer."

She looked up at the castle sitting on top of the hill in front of them. Although it was now much larger in appearance then it had been from the hotel, the castle was still nearly a quarter kilometer away. But it was the long stretch of castle stairs just south of the restaurant that made Cameron choose this route.

The old castle steps provided a direct and unobstructed ascent all the way from street level to the east entrance of Prague Castle. However, seeing the steps in person gave a much different perspective then the cartoon map they had looked at earlier.

In the middle of the night the castle stairs were bleak and eerie—almost creating the feeling that they were slowly approaching Castle Dracula instead of Castle Prague. Each step was much larger than reasonably necessary and framed by two massive stone walls at least ten feet tall. And the bittersweet hue gleaming out of the bronze wall sconces added dramatically to its chilling appearance.

"Fortunately, I don't think these stairs are off limits, even in the middle of the night," Cameron whispered as they began their climb.

Iris looked up at the giant wall to her left. "I hope not. If they are, we're in trouble. There's no way to get out." She looked over at him walking next to her. "I feel like a rat in one of those maze experiments."

Aside from there being virtually no turns, Cameron thought her description was pretty appropriate. It did feel a bit like they were trapped in some perilous labyrinth. And as they drew even closer to the outer edge of the castle, two giant towers began to rise above them on the horizon.

"The one on the left must be Black Tower," Cameron told her as they approached the top of the stairs. "I can't remember the name of the other one though. But I think I saw a poster of it hanging in the hotel lobby."

"Well it looks like a guard tower."

Skull stopped walking and pulled Iris by the sleeve until their backs were against the wall. "You got the map with you?" He looked down at her pocket and held out his hand. "Let me see it."

She handed it over and he unfolded it against the stone surface behind him. The tower in question had a small green circle drawn on it with the number 16 written inside. He flipped the map over and on the back was a legend that gave a description of each asterisk.

"Here it is." He paused and looked briefly up at the tower again. "Okay, that's Daliborka." He looked back to the map. "Shit! It's a gun tower slash prison from the 15th century."

"Yeah, but it..."

"Ssh." He handed the open map back to her and poked his head around the edge of the wall. There was a smaller brick building off to the right that separated them from the entrance to the Golden Lane.

Colonel Skull studied the area closely. A few dark clouds were beginning to close over the already dark night, but positioned at the base of Black Tower he was still able to see a young man wearing a light blue military style service uniform. The officer stood motionless with his back to the wall, almost looking half asleep. But it was the second guard who slowly emerged from around the far wall of the small building in front of him that made Cameron shaky.

That's no service uniform he's wearing.

The man walking slowly through the darkness in front of them was dressed in green combat style fatigues with a matching dark green beret. He held what looked to be a small assault weapon against his chest, and from the occasional reflection of light that bounced off the top of it, Colonel Skull guessed it was probably an attack knife model of the armies Skorpion sub-machine gun.

"Oh fuck," he whispered, and leaned the back of his head against the wall.

"What's wrong?"

Cameron rubbed his forehead. "There are two guards over there. But one of them is a foot patrol." He turned to her. "And he's wearing battle dress."

"A dress?" she asked confused.

"Not a woman's dress." He pointed to her legs. "Battle dress. It's just another word for uniform." He put his head back against the wall. "Damn it! Why the hell would they have heightened defenses right now?"

"Are you kidding?" She held out her arms, "because of everything that's going on."

Her voice was much too loud and she put a hand quickly over her lips when Cameron gave her a ferocious look. "Everything that's going on," she repeated, much quieter this time.

"But why would the President of the Republic suspect that the castle is in jeopardy?"

"They know just as much about the missing books as we do. Why wouldn't they suspect it?"

His eyes opened wide. "They know about the missing books? I was told no one outside Nightcorp and the Swedish Parliament knew about them." *Oh, and Father Matousek.* "It was supposed to be classified until I finished my investigation."

"Well it wasn't," she assured him. "I was scheduled to meet with the Czech Ambassador last night to review the libraries security tapes."

"Well that's just great. When the hell was someone going to tell me?"

"I thought you knew."

Son-of-a-bitch, he thought, although he wasn't as angry with Iris as he was with Kestner. "Alright." He took a deep breath and peered around the corner again. "We're going to have to watch for a few minutes so I can study his patrol. Maybe I can map out some sort of behavioral pattern."

Unlike the castle guard posted at the foot of Black Tower like a mannequin, this officer was very alert. His disposition reminded

Colonel Skull of one of the MP's back at Fort Benning. Keeping a steady pace, the soldier marched away from the lights of the castle and slowly disappeared into the darkness of the southern gardens.

Cameron gently pushed Iris by the shoulder.

"What the hell are you doing?" she asked annoyed.

"Get out of the light," he whispered. "Wait here. I'll be right back."

Without hesitation she grabbed his coat sleeve and pulled hard on it. "You're leaving me? Where are you going?"

"We'll never get past that guy without him seeing us." She was still holding onto his sleeve and Cameron put his hand on top of hers. "I'll be right back," he promised again.

Her eyes began to water. Skull didn't need to explain himself any further. The solemn tone in his voice projected his intentions very clearly. "Cameron don't," she pleaded. "Let's just forget it. We can go back to the hotel and figure something else out."

The orange glow from the lamps on the wall reflected off both their eyes. "I'm not going to hurt him," he assured her. "I promise. But I've got to go." He leaned in and kissed her on the forehead. Despite their rough beginnings and considering the current circumstances, the gesture wasn't nearly as awkward as he might have suspected it would be. "Just stay right here and I'll be back in a few minutes." He gently removed her hand from his sleeve and turned back towards the castle.

Slowly he crept back towards the end of the wall, and in his best James Kestner voice, he quietly mocked the audio recording from earlier. "Just investigate the cemetery, Cameron. You'll be back home in a couple days, Cameron." He blew out a frustrated breath of air. "Yeah, right."

As expected, the young guard in the light blue uniform was still standing by the tower, but by now the second soldier had completely disappeared into Na Valech Garden.

Cameron took one final glance at Black Tower before quickly ducking out of the stairway and pinning himself against the backside of a mature weeping willow tree. In the middle of the night the castle garden was nearly black, and after another deep breath he stretched his neck to look around the side of the large tree trunk.

There was still no sign of the armed guard anywhere so he searched quickly for another vantage point. There was another large willow about twenty feet in front of him and he made a quick decision to attempt reaching it. Crouching over, Skull took the first step away from his cover when suddenly his worst fear became a reality.

Never in his career, even as a rookie had

he been so careless. The notorious sound of Fransesco Ferrari's custom ring-tone — "Beep Beep Beeeeeep Beep – Beep Beep Beeeeeep Beep," Morse code for "FF" blared out from his hip pocket.

His heart stopped. And as much as he wanted to duck back behind the tree next to him, he couldn't coax his legs into moving.

The beeping continued. Finally, his heart thumped frantically against the inside of his chest and he reached down and squeezed a hand tightly around the outside of his pocket around the phone.

Shut up. Shit! PLEASE SHUT UP.

Surprisingly the soldier didn't yell out, but a flashlight clicked on and pointed abruptly in his direction, followed by the soft sound of footsteps crossing over the damp grass.

Cameron looked up from his pocket. The beam of light from the guard's flashlight was scanning over the eastern part of the garden. But fortunately it was still a good thirty yards out. Instinct told him to hide back behind the tree, but logic told him otherwise. Without question, the soldier would find him there.

He spun himself around and ran back towards the castle stairs. Iris was leaning in the shadows against the wall. "Come on," he ordered in a loud whisper.

"What happened?" she asked.

"Never mind. We've gotta get the hell out

of here. Now!" This time it was him who grabbed her by the sleeve and pulled her behind him as he hurried down the steps.

"Ne dalsi krok." The soldier's voice was stern, and just loud enough for them to hear.

Fuck! Colonel Skull put an arm out in front of Iris' chest and stopped her from running. He turned his head towards her and gave her a look that said, *"Just do as I do."* He put his hands on top of his head and Iris copied him.

"What are we going to do?" she asked frightened.

Cameron kept his eyes straight ahead. "Ssshh. Let me do the talking."

"How are you going to do that? You think he speaks English?"

He suddenly felt like he could pass out. She was right. The chances of this guy speaking English were slim. *This is bad.*

The soldier's boots scuffing off the stone steps were getting louder behind them. At any second Cameron expected to feel the barrel of the man's gun pressed against his back. Or worse — the tip of the bayonet affixed to it.

Craaap! Cameron's eyes opened wide. *What the hell is she doing?*

"Prominte dustojnik," she called out.

The soldier didn't respond, but his footsteps continued to get louder and the light of his flashlight brighter.

"Officer, we need your help," Iris lied in

Czech.

"What are you doing?" Cameron asked with his teeth locked together.

Before she could answer him, the soldier interrupted. He yelled out an order that Skull couldn't understand.

"I don't speak..."

The man shoved the back of Cameron's shoulder and repeated the command.

"I don't know what the hell you're saying!"

Iris looked at Cameron and spoke quietly. "He wants you to put your hands behind your back."

Damn it! "Distract him," he whispered.

"What?"

"Distract him. Say something. Anything."

"Um, uh..." She looked back at the man holding the gun then again at Colonel Skull. "Like what? What do you want me to tell him?"

That was good enough. The officer's attention turned to Iris and Cameron quickly spun himself out of his line of fire. With his left hand he caught the man's wrist and pulled his arm straight. Then, still holding his wrist, Cameron's other hand struck hard against the man's elbow, nearly collapsing it. The lightweight machine gun dropped from his hand and Skull quickly threw himself around to the man's back and wrapped an arm tightly around his neck.

He struggled and gasped as Cameron slowly squeezed the air out of him. Seconds later his body went limp and Cameron gently laid him down.

Iris looked like she was about to be sick. "Is he..."

"He'll be fine. But we've got to go. Someone might have heard him yelling at us." Cameron remained crouched and signaled Iris to follow him back up the steps. Although things had just played out differently than he had planned, the same outcome was reached. The military soldier was incapacitated. *Good enough.*

Again they reached the top step and again Cameron poked his head around the corner of the large wall. He looked immediately at the base of Black Tower for the other castle guard.

He was gone.

29

Frank tried again to reach Colonel Skull, but again it went to voice-mail. "Cameron, call me back ASAP. I checked out your missing pages." He paused for a second. "I don't think they've got anything to do with St. Benedict. I think... just call me as soon as you can." He hung up the phone and looked down at the open page of Cameron's book — Encyclopedia Britannica – volume A.

But I'm not sure that's it either, he thought to himself.

Kendall's movie had just finished up, but it was only a few minutes after seven and not quite her bedtime, so Frank let her stay downstairs and play as long as she was quiet. He snuck a quick peek at her over the railing before turning his attention back to the book and his computer.

His next inquiry, although also beginning with the letter A, couldn't be researched in the encyclopedia. Cameron's Britannica set must have been either a hand-me-down or bought at some neighborhood garage sale. The books were frayed and worn, and inside the front cover was the publishing date — 1963 edition.

Frank typed a name into the search bar and waited patiently for the results. "Anton LaVey," he said under his breath. "Born Howard Stanton Levey." Frank touched the screen with his finger as he read. As it turned out, Levey didn't appear to be much more than a failed musician who occasionally fiddled with amateur photography. *Yeah! And a wacko*, Frank thought. Yet all of his senses began tingling. Deep down he could feel that he was at least on the right track.

If it wasn't the written Rule of St. Benedict that once occupied the inside of the Devil's Bible, then what was it? The thought hadn't troubled him for very long. Two of Frank's unsurpassed skills were his ability to think quickly and his expertise in unconventional investigations. Although his modesty could sometimes be his own repression.

He read down the page a little further before picking up his cell and hoping that somehow he'd developed a new psychic sense, and any second now Cameron was going to call him back. But it didn't happen. The phone remained silent. "Merda," he cursed to himself in Italian.

I hope everything's alright over there.

He took another peek at Kendall downstairs. She was still playing happily on the carpet by the sofa — with what, he had no idea. He cracked a smile and checked the time on his watch to make sure he hadn't lost track of her bedtime. *Oh shoot, if she's not sleepy I guess I can let her stay up a bit late tonight.* "You doing okay down there?" he called over the back of Cameron's desk.

She stopped what she was doing and looked up at him. "Yeesss." Her voice carried disappointment and a slight hint of distress. "Do I have to go to bed now?"

He shook his head. "No. You can stay up for a while tonight if you want."

The previously frightened look on her face turned to a big smile that formed little dimples on her rosy cheeks.

Frank leaned back in the chair and looked at his phone one more time. *Forget it. I'm calling him again.* He hit send and the cell redialed Cameron's number. (Ring!) *Come on Cameron.* (Ring!) *Pick up the phone.* (Ring!) *What are you...*

"Frank," a voice answered softly.

Frank shot forward in the chair and plugged one ear with his finger. "Colonel Skull, is that you?"

"Listen Frank, I'm in some shit over here."

More than you know, I'm afraid. "Talk to me, Colonel. What's going on?"

"I'm outside the castle right now with Iris. But I had to take out a guard and leave his body detectable."

"You know the drill Colonel." Frank said quickly. "Evacuate to a non-hostile location and set up counter-surveillance."

"Christ Frank, I've already done that. I need you to try and pull up my location though. It looks like I'm in a wooded area somewhere below..."

Cameron continued to give details of his surroundings while Frank quickly opened Google Earth on his laptop. Although Nightcorp had their own private satellite surveillance, their funds couldn't compete with the billions of dollars that Google invested each year for public use. "Alright, I've got you on two different systems." Frank told him. "You're in an area called Stag Moat, just north of Daliborka. Is your position secure?"

"For a few minutes, I think. Got a lot of Vipers."

Cameron hadn't used the word "Vipers" in its literal form. The term was a generic expression used by Nightcorp to classify any stealth moving predatory enemies at night. "Just make sure you keep eyes behind you. It looks like the castle grounds stretch beyond that moat."

"I've got Iris watching the north."

"You should be okay right now then. I've got to talk to you for a minute about the missing pages."

"Go ahead."

"Well," Frank started. "You were right about the number of pages. It seems that there are either seven or eight missing. But everything else is wrong. The missing pages *do not* contain the written Rule of St. Benedict."

"You don't think so? But that would make sense," Skull argued. "Everything *I* found suggested they did. And that could explain why the white monks in Sedlec tore them out."

"NO," he insisted. "Trust me Colonel, I checked. The Rule of St. Benedict is a short text. Even if it was in there, it would have only taken up two or three pages at best. Something else is missing from that book."

Cameron answered—but it was directed at Iris, not Frank. "What? Did you hear something?"

"Colonel," Frank called.

"Hang on a sec, Frank," Cameron whispered.

The voices were faint, but Frank could just make out what they were saying. "I saw a light on top of that hill," Iris said.

"Could just be a patrol," Skull answered. "Keep low."

Things were silent for another minute before Cameron came back on the line. "Okay, Frank. So what do you think was on those pages then?"

"I'm not positive," he admitted. "But

think about it. The Codex Gigas was supposedly scribed by a monk who sold his soul to the devil. The legend says that it was Satan himself who possessed the monk — and therefore, it was Satan himself who *wrote* the book."

"Get to the point Frank."

"Colonel, why would the devil transcribe the Bible? The Word of *GOD!* Are you aware that nowhere in the world is there an actual document containing the Word of Satan? Or, more importantly, the *un-interpreted* Words of Satan."

"Frank, are you telling me you're buying into all this superstition?"

"*WE...* don't have to believe it. It doesn't matter. The point is — *someone* does."

"What about the Satanic Bible?" Cameron asked argumentatively. "There's a bunch of weird cults out there. What are *they* worshiping then?"

Frank shook his head to himself. "They're all garbage — a bunch of nonsense. Above-ground Satanism was developed by a man named Anton LaVey in 1966. These "so-called" Satanist's, the Satanic Bible, the Church of Satan, all of it is based off of opinion and interpretation. It's crap! The only doctrine they have that even comes close to historical fact is a book called the Al Jilwah."

"Never heard of it."

"Of course not, you're not a Satanist. But

these people believe that the Al Jilwah, and something else called the Qu'ret Al Yezidi doctrines, are the original teachings of Satan. It's what they base their whole religion off of. But here's the problem. The Al Jilwah was supposedly *dictated* by Satan, not written, to an Arab prophet named Sheik Adi in the 12th century. But even the Muslims admit that the documents have been altered."

Cameron's voice was confused. "So, you think the missing pages... what... contain the Book of Lucifer?"

Again, Frank shook his head aggressively. "*Lucifer* is also wrong. The name Lucifer is Latin. The bible was originally written in Hebrew."

"God damn it, Frank. *Fine!* The Book of Satan then?"

"No," he answered. "I don't think that Satan meant for his words to be... um... teachings. I think they're instructions."

"What's the difference?"

"Teachings would be meant for the whole world to follow. Instructions, I think in this case anyhow, were meant for one person."

"What makes you think that?"

"Because they were hidden inside a bible. You know that old saying—sometimes the best place to hide something is in plain sight. It's true. Think about it. Why a bible? Why not keep it simple and just have the monk transcribe a few pages?"

"Okay, I guess I'm following you so far. One wouldn't expect to find the Devil's writing inside a holy bible."

"Right. And an *enormous* bible on top of that! Why? Because no one is going to actually read a bible that size and that elaborate. Not word for word at least. They're just going to stare and marvel at it. It was the perfect place to hide them."

"Let's say you're right, Frank. Then what are the instructions to?"

"Not, *to*. The question is, *who*?"

"Huh?"

"Cameron, hear me out before you argue, okay." He waited for Colonel Skull to grunt in agreement before continuing. "Father Matousek wasn't the only one who thought we could be dealing with the antichrist."

"Come on, Frank. Give me a break alright. I don't have time for this. I've got to get going. My location's going to be compromised soon."

"Colonel," Frank said in a hard voice. "Believe whatever you want. But I think what you're looking for, the missing pages, are Satan's written instructions for the antichrist during the final hours." He paused again. "During..., the apocalypse."

—

The natural ravine of Deer Moat funneled

a harsh breeze through the castle grounds as it sliced its way between Daliborka Tower and the southern edge of the Royal Garden. Suddenly the night air became noticeably chilly and Cameron tugged gently on the zipper of his coat with his free hand.

The Devil's instructions to the antichrist? Could it be? Skulls mind slipped into a realm of confusion and disbelief. *The antichrists instructions on what to do during, and how to carry out the apocalypse?*

Colonel Skull didn't blink. "Terrible," he muttered, his mind replaying Iris' translation of the man from the books conjurations.

"What?" Frank asked.

"Nothing, I was just... forget it." His muscles became soft and the phone dropped a few inches from his ear. *But why would the white monks have buried them beneath the garden angel?* "Frank," he said softly, bringing the phone back up.

"Yes, Colonel?"

He swallowed hard. "Something was found in the cemetery in Sedlec. I thought it was... you know, the Rules of St. Benedict, but..."

"Maybe it was," Frank interrupted. "Who knows? Maybe they were in there too. But unfortunately, Sir, I think what you're really after is somewhere inside that castle."

"Along with the man that attacked me."

"Yes," Frank confirmed softly.

"Remember when I told you about King Rudolph's strange behaviors and obsessions?"

"Uh huh."

"Well," he continued. "I think it was Rudolph who removed the pages, not the monks in Kutna Hora. The man was paranoid, superstitious. If I'm right about the instructions... if he did find them... they would have probably scared him to death. I think he's the one who tore them out, maybe even destroyed them. Either way, someone out there is killing people to find out."

Cameron felt his breathing speed up and he turned his head to look at Iris—but she was gone.

"Iris!" His cry was a loud whisper at best. "IRIS," he called again louder.

"Colonel, what's wrong?"

"Frank. Iris is gone." He snapped his head quickly back and forth in all directions. "She was just here a minute ago."

"Cameron, slow down."

Skulls eyebrows went cross. "Sorry, Frank. I'll call you back later when I get a chance."

"Cameron, wait a..."

Too late. Skull shut off the phone and dropped it back into his coat pocket.

Ahhh... "Shit!"

Down in the bottom of the dry moat, and about a hundred yards to the west, Cameron caught a glimpse of the faint glow of two flashlights as they faded deep into the castle grounds.

30

Archpriest Canale closed the door to the small restroom for the third time since the flight had taken off. He leaned his head to one side in order to accommodate the curvature of the ceiling and turned on the water in the miniature stainless steel sink. Giving it a minute to heat up, he untucked his shirt and carefully peeled away the makeshift toilet paper bandage from the open wound on his side.

The man's knife had pierced through his lower right side about three inches above his belt-line. But luckily, his pain was slowly subsiding, not worsening, and there was no indication of dizziness or shock. And more importantly, there was no trace of blood during his last urination. Miraculously, the puncture seemed to miss any vital organs.

But as with any open wound, the risk of infection was high. He tossed the blood-stained bandage into the toilet and dampened a newly folded piece of paper to begin cleaning the injury.

His body flinched as the wet towel

touched down onto his bare flesh and beads of warm water began dripping down his side and soaking their way through the top of his pants. Clenching his jaw together, he continued to pat the damp piece of paper a few more times against his side until he was disrupted by the plane's intercom.

"Ladies and gentleman," the pilot announced theatrically from the cockpit. "Smart Wings flight 119, Rome to Prague, will begin making its descent shortly. Would all passengers kindly take your seats and fasten your safety belts."

Andrea looked at himself quickly in the mirror above the sink. *I still don't know how I'm going to get to Sedlec?*

The pilot's voice continued to sing out of the speaker. "Current local time is 2:33 AM, and we're looking at an outside temperature of about 14 degrees Celsius, 57 degrees Fahrenheit."

Still looking at himself, Father Canale reached up with his free hand, pulled the white collar out of his shirt, and stuffed it into his hip pocket. It had nothing to do with him trying to conceal his affiliation with the church, he just needed to free up his airway a bit.

Taking a final inspection of his side, he carefully tucked his shirt back in, gave himself a fake smile in the fingerprint smudged mirror, then walked out of the restroom. Halfway down the narrow aisle in front of him, a young brunette flight attendant, dolled up with heavy coats of mascara and cheap perfume, was pushing a thin cart in front of her collecting trash from the other passengers. Unluckily, his seat was two rows behind her and a look of awkwardness fell over his face.

"Excuse me, Sir," the stewardess said politely to an older gentleman sitting in the seat next to her.

The man looked up from his lap. "Oh, here you go." He tossed an empty plastic cup into the bag hanging off her cart.

She smiled again at him and pointed down the aisle at Father Canale. "Would you mind…?"

An eyebrow rose on the man's forehead and he twisted himself around to see what she had pointed at. "Oh, I'm sorry." He apologized as though Andrea's showdown with the food cart was somehow his fault. Then he quickly unbuckled himself from the seat and pressed himself tightly against the back of the chair in front of him, leaving just enough room for Father Canale to squeeze in beside him and let the woman pass by.

"Thank you, Signore."

"No problem. Your welcome, Father."

Making it back to his seat, Andrea situated himself back down and fastened the strap across his lap. A few bumps and shakes of minor turbulence spoiled a smooth decent, but soon he could hear the roar as the four massive Rolls Royce jet engines growled in frustration as the pilot tamed them for landing. Seconds later, the miniature city of Prague grew to its full scale and the large rubber tires touched down for the first time.

"Ladies and Gentleman." This voice was different.

Must be the co-pilot, Andrea thought.

"Welcome to Prague. Please remain seated for just a few more moments until the plane has finished taxiing and the pilot turns off the fasten seatbelt sign. We hope you have enjoyed your flight, and have a wonderful stay here in the Czech Republic."

Ignoring his request, many of the passengers on board began to rise and remove their bags from the overhead compartments. Archpriest Canale did not follow their lead. He remained seated as asked until the plane stopped and the small red light above his seat switched off. *His* luggage was still sitting somewhere in Rome.

Once allowing some of the more impatient passengers to push up to the exits, Andrea stepped slowly behind them and out onto the short sky bridge leading to the terminals.

Now inside the airport, Archpriest Canale headed past a charming restaurant with a nice view of the airport tarmac, then past the central police headquarters which he thought about stopping at for a moment. But instead he continued on, past piers A and B and the special accommodations agency until he reached a door that lead out to short term parking.

"Taxi," he yelled as he began to run towards a cab with an arm outstretched above his head.

Unfortunately the driver didn't hear him and pulled away from the curb with such urgency that it made Andrea jerk back in trepidation. But as quickly as it sped away, another pulled up on the opposite side of Aviaticka St.

Father Canale carefully calculated the timing of traffic before stepping from the curb and hailing the cabby with another hand above his head. He opened the rear door behind the driver and sat down into the rank stench of the man's brick of fried cheese that he was so indelicately shoving into his face. "Can you please take me to the nearest catholic church?"

The unshaven driver looked at him through the rearview mirror. A glob of pale-yellow Edam cheese stuck to the bottom left corner of his mouth, and he pointed a finger at the meter on his dashboard.

"Oh, yes, of course." Andrea wasn't sure why the driver had just made a point of showing him the meter. *I'm aware that this isn't a free ride.* "Any church will do." He paused a moment and tried to remember how to say "thank you" in Czech. "Dee, umm..., Dekuji," he said doubtfully.

"OK!" And without taking his eyes off Andrea, the cabby threw the transmission into drive and punched his foot down on the accelerator. Another car sounded its horn as the taxi confiscated its lane without warning.

"Would you mind slowing...?"

The cab driver shook a fist out the window and yelled a number of vulgarities at the other man.

"I don't mean to be..."

Again the driver ignored him and focused solely on being the first vehicle out of the airport. But not soon enough, the car found its way onto Evropska and finally calmed to a comfortable 60 or 70 kph. The driver, no longer angry with the world, began rattling off all points of interest along the road, clearly very proud of his native country. "Dis way." He pointed a finger north of the highway. "Dis my home as boy."

Canale feigned a grin at him before looking back through the windshield, anxiously anticipating a church on the horizon. *Any church*, he prayed.

At long last, the driver merged off the road and a much welcome shape appeared in Andreas' view. A cross. A magnificent cross in company with a sign which read, CHURCH OF

OUR LADY BEFORE TYN.

But something else also caught his attention—the lights of a giant castle glowing brightly over Vltava River a few miles off in the distance.

31

Colonel Skull took shelter under the exterior overhang of St George Monastery as the night sky began unleashing a percussion of stinging pellets of frozen water. But with a surface temperature still a few degrees above freezing, each tiny ice rock that narrowly missed his head quickly turned the previously packed earth into a mud filled wetland.

The two flashlights that he'd attempted to track only moments ago were now long since disappeared into the darkness. And without giving away his position, there was little he could do about changing that.

Keeping a low profile with his back pressed against the cold stone, he crept his way further along the outer wall towards the front entrance of the castle. God how he wished there was a way to scale the wall and drop inside somewhere between guard posts. Maybe shoot a grappling hook from his belt like Batman, then push a button on his belt-buckle and zip himself right over. But then again, if it were that simple, he didn't suspect that castles would be a major part of history right now. Still—it was a nice thought.

With one hand held as a shield above his head, he felt along the outside of his pockets with the other, taking an overdue inventory of his effects. Unfortunately, he had nothing that could be of great value at the moment. Save his most valuable asset of all—training and experience. In fact, according to one of his old unit commanders, survival could only be obtained by those with the will to obtain it. The commander spoke about it as if it were a piece of fine art. "You can't rely on anything but yourself," he would tell his men. "Any equipment or aid *can*, and *MUST*, be considered a bonus. No equipment does NOT equal unequipped."

Pulling the collar of his coat higher up the back of his neck, Colonel Skull crouched himself over and moved away from the inadequate protection of the tiny overhang above him. He guessed it to be a hundred yards or so before he would reach the main entrance, and with the sudden onslaught of hail, he also guessed that the majority of castle guards would be seeking shelter of their own. As unpleasant, and unusual as it seemed, the abrupt change in weather could prove to be a blessing.

This theory proved accurate as Skull approached a recess in the castle's fortifications. The outer wall cornered inward 10 feet or so and stretched nearly double that until it reached the cylindrical base of another tower. But it was through one of the towers narrow archer windows at its peak that he could faintly see the outline of a man in uniform turn away to escape the recent mixture of rain and hail.

Excellent.

Keeping himself hunched over he ran quickly to the base of the circular wall and hugged its perimeter until reaching the far side. Now one last stretch of straight unobstructed wall drew a line connecting him with the front entrance of the castle.

Iris still has the map though, damn it. Think Cameron, think. What was the layout of the front of the castle? Where were the optimal guard posts?

He puckered his lips and shook his head in disappointment at not being able to remember. But there was no sense dwelling on it.

With another quick glance at the towers summit, he took the first step away from its base.

"WHOA! Shhiiiittt!"

The ground beneath him, loosened and weakened from the storm, gave out from under him. He landed hard on his backside and slide feet forward halfway down the steep hillside. With each tree and shrub that he reached out for, the branches cracked louder and his body pounded harder off the earth as his slide quickly turned into a tumble.

Ultimately he landed with a final hard blow to his shoulder—the same shoulder that had struck the column earlier in the church of bones—against the rotten remains of a fallen tree. He slowly rolled himself onto his back and let out a muffled, wheezing cry of pain. With his uninjured arm he reached across his chest and choked in a second raspy gulp of air when his fingers brushed against the trauma.

His head fell to the side. His eyes rolled back. The pain nearly caused him to lose consciousness until a dull thud next to him unsettled a golf ball sized clump of mud, followed quickly by another. A second later, the report of the semi-automatic sub-machine gun echoed through the thicket of leaves above him.

They're fucking shooting at me!

With a seemingly impossible burst of adrenaline, he scrambled in a frenzied panic to his feet and barreled the rest of the way down the hill—stumbling an erratic pattern towards any sign of cover.

"Ho najit," a male voice yelled out. "Nyni!"

"Fuck FUCK!"

More shots rang out from above him, and every flutter of leaves above his head only confirmed that his escape was not advancing hastily enough. He ducked quickly under a branch then planted a hand on top of a large rock and vaulted himself over it. As his feet hit ground beyond the boulder, a chip of siltstone shrapnel broke off and shot into his wrist. He ignored the pain, thankful it wasn't the bullet that hit him.

A few steps further and the foliage around him thickened a bit, easing his fear only slightly until he realized that the next two shots were safely off target. He stopped momentarily, held a hand to his chest and took a few quick but efficient breaths. Then he looked back up at the castle and raised an eyebrow. *Could I be so lucky?*

Then something else caught his eye. Just before the northern wall met with the front wall, Cameron saw what looked to be a large doorway. And more importantly, it was an *open* doorway. At each side of the opening Cameron could also see the profile of a guard, which gave him the impression that this particular doorway was probably incapable of either closing, or locking. Whatever the case, it was not important. Two men, even armed ones, offered less of a complication than a locked door. Men had weaknesses and vulnerabilities, where a solid castle gate had none. At least none that he was capable of easily penetrating.

"The back door it is then," he said quietly to himself. *But how to get past these two clowns?*

As with interrogation, distraction techniques he knew could be executed one of two ways—lazily, or efficiently. He could opt to throw a rock into an outlying bush like they so often do in the movies. But this wasn't Hollywood. How much time would that really buy him? Two, maybe three seconds? Quickly recalling an afternoon at Fort Benning he'd spent in a cognitive behavioral therapy class, he knew that people were *effectively* distracted by either something they really like or something they really hate. So the goal of the distracter should be to provide one or the other. Or — *become* one or the other.

And Cameron knew beyond a doubt that what these men hated was not the thought of him slipping past them. That was simply the first domino. No, what they hated was the last domino. The final outcome of what would happen if he slipped past them — dishonorable discharge from the Czech Armada, and even possible imprisonment under a false treason conspiracy. Contrary, what they would like most would be to capture him alive. Become the lone soldier who could recount their heroic tale of how they subdued the dangerous intruder singlehandedly.

Remaining crouched over, Colonel Skull snuck quietly over to the concrete walkway which ran perpendicular away from the men's post. He took another look over his shoulder, a reassurance that these two guards were the only one's within a good ears distance, then jumped out from behind his cover and stood in full view about 40 feet in front of the two men.

Their eyes opened wide, delaying the reaction to raise their rifles, before each turned to the other with a look of query on their face.

Cameron held up his hands. "I'm not looking for trouble," he called out. "I'm just trying to find my friends." He spun a quick 360 on his heels. "I'm unarmed."

Both men brought their rifles tight to their shoulders and began jogging towards him.

Cameron fought off a smile. *That's a good boy. Come to papa.* "Hey, I bet you guys get medals for this, huh? What do you think?" They were now less than 15 feet away and Cameron began to hold out his wrists. "So? Which one of you gets to arrest me?" He looked to the one on his right. "You?"

Neither man could have been more than 25 years old, which was only going to make this easier. And at Cameron's last question the other taller guard on his left quickly reached to his side and unclipped a set of silver handcuffs.

Skull didn't pretend not to see him do it and abruptly turned to him. "Oh, you get to be the hero, huh? Okay then. You're probably looking at a fat promotion for this huh?" He winked at him, lowered his voice and signaled a finger towards the other guard. "Just between you and me bud, I knew this guy didn't have the stuff."

"Wait," the other guard held an arm out

in front of his comrade. "He tries to trick us. Go. Get the Master Sergeant."

The taller kid almost laughed. He wore an expression that said, "*I don't fucking think so*," and he turned to voice his objection. As he did, the barrel of his rifle dropped and took aim at the ground by his feet. Big mistake. With his left hand, Colonel Skull threw a sharp jab which caught the man in the side of the throat, just below and slightly in front of his ear, causing shock to both the carotid artery and the vagus nerve. His eyes rolled back into his head and the man dropped like a heavy sack of potatoes.

In an instant, Cameron ducked his shoulders and spun himself towards the other guard — the barrel of the man's rifle literally brushing through the top of his hair as he escaped underneath it. Again with his left, Cameron drove a hard elbow into the man's lower ribcage. He staggered for only a second, dropped the gun, and then reared up and shoved Cameron onto his back with both hands.

The guard's impulsive reaction caught Cameron off guard but he quickly picked himself back up. Once on his feet he had less than a second before the guard was hunched over charging at him. Cameron planted a boot firmly on the ground behind him, braced himself, and at the right moment when the guard was just a step away, Cameron pushed the back of the man's head down and wrapped his right arm over and around the back of his neck. He caught his own wrist with the other hand, locking the man's throat tight under his armpit and pulled up—a move known in the world of mixed martial arts as a "guillotine choke."

He tightened his grip and strained the muscles in his arms until he could feel his face turning red and the veins in his neck begin to bulge. But the guard was still conscious, and ignoring the unwritten rules of man-to-man combat, he reached down and grabbed Cameron by the testicles. Skull coughed up all the air in his lungs and panicked. Now in desperation he did the only thing he could think of. Without releasing the man's neck, he thrust his body backwards and down towards the ground behind him. The guard's forehead struck hard against the wet concrete and slowly his grip on Cameron relented.

Colonel Skull laid there for a minute. He was sweating despite the cold and felt sick to his stomach from the devastating crush on his manhood. Finally he forced himself back to his feet. He brushed off the back of his pants, examined his crotch for a moment then looked down at the man behind him. A pool of blood was forming slowly around the man's downturned face, dispersing over the water blanketed sidewalk like a storm cloud creeping over a clear sky.

He was dead.

A sudden terrible feeling of remorse tugged at Cameron's heart. *Just a boy.* He had never meant to *kill* him, and now he found himself thinking of the young man's family. His parent's faces when they heard what had happened, his brothers and sisters preparing themselves to bury their sibling.

Cameron stood there for another minute thinking to himself, ignoring the cold and the rain that was now dripping from his hair and onto his face. *He was probably in his mid or late twenties. Just doing his job.* Then Cameron realized something else. *My father was 24 when I was born. Oh my God. This kid…, even if he was only twenty-two, could have been someone's dad. What if I just…*

This was not the first time he'd killed a man. But why this time it was hitting him so hard was a mystery, however an emotionally painful mystery none the less.

He bent down and picked up the rifle, checked to make sure it had a serial number and full magazine then saluted the soldier's body before turning towards the open doorway.

He crossed the threshold to the interior of Prague Castle which was dimly lit by intermittent accent lights hung from opposing walls. Although a poor alternative for sunlight, the semi-modern wall sconces provided enough ambient light to make Cameron pause briefly for his eyes to adjust. He blinked a few times then noticed adjoining corridors to both his left and right. And straight ahead was another opening that appeared to exit into the castle's main courtyard.

He began to jog a few steps until he came to a brass placard and stopped. He paused to read it silently and suddenly his lips turned up in a slight grin.

On the sign read: THE GALLERY OF THE PRAGUE CASTLE. ORRIGINALLY USED AS STABLES DURING THE RENAISSANCE PERIOD, THE GALLERY WAS REBUILT IN THE 20TH CENTURY AND IS NOW HOME TO EXHIBITS FROM BOTH THE RENAISSANCE AND BAROQUE PERIODS. INCLUDED IS SOME OF THE ORRIGINAL WORKS FROM THE COLLECTION OF RUDOLPH II.

32

An odd expression painted the tanned face starring at him from the wall. The eyes of the man were nearly crossed, his beard uncombed and dirt stricken, and his mouth hung agape.

Still in half darkness, Colonel Skull leaned to his left and squinted at a small metal plate next to the man's face. The oil on panel painting was titled "The Mocking of Christ;" created in the beginning of the 16th century by an anonymous Dutch artist. Correspondingly, the next painting along the wall was from a Flemish painter during the 17th century — "Assembly of the Gods on Mount Olympus." But nothing suggested so far as to which pieces of art were part of King Rudolph's original collection.

Cameron looked further down the hall to his right. The gallery of Prague Castle was astonishing, architecturally as much so as artistically. Even in the dim light, the bright persimmon shade of orange twinkled off the walls with each turn of his head. The floor was a polished hardwood and the ceiling..., *WOW*, was the only word Cameron could find to describe it. As bright white as any fresh snow he'd ever seen. And the way the arches crisscrossed created an illusion of silk sheets being gently waved overhead.

Slowly Cameron moved towards the center of the wide hall. He crept quietly towards a small room on the far side which appeared to contain pieces from a different period. Too focused on the room ahead however, he failed to notice that the wet rubber soles of his boots were squeaking across the wood floor with each step.

Those pieces look... He turned his head quickly.

A muffled voice echoed quietly through the hall, seeping in from under a partially closed doorway at the end of the gallery, but it was too distant to make out each word. "Keep..., minuta..., those...,"

Cameron froze in mid stride and leaned an ear towards the voices. Although still faint, he could tell from the casual dialect and crude vocabulary that whoever was outside talking was definitely no military man. And strangely, the dialogue changed from Czech to English and vice versa every couple words or so.

He took another glance at the room in front of him. It was only a matter of a yard or two in front of him and he listened again for the voices before picking up his back foot. They seemed to be gone. One cautious step at a time he eased his way out of the center of the gallery until an undeniably familiar sound brought him to a quick halt once again.

"Sssshhhhh," came the sound.

Crap! He clenched his jaw and waited, but there was nothing but silence.

Something was wrong. He wasn't sure how he knew, but deep down he could feel it. The shush from outside hadn't been delivered on account of someone's over enthusiastic tone. It was a shush for total silence — to listen.

He didn't wait for what he knew was about to happen. Two men, if not three or four, were about to enter the gallery with guns at the ready. Instead, Cameron sprang off his back foot and ran opposite the direction of the voices. He came back quickly to the corridor that he had entered from. The bodies of both young guards still lay sprawled out across the outer walk. Turning his back to them, he shifted left and ran out into the open courtyard.

At first glance it appeared to be a dead end. Through the rain and darkness, the courtyard had no other visible exits. Just an open arena boxed in by giant gray walls, giving him the sensation of a Roman gladiator thrown into the coliseum to await an army of unknown opponents.

He hesitated only a second then ran through the center of the square, past a large stone fountain and up a short flight of steps to the first small door he found. Not bothering with the handle, he rammed the door twice with his good shoulder. It didn't budge.

Un-slinging the submachine gun from his shoulder, he raised it above his waist and slammed the butt of it onto the top of the door handle then once into the jamb until the latch bolt snapped and the striker plate splintered free from its frame. He stumbled into the dark room and pinned his back against the inner wall trying to catch his breath.

Surprisingly, all he could hear from outside was the sound of rain and distant thunder. No voices, no footsteps, and most importantly — no gunfire. He regained himself and instinctively slipped into stealth mode. Silent and covert, he navigated through a series of rooms and out another door to the castles second courtyard. From there he stared up at the brilliant front face of Saint Vitus Cathedral. Without question it was the largest, most extravagant, and majestic building he had ever laid eyes on.

After a brief look up at the soaring towers that flanked each side of the main entrance he decided however that what he was searching for was not likely inside. So instead of exposing himself further in the unprotected span of the courtyard he slipped into the narrow passage running along the northern wall of the cathedral. Rounding the back corner of the building he could see two men up ahead. Quickly he raised the rifle and peered down the iron sights at the man on the right. Neither had heard nor seen him and were keeping a steady pace in the opposite direction.

Toying with the gun, Colonel Skull slowly aimed at one man then at the other before gently pulling the front of the barrel up and pretending to fire.

"Bang," he whispered.

After waiting a minute to let them put some distance between them and him, Cameron jogged ahead a few yards, stopping when he came to one of the castles guard towers. Calculating his position in his mind, he determined that this was probably the same tower he had circumnavigated from outside. If so, then there was at least one guard inside. He remembered seeing the man's silhouette as he had turned from the window to escape the rain.

At the towers base was an open doorway which lead directly to the base of a circular staircase. Keeping his guard up, Cameron began the ascent to the towers summit, stopping again momentarily to scan quickly over another visitor's plaque mounted to the wall a few steps up.

Powder Tower, as it was called, had a rather extensive history, as did much of the castle. But interestingly, the name Rudolph appeared again towards the bottom of the paragraph. Aside from being the largest of the castles gun towers, this one was host to an alchemist's laboratory under the command of King Rudolph.

Getting warmer, he thought to himself.

He continued up the staircase. Slowly winding himself around the inside perimeter of the tall tower. The steps seemed never-ending and Cameron paused for a second to take in a deep breath. As he did, he leaned to his left and looked further up. Something was there. Not an end to his climb, but an object situated on one of the steps.

What the hell is that?

He knelt and readied the submachine gun to his shoulder — his left elbow braced on his upper thigh and his right finger pulling slight tension on the trigger. The object didn't move but he remained cautious as he crept near it.

In the darkness of the staircase, Colonel Skull couldn't tell that it was the body of a man until he was right on top of it. What he had seen from below was just the bottom tread of a Czech combat boot. The castle guard was sprawled out in an unnatural position along the steps. His left leg was folded up around his back and his neck was stretched and broke to a near 90-degree angle. To Skull's relief however, his face had not been torn off.

But what had happened? Had he fallen down the steps? Doubtful.

Cameron flicked the safety switch on the

side of the rifle with his thumb to assure it was off. Keeping tight and low to the wall, he rounded a few more bends in the staircase until he could see the edge of an open door up ahead.

Waiting patiently, he listened for voices or footsteps. At first there were none, but seconds later he could here both. And the acoustics of the tower funneled the noises down to him from recognizably separate decibels and frequencies.

There's two of them.

He felt along the curvature of the wall to his left. The sweep was shallow, giving him a rough estimate of the tower's radius. *Roughly 30 feet. That gives me an upper floor size of…, what, around 190 linear feet, and like 1,400 square feet. Assuming each man is at opposite ends of the room…, shit, I'm going to have to be really fast about this.*

Focusing momentarily on controlled breathing, Colonel Skull inched forward towards the door. As guessed, as the backside of one man came into partial view, a footstep from the other confirmed that he was indeed on the opposite side of the room.

Cameron steadied the rifle against his shoulder, keeping both eyes open. Unlike traditional shooting styles, Cameron was trained to aim and fire without closing his subdominant eye. For multiple targets, or a single moving target, it was more efficient to leave both eyes open, once teaching yourself to keep primary focus through one eye. That way, if the target moved or another appeared, one eye could keep aim while the other did the tracking. This wasn't a lesson he'd learned in the military though. This was taught to him by an old-time hunter nicknamed "Grizzly" back home in Oregon. "Try following a fleeing buck through a scope with your other eye closed," Grizzly would tell him. "You can't. You'll keep dropping the gun to see where he went."

Skull inhaled through his nose and began to slowly exhale through his mouth when another movement caught his eye — a movement he would have missed had his *left* eye been closed. Silently he swung the barrel over and readjusted his sights. It was an unexpected third man in the room, this one facing directly at him.

Cameron blinked and dropped the rifle about a half inch to look clearly into the man's face — to look him right in the eyes.

33

Frank held the small baby monitor to his ear and listened for Kendall's breathing. Although some people chastised Cameron as being to over-protective as a parent, he still kept a baby monitor in her room while she was asleep.

Frank was glad he did. Over-protective or not, the piece of mind allowed for a good night's sleep — or in this case, a good night of research.

He went back and forth from Cameron's library to the computer and from Nostradamus to the antichrist, occasionally toggling back over to Google Earth to make a guess as to where Colonel Skull might now be.

Maybe that's what I should be focusing on, he thought while doing another virtual flyby of Prague Castle.

He shifted in his chair. About an hour earlier he had become frustrated with the single 19-inch monitor on Cameron's desk, and so using an application called iDisplay, he had set up his new Apple iPad as a secondary wireless screen. Now with an additional 9.7 inches of high-resolution display, Frank was able to comfortably keep multiple windows open, one of which was Safari Explorer, another Goggle Earth, and the third was a small pop-up window with an encrypted chat linkup for General Kestner's Verizon Droid. Frank's orders from the General — "You inform me on every detail. If you or Cameron so much as get up to take a *shit*, I want to know about it. I'll be on a plane for the next three hours, but any Intel on the Colonel comes to me directly."

Frank leaned back in his seat wishing there was a way for him to accurately live track Colonel Skull. Knowing that that was an impossibility however, he concentrated again on the castle. "Where did you hide those pages?" he asked the late King.

The likelihood that Rudolph had destroyed the pages seemed doubtful. The man was too intrigued by things of the unnatural. His collection was known publicly to contain pieces exceptional enough to challenge Peter the Great's Kunstkammer museum in Russia.

With paintings being only a small portion, Rudolph's Kunstkamera contained coins, medallions, works of bronze and ivory, colossal pieces of uncut gemstone, botanical gardens, exotic animals, and even some scientific instruments of the highest rarity. His passion was so extreme that it drove him not only to collect, but to physically exploit the talents of some of Europe's finest scientists, architects and philosophers.

And all that was excluding his private collections which were even more bizarre — arcane items of the supernatural, some of priceless value and some foolishly bought in obsession despite their worthlessness. The tooth of a narwhal whale was purchased under the false belief that it was the horn of a unicorn. There was a marble sarcophagus found near Athens after the battle of the Amazons, the supposed teeth of a mermaid captured in the Aegean Sea, and of course, the Devil's Bible.

He rolled his head from left to right, cracking the bones in his neck loudly. The problem now he realized was even worse than it had been five minutes ago. What they were trying to find was something that had been deliberately hidden, not just simply withheld from his public exhibitions. As a matter of fact, many of the items in Rudolph's "cabinet of curiosities" were either no longer in existence or based on hearsay and legend. A magnetite lodestone, said to increase in size while resting on the shelves in his cabinet, was clearly a myth, while a human skull carved from yellow agate was very much real, and in fact well preserved in Vienna Austria at the royal museum.

Frank looked down at the baby monitor. Two quick coughs followed by a sniffle came out of the speaker while a stream of tiny green lights flickered up and down like the treble waves on a stereo equalizer. He waited before getting up, knowing from experience that she'd most likely fall right back to sleep. She coughed once more then did indeed slip back into dream.

I hope she's not catching a cold, he thought. But again his mind was put to ease, knowing that Cameron, the over-protective parent, kept a fully stocked first aid kit ready to treat anything from a runny nose to a broken leg.

Frank knew this first hand. Two summers ago he had accidentally stepped into an abandoned porcupine burrow in Cameron's backyard after downing a few Red Frog Ale's that he'd stocked up on at the Oregon Beer Festival the week prior. The fall had fractured his shinbone, and before he could even hobble himself back over to the house, Cameron had already diagnosed the problem as a tibial shaft fracture and was halfway through splinting his leg with duct tape and a stiffly rolled up newspaper. To this day Frank owed his un-staggered step to the Colonel's preparedness and ingenuity.

Getting back to business, he blinked his eyes a few times and leaned forward again in his chair. He returned to a website that he'd previously visited and began cross-referencing locations, dates and names. What he found was not surprising. Rudolph II had ties to most areas of Castle Prague, many of which had undergone radical changes since his time.

Once used as stables, the Spanish Hall was now a gallery and convention center — once home to horses, now home to the country's presidential elections. Powder Tower, which was Rudolph's alchemist workshop, later turned gunpowder warehouse then eventually living quarters for the sextons of Saint Vitus Cathedral. The Golden Lane and Daliborka Tower was once a prison, but today it could be argued that it was possibly the most romantic region of the castle.

By chance, Frank happened to glance down at the small digital clock on the lower right side of the screen. "Oh crap!" he said aggravated. The last time he'd given Kestner an update was over an hour ago. Quickly he clicked into the chat window and typed, NO WORD YET FROM COLONEL SKULL. LAST CONTACT REMAINS MINUS 1.25 HOURS.

Within seconds a reply popped up. CAN WE CONFIRM PENETRATION OF OUTER WALLS?

NEGATIVE, Frank replied. I'LL ATTEMPT RECOMM NOW. He reached over for his cell phone and dialed Cameron. What else could he do? There were no other active lines of communication with the Colonel.

In nearly any other part of the world, Nightcorp would have had an operative available locally to provide B.A.R., or, Backup Alert Reinforcement, but not in the Czech Republic. In fact, certain areas of East Asia, particularly North Korea, was the only other place that Frank could think of where someone was not readily available. Even in hostile areas of sub-Saharan Africa like Somalia, where the Al-Qaeda inspired Shebab militant group was growing at an alarming rate, Nightcorp could still provide additional ground support should the enemy engage.

The phone in his hand suddenly went to voicemail. It was not to his surprise that Colonel Skull didn't answer.

Frank set the phone back down. *I'll try again later before I tell Kestner*, he thought.

It was then that he noticed something else on the screen and the wheels began turning faster in his mind. It was the word—*oldest*. He leaned in for a closer inspection.

Oldest what? He thought, questioning the webpage.

He right clicked the mouse, then scrolled down and enlarged the image and its caption. What popped up were actually multiple images along with a brief description of the building.

The first picture he saw of St. George Monastery was a beautiful shot taken just after a light snowfall. Reminiscent of its time, the monastery had an alluring and almost magical look to it. It was built as the first convent in the Czech lands during the first part of the 10th century. And even more interesting—it had been established for the Benedictine order.

"Of course," he said out loud. "I'm so

damn focused on Rudolph that I've been neglecting everything else." He pinpointed the monastery's location on a map of the castle. It was very close to Colonel Skull's last known location.

That's when it occurred to him. If St George Monastery was the oldest Benedictine monastery in what used to be Bohemia, was it possible — *IS it possible* — that what he was looking at was the actual site where the condemned monk had scribed the Devil's Bible?

34

Colonel Cameron Skull peered over the gun metal blue barrel of his confiscated submachine gun and into the ocean blue eyes of the figure across from him. The Englishman was seated on the ground with his wrists bound to the leg of a table.

Jake

Skull pressed a finger to his lips. Now he understood what was going on. The two men holding Jake hostage were STB. That also explained why the broken body of a castle guard laid stiff and cold eight steps below him.

Off to Jake's left, the large Czech with his back to Cameron was pacing back and forth along a ten foot stretch of wall. A slow stagger was more like it. Even from his current vantage on the stairs Cameron could see the rectangular imprint of a flask protruding from the man's hip pocket. The early effects of cheaply made vodka were beginning to take their toll on his balance, and Colonel Skull had no difficulty remaining hidden as the man switched directions.

By pivoting on the ball of his right foot,

Cameron now had his back to the opposite wall in the stairwell. This not only put him out of sight with the drunk, who was now walking towards him, but also gave him a new angle to view the room's interior. Still no sign of the other man though.

Cameron glanced again at Jake over his right shoulder. Jake was staring back at him — a sad look in his eyes, like that of a lost puppy dog. He had been gagged and taped. A small corner of the fabric, now soaked with saliva, hung out from under the bottom edge of the silver tape across his mouth.

Once the sound of footsteps changed direction again, Cameron rotated back to his original position along the wall. After wiping his palm across his pant leg, he quietly eased the rifle back to his shoulder then took aim at the man's robust backside and gently rested his forefinger on the trigger. Easily and gently he started to apply pressure when a dark blurry object suddenly crowded his field of vision.

Cameron jerked back, barely catching himself from tumbling down the stairs. As he did, his finger depressed the trigger and the Skorpion submachine gun blasted off a quick three round burst into the room ahead.

His eyes grew wide and he reached out frantically for a hand rail to help pick himself back up. He didn't find one in time and had to jump back again as the other STB swung the butt of his rifle a second time at Cameron's head. It narrowly missed him but smashed hard into the stone wall of the stairwell less than two inches from Colonel Skull's face. The back of the gun shattered and splinters of its wooden stock exploded all around him.

Somehow this guy was even bigger than his drunken compatriot. He must have stood at least six foot six and could weigh no less than 300 pounds. Dressed head to toe in black drag, including a bomber style fur hat, he looked and smelled like an Oregon black bear—a second later and he sounded like one. The man let out a deep roar as he hunched over and charged. Shoulder to shoulder, his massive physique took up nearly the whole stairwell and Cameron found himself being lifted onto the man's shoulder as he crashed into him.

With the bottom of his fist, Colonel Skull hammered down repeatedly onto the back of his thick neck. It didn't faze him.

Finally the giant lost his footing and they fell hard onto each other. Cameron struggled beneath him. Able to use his smaller and more limber size to his advantage, he freed himself and quickly rebounded up two steps.

The wounded bear was still trying to right himself. Cameron turned. Tucked into the back of the man's belt was an 8-inch serrated combat knife and Skull grabbed for it. It pulled free of its sheath and he tossed it from his left hand to his right, then flipped it over and plunged it deep into the man's back. The blade deflected off a vertebra and punctured through the spongy tissue of his right lung—a soft whistle escaping as the air squeezed passed the edge of the blade. He groaned softly in agony before falling limp, his body landing face down with both arms and both legs outstretched till they hit wall.

"Holy shit," Cameron said, whipping off his brow.

He left the knife sticking out of the man. There was still another STB in the room with Jake to deal with.

Leaping two steps at a time, he quickly reentered the room above. Jake, still tied to the table, began mumbling gargled noises from beneath his gag. And in the center of the room, the drunken mercenary lay face down in a pool of blood.

"Aagg rrrsspppll."

"Jake!" Skull said irritated. "I can't understand a word you're saying. Give me one minute, will you?" He walked over and knelt by the man on the floor, then raised an eyebrow. "What the hell?" He looked over the body. Indeed, one of the rounds from Cameron's gun had struck the man, but it had caught him in the upper thigh. A disabling shot, yes, but certainly not a kill shot.

Cameron reached down and placed two

fingers against the side of the man's throat. There was a pulse. He was still alive.

Skull was confused. He stood back and scratched the top of his head. *Was he just that drunk that a little bit of blood loss made him pass out?*

Jake started squirming again.

"OK OK, I'm coming. Are you alright?"

Muffled garble came out from under Jake's gag once again.

Unwilling to continue listening to it, Colonel Skull reached behind Jakes ear and tore the tape from his mouth with a single yank.

"Oww," Jake moaned. He wiggled his jaw back and forth a few times as Cameron finished cutting through his wrist restraints. Once free, he reached up and massaged both cheeks. Then, as if his capture had never happened, he stood and essentially picked up conversation where he and the Colonel had left off. "So, did you find what you were looking for in the Church of Bones?"

"What? That was..., did they...," Cameron paused and pointed at the man on the floor before continuing. "Never-mind." He turned around and waved a hand over his shoulder for Jake to follow. "You're a strange guy Jake. You know that?"

Jake Evans hopped up alongside the Colonel. "You found me pretty quick," he exclaimed. "How did you know where I was?"

Cameron stopped and looked at him.

"Listen Jake, I'm going to be honest with you. I *didn't* know you were here." He put a hand on Jakes shoulder. "Your sister and I tried to…"

"My sister?" Jake questioned abruptly. "Are you talking about Iris? She's here?"

"No, she…" Again, Skull was stopped short. More footsteps and another deep baritone voice sounded in through one of the windows.

Jake had heard it as well. And to Cameron's surprise, he kept quiet and continued to follow him down the stairs and over the two bodies laid upon them. They reached the lower landing and Colonel Skull signaled for Jake to keep low and to the wall.

Peeking out the doorway, all Cameron could see were the same two men from earlier still patrolling the perimeter of St Vitus Cathedral. Their rounds had taken them a full revolution, maybe two or three, around the massive building and they were now headed away from him as they had been earlier.

"Come on," he whispered to Jake.

This time, instead of backtracking out the way he came, he led Jake East and silently followed twenty yards or so behind the two men. Whether they were STB, royal guards, or Czech Armada made little difference at this point.

"Where are we going?" Jake whispered, keeping tight to Cameron's heels.

"We have to find those pages before…"

He cringed at the remembrance of the creature's face. "They're somewhere in this castle."

Jake had no idea what he was talking about, but held any further questions till later.

Ahead, the two patrols slipped around the back corner of the cathedral, exposing a large statue of a horseman impeding entrance to another building. Cameron pulled Jake along silently until they were able to crouch alongside the statues base for cover. He held a hand pressing down on Jakes shoulder as they kept watch on the two men.

"Okay, let's go," Skull finally whispered.

He turned for the open doorway. Overhead, a violent bolt of lightning suddenly erupted, turning the darkness into an electrified shade of blue. The vivid flash of light gave Cameron pause.

"What are you doing?" Jake questioned apprehensively.

Colonel Skull didn't turn to look at him when he answered with a suppressed *hush*. He was waiting — and watching. Finally, another flash of lightning boomed in the distance, and above the open doorway, Colonel Skull saw it — a relief sculpture carved into the rock frontispiece of the building.

Like the statue now a few steps to his rear, this too portrayed a man on horseback. But this time the man brandished a sword and was preparing to strike at a dragon-like creature stooped at the horse's forelegs. Yet despite the carving, it was the inscription below it that drew Cameron's attention.

Written in Romanesque style calligraphy, the inscription began with the words SAINT GEORGE—the "S" in Saint characterized by a Taijitu, the ancient Taoist symbol representing the "Yin Yang" philosophy.

Cameron was well familiar with the symbol, although he'd only learned of its ties to Celtic art three years ago when he and Kate had vacationed in the Cook Islands off the South Pacific. Before an evening visit to Aitutaki Lagoon one night, his Irish lass had gotten the symbol henna tattooed on her right ankle.

But what is it doing here? He wondered. *And why is it turned sideways?*

Generally, the Taijitu was positioned as two equal opposites of a divided circle—one half on the left, the other on the right. Representative of coexistence, the symbol could stand for many things—night and day, hot and cold, male and female, and to some—good and evil. But this taijitu was not two harmonious equals. It clearly displayed one half of the circle dominantly above the other. But which half was the dominate one? Light or dark? *Good or evil?*

He couldn't wait for another lightning strike. Even if he had, there was no color to the relief sculpture to give away the secret. It remained the solid sandy hue of aged stone.

Tapping Jake on his elbow, they continued and disappeared from view through the southern entrance and into a hallway adorned by more stone tablets hung frequently along one wall.

"Where are we?" Jake questioned.

"I don't know," he admitted, taking a moment to scan down each opposite end of the hall. As he turned back around, a man's shape suddenly emerged from beyond the corner up ahead. "Get down," Cameron ordered to both Jake and the strange man.

Colonel Skull pinned Jake to the wall and shouldered the gun, taking aim at the man's head. He hesitated. The man before him seemed calm. He began approaching them but kept his hands peacefully to his sides as he did.

"Hold it right there," Cameron yelled to him.

The man stopped. He was close enough now for Cameron to identify a small square patch of white just below his chin.

He lowered the gun. "Who are you?"

"My name," the man started, "is Andrea Canale. I am Archpriest of Saint Peter's Basilica in Rome. And to answer your first question, this...," he held out his hands to display the room around them, "is the Convent of Saint George."

—

"I am a senior member of the Vatican," Father Canale said in response to Cameron's last question of, "How did you get in here?"

The three of them were now standing in the depths of the chapel, just below the altar. They were circled around a large stone chantry which disturbingly had another piece of stone, roughly the size of a body, resting atop it. And further, to Skull's left was a niche that only moments ago the Archpriest had confirmed was the tomb of Prince Vratislav — the church's founder.

"Oh bloody hell," Jake suddenly wailed. "That's disgusting."

He was looking at a tarnished ebony statue, morbidly named "Brigita." It was at first glance just a skeleton. But upon further inspection, the statue depicted flesh on the woman's hands, a skeletal head and ribcage, and exposed organs spilling out of her midsection.

Cameron glanced at it quickly then returned his attention to the priest. "So, father," he began, still skeptical of whether or not to trust this man. "What are you doing here?"

Andrea wasn't sure how to answer that. What was he doing here? Originally his intentions were to travel to the ossuary in Kutna Hora. He looked curiously at Colonel Skull and thought, *what is he doing here?* "I received news from the town of Sedlec," he finally admitted.

"But shortly after arriving here in Prague, I...," He glanced up at the ceiling. "I'm not sure. Something just..., I don't know. Something just drew me here."

Cameron leaned over the altar. "Excuse my language father. But that sounds like bullshit to me."

"Clearly I can see the reasoning behind your mistrust." He paused, not knowing how to address this man. "Um, how should I call you?"

"Skull. My name is Cameron Skull."

"I'm Jake Evans," an accented voice chimed in from the background.

Neither Andrea's nor Cameron's gaze shifted. Finally, the priest acknowledged. "Cameron?" he asked, thinking out loud. "Not by chance, *Father* Cameron?"

"Pardon me?" Skull questioned bitterly.

Andrea eased up, confident in his assessment. "You were at the ossuary in Sedlec, were you not?"

Cameron didn't answer. *Who the hell is this guy? And how does he know that?*

The Archpriest continued. "I departed from Rome once I heard the news about what happened to Father Matousek. Quite honestly, if what I heard was in fact truth..., it frightened me."

"And why is that?"

"Is it true? Was the priest's face...?" He couldn't finish his sentence.

Colonel Skull took a step back—a cold shiver running down the length of his spine. Shaking his head, he answered. "You don't want to know."

"But I'm afraid I must."

"NO!" the Colonel yelled. "Trust me, Father. No one needs to know the things I saw." *Or heard, or felt, or smelled*. He remembered the creature's breath as it had bent over him. He turned and paced a few steps, then altered directions quickly when noticing he was headed towards the founders open tomb. "What was there…," he started to say, his voice softened a bit. "Whatever it was, it was *terrible*. That thing just…" He shook his head again and looked up at the archpriest. "I don't know. I've never seen anyone so…, it was like, some sort of demon."

"I'm afraid not," Andrea corrected. "It was no demon that killed Father Matousek."

"And how the hell would you know?" Skull asked with anger in his voice. "You weren't there. You didn't see what I saw." He turned his back to the priest. "*Be thankful* you didn't have to see what I saw."

"The one you are seeking," the Archpriest said with confidence. "Likewise, the one who is seeking you—*is not* a demon."

Cameron turned back around.

"She is — a *demoness*."

35

Everything was dark. Although the blindfold around Iris' face felt loose enough to shake off, she didn't dare. She was not alone — two of the three voices were still in the room with her.

Above her head, her wrists had been tied and secured to a support on the ceiling with a thick bristly rope. And had another inch of slack been pulled to tighten the knot, it would have probably left her toes dangling just above the cold floor.

She leaned her head back and tried wiggling her fingers to keep the blood flowing. They were beginning to lose feeling as her body was slowly stretched.

"Go see what happened to Imrich," the older of the two voices said in Czech.

"Ah, he's probably just wandering around. Stupid fool. Did I tell you that I caught him eating a streusel by the men's room earlier?"

"Doesn't matter. Go find him. We need to be getting to Brevnovsky klaster soon."

The man rose. Iris could hear the legs of his chair chafe across the hard floor, followed by a door opening. The sound of the night's rain and thunder grew strong, almost deafening, until the door closed again behind him, reducing it back to a soft white noise.

Then the sound of a second chair, this one followed by the creaking of the floor as heavy footsteps approached her. The man didn't speak, but a husky bovine-like stench alerted her to his close proximity.

Something brushed against her hip and her body jerked to the side. "What do you want?" she asked, trying to pinpoint him through sound—like a bat navigating with echolocation. "To, co chces?" she asked again.

"Oh, I speak English, Ms Wilhelmsson."

Her tracking was off and she spun her head around to face the voice. "What do you want with me?"

The man sucked in a deep breath through his nose, as if smelling a freshly baked pie. "Oh no, it's not me who wants something from you." He chuckled softly. "Well…, maybe I do want *one* thing." He reached down and slowly ran his hoof in between her legs, forcing her thighs apart.

She locked her knees together and pulled away as best she could. "Keep your fucking hands off me," she demanded forcefully.

The ox struck her hard in the jaw with the back of his knuckles, then reached up and grabbed her by the cheeks with one hand. He squeezed tightly, causing her lips to pucker under his grip. "That's big mouth for such tiny woman. Maybe I fill it with something. Eh, you like that?"

Her eyes began to water, partly from fear, but mostly from the pressure that was being applied to her face.

"Nothing more to say?" he asked, releasing her and then slowly walking a full circle around her helpless body.

Although see couldn't see him, she could still feel his eyes as they scanned up and down the length of her petite frame.

Standing back in front of her now, he suddenly took hold of her top with both hands and tore the Abercrombie shirt down the middle. He paused for a moment to gaze at the lacy white bra covering her ample breasts that he'd just exposed.

His breathing began to get heavy. Long deep panting that warmed her skin with a disgusting embrace on each exhale. Then, finishing what he had started, he violently shook, pulled and yanked on the fabric until the shirt was left to nothing more than shreds of cloth thrown about the floor.

Iris shivered, trying to both rid herself of the sudden goose bumps, and to give an inconspicuous strength test to her restraints. They held firm.

The ox was taking a sickly delight in each

second of his siege. Especially in the way his attack caused her larger than average bosom to wildly bounce up and down, inducing an almost painful arousal in his pants.

He wasted no time continuing. He reached down and unbuckled her belt, then unzipped the front of her jeans and tugged them to her ankles. With a finger the same size and texture of an overcooked sausage, he slowly stretched the elastic band around the waist of her matching white panties, then released it and allowed it to snap back against her skin.

Iris flinched.

"Do you like it when it hurts?" he whispered in her ear. "I do." He held the back of her head tight with his right hand and firmly squeezed each of her breasts with the other. Still whispering in her ear, he said, "How goes your American song? Hurts so good?" He chuckled. "Do you want me to, *Come on baby, make it hurt so good?*"

Sick fuck! Iris thought.

It was a sadistic reference to John Mellencamp, but he was right. She did indeed want it to "Hurt so good." "You bet I do," she answered mockingly. "As long as I'm the one doing the hurting." And with her legs bound together by her pants around her ankles, she picked up both feet and drove both her knees straight into the man's crotch.

He buckled over, barely catching himself

from falling with one hand on a shaky knee and the other on his testicles. He tried to speak, but his words came out as garble and spit.

Iris pulled up on her wrist restraint, lifting herself off the ground. She swung her body backwards then shifted her weight and flew forward, catching the oxen under the chin with the pointed tip of one of her brown leather ankle boots that he had failed to remove. He squealed in pain as his body tumbled backwards and landed unconscious on the ground behind him.

Knowing she didn't have much time before he woke again, she shook her head furiously side to side until the blindfold dropped over the bridge of her nose. She took one look at the man then up at the ceiling. The other end of the rope around her wrists was looped over a metal J-hook screwed into the drywall. It then ran down at a 45-degree angle where it was tied to a cleat anchored to the wall.

She cursed out loud to herself, "Shit," then took another look at the man on the floor. He was still out — at least for the moment.

Again, she looked back at the ceiling. *Maybe I can jump high enough to flip the rope over the edge of the hook*. She had to try. Pushing off her toes, she jumped and tried to fling up the top of the rope. Not even close.

She tried again, then again, and again a fourth time. Still nothing. With each attempt the rope settled back to its previously comfortable position on the J-hook, leaving her to fall back down and nearly dislocate her shoulders from the sudden jerk when the rope pulled tight again.

"Come on Iris," she encouraged herself. No matter what, she just couldn't seem to manipulate it in such a fashion as to get it to flip over the hook.

Once more she jumped, and once more the rope failed to overcome the hook. Her eyes closed tightly as again she came back down and the rope pulled tension. But this time something snapped. Her feet hit ground and her knees buckled. She fell forward, catching herself just before landing her face on the boots of the downed man in front of her.

Startled, she looked up. The rope had not broken, but instead the hook itself had pulled free from the drywall under the stress of her weight being dropped on it. Although she was happy to be free, she was unhappy about how it got accomplished.

That's it. My new diet starts as soon as I get back home.

She rolled over onto her butt, yanked the rope from her wrists with her teeth, dusted some of the chalky drywall off her legs, and then pulled her pants back up and stood. The man on the floor began moaning softly. "Fucking asshole," she whispered as she refastened the belt around her waist.

For a moment she played with the idea of kicking him in the face, but instead she dredged up a loud wad of phlegm from her nose to her mouth and spat it onto his forehead.

Lastly, she bent over and picked up a shred of what was left of her top. It wasn't but a fraction of a sleeve.

"Oh that's just great," she muttered, tossing the piece over her shoulder.

Not much I can do about it.

Topless now except for her bra, she jogged quickly over to the building's single door. Slowly turning the handle, she cracked it open and peered out into the darkness. There were lots of places for someone to hide out there, but from what she could tell, her surroundings appeared deserted.

Taking in a deep breath, she slowly abandoned the small building and ran out into the night.

36

Jake's eyes were the size of dinner plates. "A demoness?" he asked in panic.

Father Canale looked over at him. Jake was standing on the bottom stair of a curved set of steps leading up to the altar. "Yes," the Archpriest confirmed. He turned back to Cameron. "She goes by the name Lilitu."

"Lilitu," Cameron repeated, caught in amazement by the thought of his earlier attacker being a woman. "And she's a demoness?"

The archpriest hesitated. "Lilitu, or Lilith, is the bastard child of Giovanni Santalla — born on the Sabbath, prematurely to a Jewish peasant in Jerusalem." The priests gaze stiffened. "On the 6th day of June, nineteen hundred seventy-six."

June 6, 1976? Skull thought. He gulped down a hard breath. Whispering, mostly to himself, he said, "six, six, six."

"The number of the beast," Andrea professed quietly. "She…"

"Wait. Who is Giovanni Santalla?" Cameron asked before the priest could go any further.

"Padre Generalle. He is the superior general of the society of Jesuits. The Black Pope."

"Black pope?" Jake asked.

Skull held up a hand to silence him. "Jake, please? Just sit tight and let me finish talking to Father Canale for a minute, okay?"

"Sorry." Jake's tone—like his haircut—was disappointment with a side order of attitude.

"It's okay, just…" Cameron turned back to the archpriest. "So, what happened? Why is she…?" He waved a hand over his face. "You know."

Andrea fought to explain. He knew he had to, but he also knew that time was running short. "On the day of her birth," he began, "the father general had been overseeing an excavation of King Solomon's well in the City of David. When news of the child reached him, he fled from the site and wasn't seen again for six years. The church temporarily disregarded him…, but only hours after his disappearance, someone set fire to the mother's home."

"Burning everyone inside. Including the child," Cameron finished for him.

"Not exactly," Andrea corrected. "There were two other peasant women who shared the home with the child's mother. One was burned to death, but the other escaped relatively unharmed. She ran to get help. But by the time she returned with men from the village, the flames had consumed nearly the entire structure."

Cameron squinted. "I don't understand. Then what…"

"The peasant woman and the men stood helpless. Then just before the final timber support gave way, a being appeared through the flames." Father Canale held back for a moment. "It was the child's mother—engulfed in the flames from head to toe." Andrea quickly looked over at Jake, then back at Colonel Skull. "The woman screamed," he continued. "Her hair and clothes had been lost as embers, and her flesh…, and the flesh of the babe cradled in her arms, was beginning to blacken and rupture." He closed his eyes. "She collapsed to the ground, trails of foul black smoke emanated from her charred skin, and she dropped the child at the feet of one of the men." He sighed and his eyes closed even tighter together. "Dropping the child…, at *my* feet."

Cameron and Jake gave the priest a respectful moment of silence.

Andrea opened his eyes and feigned a smile. "Of course, that's back before I was a priest."

My God. Colonel Skull started pacing again. "And you named her Lilitu?"

"Oh no no. She was never given a name." Andrea walked to the other side of the stone slab and stepped in front of Cameron. "There was no hope for her survival," he said gravely. "There was just no way she was going to make it."

"But she did."

"She did indeed." Father Canale now had fear in his voice. The same fear he'd had when first hearing from Sacristan De Luca. He placed both hands on Cameron's shoulders and a tear suddenly filled his eye. "It was a miracle," he said. "It's what led me to join the clergy. For surely it had to have been the hand of God that saved the child."

"What happened, Father?" Cameron asked softly. "What happened to her that changed her?"

The priests head lowered. "As she grew older, she started seeing the signs."

Cameron pulled Andrea's hands off his shoulders and leaned his head down and to the side so he could look him in the eyes. "What signs?"

The archpriests lip trembled, and he quoted, "So I threw you to the earth; I made a spectacle of you before kings. By your many sins and dishonest trade you have desecrated your sanctuaries." His voice got louder. "So, I made *a fire* come out from you, and it consumed you, and I reduced you to ashes on the ground in the sight of all who were watching—Ezekiel twenty-eight."

"So what?" Cameron asked. "That can't

be all." Andrea didn't respond and Colonel Skull took him by the arm and shook lightly. "Father..., you know as well as I do that that passage is referring to the Devil, not her."

"Is it?" Andrea wasn't so sure.

"Of course. That's..."

"There's more," Father Canale whispered, interrupting him. "The date of her birth — 666, the Vaticinia Nostradami, the..."

"Wait. The what?" Cameron shook him again. "What was that last thing you said?"

"The Vaticinia Nostradami? It is the Lost Book of Nostradamus."

Cameron inhaled loudly. *The Lost Book of Nostradamus!?*

"Not of Michel de Nostradame," Andrea clarified. "But of Cesar de Nostradame — Michel's first-born son. The book had been lost to the ages, until rediscovered in 1982 hidden deep inside the National Library in Rome. It contains a collection of watercolors which are said to predict the Armageddon."

Jake was now standing directly beside the Colonel but neither man spoke.

The priest continued. "One of the apocalyptic images depicted by Cesar is that of a Pope." He paused momentarily. "A *black* pope."

Cameron was staring blankly, his eyes facing Andrea but his gaze focused somewhere in the beyond. Likewise, Jake had gone back and taken a seat on the step — his lower jaw hanging partially open.

"The name Lilitu," the archpriest continued, "was chosen by her, after she dismissed God as her savior. She began to believe that it was not God, but his expelled guardian cherub who had saved her on the day of her birth."

Andrea brushed a hand over the large stone slab as he walked back around to the other side of the altar. "According to the Alphabet of Ben Sira, Lilith was the first wife of Adam."

"The first wife of Adam?" Skull asked suspiciously. "As in — Adam and *EVE*, Adam? Is that the Adam we're talking about?"

"Yes. That *Adam*. It is in the Alphabet of Ben Sira, and in the Dead Sea Scrolls, "Songs of the Sage," that Lilith is pronounced as Adams first wife — before Eve. She is even referenced in several midrashic texts of the Torah — the Five Books of Moses."

Andrea looked to Colonel Skull for a reaction, but got none.

He continued, "It is said that Lilith refused to lay beneath Adam, and so Adam told God of her disobedience. She then fled from the Garden of Eden, and God sent down three angels to retrieve her. The angels, Senoy, Sansenoy and Semangelof found her in a cave. She was bearing children, despite her defiance with Adam, and yet still refused to return to the Garden. The Angel's then told her that for each day of her insubordination they would strike down 100 of her children. So, it is out of revenge for God and his Angels that Lilith turned to Satan, becoming his demoness."

"So, she thinks she *IS* Lilith," Cameron asked bewildered.

Andrea shook his head. "No. She *BELIEVES* that she is something more."

The signs. Colonel Skull remembered and his eyes widened. "She's...," He gulped. "She's the antichrist."

—

The room was silent. Jake had risen from his seat, but now stood with a trembling hand gripping the banister.

Archpriest Canale also remained silent. He was not unconvinced enough of the accuracy of Cameron's last statement to offer dispute. Although he wanted with all his heart to propose an alternative—there was none. For the last two decades, Andrea had feared the day when someone else would voice those words. *"She is the antichrist."*

Colonel Skull saw the painful fear in the priest's eyes. It was a look of torment, but also one of salvation. However, his own mind was still racing—evaluating possibilities and flashing through still framed images like they were being spun on a projection reel.

He looked over at Jake who was silently begging him for answers. One if the images in Cameron's mind had been of Iris. What had happened to her? Where was she now? *How am I going to save her?*

Archpriest Canale finally broke the silence. "We should…"

Cameron's head snapped to him. "We can't let her find those pages."

Andrea leaned back confused. "What pages are you referring to?"

"The one's missing from the Devil's Bible."

Suddenly Cameron realized that Father Canale was unaware of everything that had happened in Stockholm. He gave him the abridged version of the story, omitting the less substantial details, and at the same time, satisfying Jake's lust for answers.

"Colonel," Jake interrupted.

Cameron turned to him. "What?"

Jake was pointing to the side pocket of his pants. Skull looked down and saw the light from his iPhone penetrating through the thin fabric of his jeans.

He reached a hand into his pocket to retrieve it. He'd forgotten that earlier he had shut off the ringer to avoid another mishap like the one he experienced earlier. "Sorry, Father. Give me just one second," he said, looking from Andrea to the flashing screen of his phone. It was Frank calling him again. He looked again at Andrea. "I've got to take this," he told him.

Turning around and taking a step away from Jake and the priest, Cameron answered, "Hello? Frank?"

There was static on the line.

"Frank, can you hear me?" Skull asked, plugging an ear with his finger.

"Colonel," Frank finally answered. "What's your position?"

"I'm inside Saint George's Basilica," Skull answered.

"Colonel? Colonel, are you there?"

"Yes," Cameron pushed the phone harder to his ear. "Frank can you…?"

"Sir, if you can hear me," Frank said over him. "I think you need to get to Saint George's Basilica. It was used by Rudolph II, and it's the oldest monastery in the Czech Republic. I think it's possibly even the site where the Devil's Bible originated—where Satan possessed the condemned monk. If I'm right," Frank concluded. "Then that's where you're going to find the missing pages."

—

"What was that?" Jake asked in a frightened whisper.

Archpriest Canale had heard the sound as well. Colonel Skull on the other hand was still calling Frank's name into the mouthpiece of his phone and walking circles around the altar to try and better the reception.

Jake hopped up and jumped a few jittery steps over to Cameron. In his fright, his English accent grew stronger, almost to the point of overpowering his clarity. "Colonel, eh sir?" He drummed Cameron's shoulder repeatedly with the open palm of his right hand.

Colonel Skull tried shooing him away.

"Eyy," Jake protested. "If you fancy your arse, stop pissing about and listen to me."

Surprised by the Englishman's sudden aggression, Cameron lowered the phone and turned to him. As he did, he saw Father Canale peering over the pews towards the front of the chapel.

Just as he was about to question Jake's choice of words, a second faint *"click"* came from the front of the basilica.

Cameron slid the phone quietly back into his pocket and crouched over. "Jake," he whispered. "Get back."

He and Jake slowly crept backwards, but Andrea remained poised.

"Father," Cameron called in a whisper. *"Father."*

Andrea turned his head but not his body. Cameron signaled to him with his hand to "get down." He understood the gesture and knelt, then followed the Colonel's lead and inched backwards until the three of them were huddled next to a wall in the shadows of a small secluded room—inside the tomb of Prince Vratislav.

Nearly a minute passed before the archpriest broke the silence with a low voice. "What do you suppose it was?"

"I don't know," Skull answered, not taking his eyes off the front of the church. "It... wait, what's... ssshhh."

A figure slowly emerged at the opposite end of the room. It's silhouette only slightly darker than the moonlight coming in from one of the cathedrals narrow windows. The form was hunched over, carrying its body as if it bore the weight of Jesus' cross on its shoulder. With each step the figure grunted and pulled a leg painfully behind it.

"*Zombie,*" Jake thought out loud.

"No." Suddenly Colonel Skull stood and darted out of the tomb. He swerved around the altar and hurdled the first set of pews, then ran up to the man and put a hand on his back. "What happened to you?" he asked the man. "Are you alright?"

The man didn't answer, but his body began to ebb forward.

Cameron quickly placed his other arm under the man's torso to catch him before he fell. The man's shirt was wet with something and he moaned in agony as the Colonel eased him upright. "What the hell?" Cameron muttered.

Jake and Archpriest Canale approached from the rear, stopping abruptly when the man's head lifted off Cameron's forearm. "Ugh." Jake doubled over at the waist and gagged. Father Andrea too felt ill, but it was more of an emotional sickness and he traced the sign of the cross over his heart.

"Dear God," Cameron said, his eyes growing wider in the darkness. The wetness on the man's shirt was blood — spilt out from the carnage that once was a face. It coated Cameron's hand and began running slowly down his arm and into the sleeve of his shirt.

The man in Skull's arms suddenly inhaled a loud, long breath, then exhaled slowly. The process did not repeat. He was dead.

Jake choked another dry cough onto the ground in front of him.

"May you rest in peace, my son," Andrea whispered.

Cameron turned to the priest while still cradling the man's body in his arms. "Why?" He asked softy. "Why is she doing this?"

Andrea understood that Cameron's question had been rhetorical. The Colonel knew why. But still, the archpriest offered some solace in an explanation. "And I will bring thee to ashes upon the earth in the sight of all that look upon thee — and behold, the great red dragon."

"That's why she's fucking cutting off people's faces?" Cameron said angrily as he laid the body on the ground. "What the hell does that even mean, huh? She's trying to make her victims look like Satan? Or is it that she's just pissed about her own fucked up childhood?"

"There is something more important to worry about right now," Andrea told him. The priest looked again at the remains of the man now lying on the ground. "She's here."

Oh shit. Cameron realized that Andrea was right. She *was* here — *Lilith* was here — somewhere.

Jake tried standing up straight. His eyes watered. "We've got to get out of here," he said urgently.

"Not yet," Cameron insisted. "Not until we find the missing pages." He began scanning over the large room. Searching for something, ANYTHING, that could reveal King Rudolph's chosen hiding place for the lost pages of the Devil's Bible. *Christ, I have no idea.* He thought. *They could be anywhere.*

He frantically searched everything and everywhere as he headed back towards the altar. Examining and feeling everything as he made his way forward — the painting of St. Ludmila, the deacon's chair, a small wooden tabernacle. Then he looked left, into one of the open crypts, and saw again the gothic stone allegory of the woman — Brigita. The statue seemed as though it was looking at him. Slowly, he walked over to it and tilted his head.

"What is it?" Jake asked.

Skull tilted his head to the other side and squinted. "It's – *a woman,*" he answered to himself.

"Colonel," Jake called again.

Cameron turned around and looked at Father Canale. "Frank was wrong," he said. "Father, when we first met you told me that this was the oldest *convent* in the Czech Republic."

"That's right," Andrea agreed.

Cameron took another step towards him. "But aren't convents for nuns?" He didn't allow time for a response. "That means that there never were any monks here. The Codex had to have been scribed somewhere else."

"I suppose," Andrea said. "But does that mean…"

Suddenly Colonel Skull had an epiphany. *If a convent is for nuns, then what I need to find is the first "friary" in Bohemia.* He looked at Andrea. The priest had just finished speaking, but Cameron was still lost in his own thoughts. *Wait a second – convents and friaries – two different places – opposite but equal.* "Shit, come on," he said, quickly turning for the door. "Follow me."

"Where are we going?" Jake asked.

"Rudolph believed in diametrics," he said, looking at Jake over his shoulder as the three of them headed for the churches southern entrance. "Extreme polar opposites like life and death, good and evil."

"So what?"

"So," Skull answered. "I think I might know where he hid the pages."

37

The deep rumble of a thunder cloud resonated through the night sky, trailing only seconds behind another intense bolt of lightning. "Did you see it?" Colonel Skull asked.

Nobody answered.

He looked over his right shoulder at Jake, then over his left at Father Canale. "Father," he called softly. "Did you see what I'm talking about? The taijitu?"

Another burst of light suddenly shot from the sky and revealed the priests face. Andrea had not seen the ancient Taoist symbol. Instead he was still keenly watching the corner of St. Vitus Cathedral where the two foot patrols had just circled round.

The three of them had waited inside the

basilica until Colonel Skull had given them the thumbs-up. They had then silently entered the castles courtyard, but were now standing fully exposed. There was nothing, save the rain and darkness, to conceal them. And should the two castle guards decide to double back, Cameron and Jake would have to make a run for it.

"See the what?" Jake asked.

Cameron turned. "The taijitu," he said, pointing a finger above the basilica's doorway. "I can't reach it on my own. One of you is going to have to boost me up there."

"No problem," Jake said with a little too much enthusiasm. "Let's do this."

Cameron nodded then repositioned the sling of the submachine gun so that it went around his neck and crossed diagonally over his chest. "Okay Jake, just watch you're footing on this wet ground."

The Englishman nodded back at him then took a knee just below the relief sculpture. He interlaced the fingers of both hands together and held them a few inches from the ground as a stirrup. "Ready when you are," he whispered.

Skull walked up next to him, braced a hand on his shoulder, and then rested a foot into the basket of his hands. He took a quick peek above him at the stone carving. Between the horse, the rider, the dragon-looking creature, and the boundary itself, there were at least a dozen good hand holds. And all he needed was one. "On three," he said, starting to put some of his weight into Jake's hands. "One..., twwoo..., *three*."

The strength of the lanky young Englishman was surprising. He easily propelled the colonel several good feet into the air above him. Cameron reached up. His fingers quickly found an edge and he grabbed for support. But the wet stone was too slippery, and just as fast his fingers were pulled loose. *Oh crap*. He thought, and began scrambling to find purchase on another hold.

Feeling it hopeless, Skull braced himself for a landing back onto the paving-stones of the courtyard. But unexpectedly, his left hand suddenly caught onto something—leaving his body and right arm dangling a considerable distance off the ground. He looked up. Literally, he had "caught the dragon by the tail."

"There ya go mate," Jake said.

Cameron ignored him. He reached up with his right arm and grabbed his left wrist, then pulled himself up until he could get a good fix on the dragon.

The sculptures inscription ran horizontal, nearly level with his chest. He glanced down between his shoulders and could faintly read the letters E-O-R-G-Y carved just in front of him—the end of the Latin spelling of *Saint George*. This meant that the taijitu wasn't very far to his left.

"Can you reach it?" Andrea asked.

Colonel Skull tightened the grip of his right hand before letting go and reaching out. His fingertips could just brush the edge of the symbol, but not enough to do any good. "No," he answered frustrated.

The priest called up to him again. "Drop down an inch or two. There's a small ledge below you, just above the inscription. From there you can shimmy yourself over."

"Oh sure, no problem. Just like that huh?" he mumbled sarcastically.

"What?" Andrea asked. "I'm sorry, I couldn't hear you."

"Nothing," Cameron answered louder. He looked down again. The ledge in mention was maybe an inch and a half wide—if he was lucky. And by the looks of it, very slippery. If he were to slip off and fall right now, they would have to find a place to hide before trying again. Sooner or later the two patrols would be making their way back around to this side of St Vitus.

"Well?" Jake asked. He was starting to get nervous. "Come on? What are you going to do?"

Shut it Jake. Cameron thought. He looked again at the ledge and blew out a breath. *Here we go.* He relaxed the muscles in his arms slowly until he lowered and was able to test the ledge with one hand. A moment later and he was fully committed.

"Okay," the archpriest encouraged. "The symbol is less than a meter to your left."

Jake jumped up and pushed Skull's foot lightly in the right direction to encourage him further.

Cameron kicked him away. *"Don't,"* he said sternly then shuffled himself slowly and carefully over to the stone symbol.

Both men on the ground remained silent as they watched as Colonel Skull pushed and pulled on the rock. He tried turning it — first left, then right. Nothing was happening.

Growing discouraged, Cameron felt himself start to panic. Was he wrong about the symbol? Had the last ten minutes all been for nothing?

The fingers on his right hand were now burning in pain from holding up his 190 pounds. He had maybe another two or three minutes before they involuntarily let go.

He looked again at the symbol. *No.* He thought. *I'm not wrong. That symbol is wrong.* He reached a hand into his shirt and pulled Kate's Christmas necklace from around his neck. He stared at it momentarily — *Knight* — then kissed it and began digging at the stone circle surrounding the symbol.

Pieces began flaking off and his digging turned to aggressive hammering. "It's not solid stone," he called down optimistically. "Ha ha!" He couldn't contain his laughter. "It's some type of mortar," he announced. "The mason packed some kind of a mortar around the symbol."

The archpriest wasn't as relieved. "Please hurry, Colonel. It won't be long before those men return."

"I'm almost through," Cameron lied. He paused to look closely at the taijitu. The craftsmanship was phenomenal — almost otherworldly. Even modern CNC precision laser cutting machines would have had a hard time duplicating the intricacy and accuracy of the work. As Colonel Skull was quickly finding, the round outer circle of the taijitu was fit into the surrounding sculpture with pinpoint accuracy — possibly within a few thousandths of an inch.

"Hurry, Sir," Jake said quietly, interrupting the Colonel's thoughts. "I think I hear someone coming."

Cameron finished chipping away a few last bigger pieces of mortar before tossing the necklace back over his head. He brushed off the symbol then stuck his thumb into one of the holes and grabbed the swerved line in the middle with the rest of his fingers. Taking in a deep breath, he applied the first bit of pressure. It shifted.

The movement was less than a degree, but it had moved nonetheless. He turned again harder but it stuck. "Damn it," he said to himself.

"Hurry up Colonel. I can hear the two guards coming."

"Come on, come on?" he begged the

stone. It still wasn't moving. He tried reversing, spinning it the opposite way. It moved. *Thank you.* Every inch or so the rock circle wedged itself in again. But by being gentle and patient with it, Cameron slowly began pulling it from the rest of the relief carving.

"Colonel." This time it was Father Canale calling to him. "We must get going."

"Just two more seconds," Cameron insisted.

Suddenly a light flashed on. "VETRELEC!" one of the men shouted and began running towards them.

"Bloody hell," Jake said frightened, "We need to clear off." And he began jumping excitedly where he stood—unsure if he should wait or flee.

Skull looked at the flashlight quickly then yelled a loud grunt and pulled heavily on the stone cylinder. It slowly slid free and crashed to the ground, shattering upon impact when Cameron couldn't hold up its weight.

"Hurry up," Jake yelled again.

It was dark inside, but Cameron gazed into the open cavity now exposed behind the taijitu. It was solid black, except for a single small pigment of burnt calfskin parchment rolled up tightly against the left side. Skull quickly reached in, grabbed it, and pulled its length from out of the stone tube. He held it before him for a moment, staring at it in wonder.

Roughly three feet long, the rolled-up paper felt think and heavy. Its edges were frayed at each end and it smelled of mold despite its dryness and thick coat of dust.

"Toss it down to me," Andrea yelled.

Colonel Skull wasn't about to let the pages go. Instead, he held onto them firm and released his dying grip from the ledge. He dropped down, landing solid on his feet.

"Do not move," one of the castle guards ordered in obscured English.

Both guards had their rifles pressed against their hips as they closed the distance between them and the three other men.

"What do we do?" Jake cried panicky.

"We *run*," Cameron said as he turned away from the approaching men.

"Wait." Archpriest Canale grabbed Cameron by the arm. Cameron turned back to him surprised and Father Andrea gently touched him once on the forehead then on his chest. "May God be with you," he said.

Cameron looked at him confused.

"Go," the priest instructed. "I will stall these two men, but also, I will pray for your safe return."

"Father…" Cameron said softly.

Andrea pushed the colonel back by his chest. "GO," he commanded.

Cameron bowed his head in thanks then turned to Jake. "You heard him. Let's get the fuck out of here."

38

Jake followed close on Cameron's heels every step of the way as they traversed the castles many courtyards. And even as they passed through a few of the smaller buildings that had been either left unlocked, or that the colonel was able to "open."

So far, escaping the castle was going much smoother than Cameron had expected. So much so, that it was actually beginning to make him uncomfortable. He couldn't help but feel that he was somehow being led into a trap. And adding to his discomfort, the weather had taken another abrupt turn for the worse. The previous rain had again turned to hail. But unlike the hail a couple hours earlier, the ice now fell much more aggressively and at a sharp angle, striking both men painfully in their sides whenever exposed.

Cameron held his left hand up in a loose fist and pumped it vertically a few times — a signal for Jake to hurry up. And much to Cameron's delight, Jake was actually catching on to Nightcorp's hand gestures fairly quickly.

The Colonel had only given him a *very* brief introduction to S.C.R.E.S.—pronounced jokingly by Nightcorp as, "Screams." It stood for, Standardized Close Range Engagement Signals. One hand grabbing the other arm just above the wrist meant ENEMY, usually followed by a finger pointing in the direction of the threat. An open palm pushing downward meant CROUCH, repeating the gesture a second time meant GO PRONE. Tracing three sides of a box with a finger in front of you was DOOR, while completing all four sides of the box was WINDOW.

Cameron excluded the more technical "screams," like how to describe different formations or points of entries. And then there was always common sense. If Cameron pointed a finger at Jake, it obviously meant YOU.

Jake sped up. He had fallen slightly behind after Colonel Skull ducked into a narrow passage just west of café Franz Kafka. "Do you know where we're going?" he asked.

Cameron answered him quietly while still guiding them low through the corridor. "We're somewhere in the Golden Lane. If we can get past those two towers..." He pointed up at the tall peaks of Black Tower and Daliborka. "There is a long staircase that leads down into Prague."

"How do you know?"

"God damn it, Jake." Skull stopped and turned to him. "Why do you always have to question everything? Why can't you just take my word for once? Christ almighty!" He remained in his crouched position and turned back to the west. Then his voice softened. "That's how your sister and I got up here, okay."

"Oh," Jake said. He was starting to get the feeling that the Colonel was taking a liking to his sister. The emotionally strong man seemed overly distressed at every mention of her disappearance. Not the kind of distress one shows when car keys get misplaced, but the kind of distress like when a platoon brother is captured as a P.O.W., or a beloved dog is hit by a car. A deeper and more personal kind of cut that tears at your heart and soul and can make it difficult to speak or even breath. That was the sort of distress the Colonel was showing. He was unsure of her wellbeing. Only God knew what sort of horrors the STB would put her through. But worse — would they even keep her alive?

But Jake certainly wasn't the type to let personal matters of gossip drop that easily. "You fancy her, don't you?"

Cameron's face turned bright red from anger, not embarrassment. He turned again quickly to Jake and zipped his fingers across his lips. Nightcorp had no "scream" for SHUT THE FUCK UP, but the mouthy Englishman got the idea. Then he waved a hand for Jake to follow and they moved quietly to the end of the narrow passage.

The alleyway emptied into a much wider area, lined by some of the castles original rock walls. In the center of the square was a bronze statue. And as with seemingly everything else in Prague Castle, this statue was equally unusual. It was of a naked man crawling on all fours with a gigantic human skull riding on his back.

"Look at the size of that…"

Cameron's head began to spin and Jake stopped talking. They were now less than a football field away from the outer edge of the castle.

Skull started thinking to himself. *We could just make a run for it. It's not that far, and Jake's in decent enough shape.* He scratched at his stubble. *Damn it though. Once we hit the stairs we're screwed.* He pictured Iris' face as she joked earlier about feeling like a rat in a maze.

He came up with a plan B. "Alright, Jake. Here's what we're going to do. I know there's at least one guard positioned at the base of that tower." He pivoted around. "Hey, are you listening to me?"

The Englishman didn't answer.

"Jake."

Still nothing.

"Jake," Cameron repeated a little louder. "What the hell?" He snapped his fingers. Then he realized that Jake wasn't ignoring him out of disrespect, but out of fear. His big blue eyes were staring wide at something just over and beyond Cameron's left shoulder.

As Jake's bottom lip began to tremble, the colonel slowly started rotating back around, gripping the large medieval pages tight in his left hand, and reaching carefully and inconspicuously for the submachine gun on his back with his right.

His eyes led as his body slowly followed, cautiously, carefully. His fingertips felt the cold steel of the rifle and he gently pulled it forward as his gaze focused on the dark contour of a body lurking behind him.

Like a shadow burned into the buildings of Hiroshima, the figure was black in the night and stood eerily motionless, not more than ten feet behind him. Suspended in a seemingly purposeful, nightmarish stance, the form was slouched in a deceitful manner, almost as if it were in tonic immobility. The same way a grass snake will feign apparent death as an anti-predatory defense, only to strike the moment its prey nears.

Cameron recognized the deception and continued to pull the rifle slowly to his side. Although the only thing distinguishing the forms shape from the truly lifeless statues throughout the rest of the castle grounds was a sparse twinkle of light from off its chest— moonlight reflecting off the rain covered breast as it rose and fell to the slow rhythm of heavy breathing.

He knew who it was. It was *her*. It was Lilitu. And as soon as the realization came over him, the demoness slowly lifted an arm and pointed a crooked finger down at the rolled-up pages held tight in his grip.

He clenched harder onto the parchment, pulling the papers close to his side to protect them from both her and the rain.

"Ca ca colonel," Jake stuttered in a frightened whisper.

Cameron ignored him, refusing to take his eyes off the woman apollyon before him. "You're not getting these pages," he called out to her.

Her head tilted back and she made a sound that almost resembled laughter. Then she spoke to him through a coarse voice in a language that was unrecognizable.

"The man you killed this morning was a priest, and a good man," Skull said while feeling for the trigger of the submachine gun. "And how many others?" he asked. "For what? Because you had a rough childhood? Well guess what…"

She laughed again, not giving him the chance to finish.

Cameron ignored her mockery. His trigger finger rested on its perch and he quickly swung the rifle up to his side. "Game's over," he said assuredly. But he didn't pull the trigger.

Her laughter ceased. She lowered her brow and brought her hand back to her side. She spoke again through the same monstrous voice, this time in English. "Nnoo gaammmeesss." Her words were long, and resonated coarsely throughout the small courtyard.

Suddenly the roar of a thunder cloud boomed through the night, followed close by two simultaneous bursts of intense lightning. The bolts of electricity lit up the courtyard and everything in it, including the disfigured appearance of the devilish woman across from them.

At first sight of her, Jake's knees began to tremble and he nearly collapsed. The scars over her face were so extreme that they left no skin unblemished. And the remaining tissue had not healed the color of flesh, but instead gave her a putrid red complexion—almost as if she were still on fire.

She wore a long black coat, dusted with spots of grayish dust. It was unbuttoned down past the curve of her breasts, which too were scarred, if only slightly less than her face.

She twisted her head a few degrees, then stepped a short step forward.

Skull pushed the barrel of the rifle further towards her. "Don't even think about it."

Jake must have noticed something. "Colonel," he said quietly. "Get back."

Cameron's eyes squinted in confusion. "What?"

"Please colonel, let's get..." Jake was cut

off by the monster leaping into the air in front of him.

Lilitu sprang towards Cameron. She landed in a crouch then quickly vaulted a second time, closing the distance.

Skull jerked back. His eyes followed the creature much faster than his hands and the gun fired unsuccessfully. Three hot empty shells ejected from the machine guns magazine as three 62 grain semi-armor piercing rounds buried themselves deep into a stone wall.

"Colonel!" Jake shouted.

The ancient pages of the devil's bible dropped from Cameron's hand. Lilith leapt forward again and clawed at his face. He leaned back quickly, avoiding the sharp talons by mere inches. But saving his face, Skull was unable to protect his midsection and her sharp nails cut through his shirt and deep into his chest.

He screamed out in pain and stumbled backwards. His hand holding the rifle went limp and the gun dropped and deflected off the ground, landing half submerged in a quickly deepening pool of rainwater.

Lilith leapt forward again, ferociously and without hesitation. She clawed and bit at him with the speed and wrath of a hundred enemies. Like a school of piranhas devouring a capybara more than 5 times their size.

Skull fought to avoid the onslaught of attacks. One after another they grazed his clothing, shredding easily through the weak fabric. He weaved right and made a run for the drowned rifle, but was quickly knocked to the ground. "Jaa..." He choked and had to gulp down a mixture of rain, sweat and blood before trying again. "JAKE," he called.

Lilith had finally slowed her assault, leaving Cameron to crawl backwards on his elbows while she slowly crept towards him.

"Jake," Cameron yelled again. "Get the gun!"

Again lightning blew up the sky.

The colonel inched himself backwards, inconspicuously snatching up the pages as he went, but also trying desperately to recall and utilize some of his training in the process as well. 6 weeks of basic conditioning, 2 weeks of airborne and air assault scenarios, 8 weeks of land warfare—including hostage negotiation, navigation and demolition, 2 weeks of phase three mountain exercises, 1 week of physical fatigue training, and lastly, one *hell* week—all to find himself right now overcome by a petite woman somewhere in her mid-thirties.

Lilith reached an arm forward and pointed again at the pages rolled up in Cameron's hand.

He squeezed them tightly. Water dripped out from the wet parchment but he refused to release them. He shook his head at her. "I told you, you're not..."

Lilith roared out in a high pitched but also somehow contradictory masculine tone. Her chest bowed out in anger and she looked back down at the colonel. "You presume what I want is of the physical world?" she asked. "Foolish. What I want…"

She suddenly collapsed, hitting the ground hard just in front of Cameron.

Jake stood behind her, holding the submachine gun upside down in his hands like a baseball bat.

"Thanks for not hesitating," Cameron said, picking himself up from the ground. He looked down at himself. The cuts across his chest hurt worse than they actually were.

"Are you okay?" Jake asked. "You're bleeding pretty bad."

"It's shitty alright. But it looks worse than it is." Cameron curled his lip at Lilith, who was already starting to squirm a bit. "I'll be fine."

Lilith moaned.

"We should chivvy along," Jake pointed out anxiously.

"I don't know what the hell that means," Cameron said, "but yeah, let's get the heck out of here."

The Englishman handed him back the rifle. He then took the first cautious step around the body of Lilith when something grabbed hold of his ankle and pulled. Jake screamed out as he lost his footing and stumbled to the ground.

Skull spun back around.

The demoness was back on her feet, posturing up for another attack.

"Fuck!" Cameron tried again to bring up the rifle fast enough. But a shot fired before he had the chance. "What the…"

The shot had not come from his gun. And worse, the round had nearly struck him in the leg.

Lilith looked up. Two more shots fired quickly at them, followed by a voice.

"Hold your fire," the colonel yelled out to the guards.

They ignored him and another round sliced through the air, this time coming closer to Lilitu than him, but he wasn't about to press his luck. He slung the rifle over his shoulder and grabbed Jake by the wrist. "COME ON."

Jake scrambled and sprinted alongside the colonel, ducking and weaving to avoid the barrage of gunfire raining down on them.

They reached the base of black tower and Cameron easily crippled the young guard with a forearm to the bridge of his nose when the young man stepped in front of them. He looked back quickly over his shoulder before continuing their run towards Prague. Lilith was gone.

"Colonel, what the bloody hell are you doing?" Jake cried.

More relentless gunfire shot at them from above. Cameron uselessly held a hand over his head to guard himself then turned back and ran with Jake for the castle stairs.

"Aahhh!" Jake screamed out in pain. "I'm hit!"

Skull's stomach knotted up and he turned. A round had caught Jake in the shoulder. "You've got to keep moving," he ordered. "Let's go." He grabbed him again by the wrist.

Damn it. Cameron thought. He was beginning to panic. There were just too many shots coming at them. "Just keep running," he yelled to Jake.

"We're not going to make it," Jake answered fearfully.

Then suddenly a deep rumble resonated from the hillside just east of the royal staircase.

39

The headlight was quickly growing brighter, bouncing up and down over the rough terrain as the BMW scaled up the incline.

"What the..., is that...?" Cameron continued to run with Jake but squinted at the motorcycle coming straight at them.

"IRIS!" Jake yelled, and began waving his arms in the air.

The BMW bucked over another small pile of deadfall before Cameron got a clear view of the long blonde hair, wet and matted from the rain, tracing the outline of Iris' face. He also saw that her shirt was gone and her once lacy white bra had now become semi-translucent. He didn't have time to dwell on it, but his subconscious captured a mental image of the moment as without a doubt the sexiest sight he'd ever seen.

The bike sped forward then slid sideways to a stop in front of Cameron. Iris waved a hand towards herself. "Get on," she shouted.

"We can't all fit," Skull told her.

She reached out and grabbed a fistful of his shirt and yanked him towards her. She kissed him once hard on the lips then pushed him back. "Just shut up and get on the damn bike." She released her grip. "Hurry up."

Skeptical, he threw a leg over the seat behind her and wrapped his arms around her waist. Jake bounded up behind and quickly straddled himself uncomfortably over the saddlebags, then in turn put his arms around Colonel Skull.

Another blast from a guard's rifle pinged off the rear fender. "GO GO!" Cameron instructed.

Iris pulled down on the throttle and the rear tire spun in the mud before finding traction and launching them back in their seats. The motorcycle raced down the hill, tracing the outside of the long staircase until the three of them were safely away from the castle.

—

They stopped once reaching a hairpin curve on Chetkova St. Iris pulled the bike under the cover of a large oak, yet close enough to a neighboring street lamp to have some usable light. She dropped the kickstand and Cameron wasted little time removing Jakes hands from around his waist.

"Here." Cameron took off his coat and wrapped it around Iris' shoulders as soon as she dismounted the motorcycle. "Are you alright?"

She squeezed it around her, nodded, and smiled up at him.

"Colonel," Jake asked, "what happened to the pages?"

"What pages?" Iris asked.

Cameron lifted up the front of his shirt and pulled out a three-foot-long roll of parchment that was tucked into his pants. "It wasn't easy trying to cram these in there while I was running," he said.

The paper was damp, bent and wrinkled but he pinched the edge of the top sheet with his fingers and slowly began to unroll it.

"You found them," Iris whispered in amazement. She walked over and nestled herself close to Cameron, starring awestruck at the lost pages of the Devil's Bible.

As the top line of script began revealing itself, all three heartbeats gathered around began to race. The text was faded. And even the water-resistant calfskin paper was unable to hold back the full fury of a Czech hailstorm. The insect ink was smudged around the edges and beginning to run down the page.

Although it was still legible, it was not decipherable—at least not to Colonel Skull. It was a text unlike any he had ever seen. Even Iris looked bewildered at it.

"I've never seen anything like this," she said softly. "Finish unrolling it."

Cameron continued to open the page.

About a third of the way down the text changed abruptly from one line to the next.

Iris gasped.

Again, at the bottom third of the page, was another sudden change in text. "What is this?" Cameron asked.

"I have no idea," she admitted. "I don't recognize any of this." She reached out for the paper. "Let me see the next page."

Skull handed Jake the top sheet, exposing the one beneath it. "Hold onto this, please."

Jake took it from him carefully.

The following page was expressed in a similar pattern—divided three times by sudden changes in script and language.

"Wait a second." Iris grabbed the corner of the paper and pulled it towards her. "This one looks familiar." She leaned in for a closer look. "I recognize this one," she said, tapping a finger onto the bottom third.

Jake asked the question before Cameron got the chance. "What is it?"

"It looks like…"

"What?" Cameron begged.

"Well," she started. "I can't be sure, but…, it almost looks like it could be Phrygian."

"What-*the-hell* is Phrygian?"

"*Phrygian,* is what some consider to be the first language. It's similar to Greek, but older. It's predated only by un-translated and undocumented codes and signs—languages with no pronunciations. Some people say that…" She stopped and lifted the edge of the paper.

"Some people say what?" Cameron asked.

Iris didn't answer him. She leaned down further and quickly studied a few of the pages below. Finally, she looked up. "Oh my God!"

"What?" Jake asked angrily.

She pointed at another section of text on the following page. "Look. I think this is Ancient Macedonian."

"So, what?" Cameron said.

"And this one…" She pointed at another text, again on the page behind. Then one by one started going through the pages. "I think its Ancient Sumerian. And this one looks like some form of Tamizh. The point is that these are all the oldest languages known to man. Even predating Hebrew and Egyptian. Most are Indo-European, but together they cover nearly the entire world."

"And what do they say?" Cameron asked.

"I have no idea," she admitted. "There are maybe a handful of people in the world who could translate most of these. I only recognize them from…" Again, she stopped.

"What's wrong?"

She stared blankly at the final text on the last page. "This one…, this one might be Adamic."

"Okay."

"Adamic has never actually been documented as a factual language. But certain traditions suggest that it's the language that God used to speak with Adam and Eve in the Garden of Eden."

Colonel Skull's eyes widened. He thought in silence for what seemed like minutes before speaking. "And if God spoke to Adam in this language, then..." It was now his turn to pause for a deep breath. "Then the serpent must have also spoken the language."

"Yes," Iris agreed. "That's how Satan was able to trick Adam into eating the forbidden fruit."

Skull looked down at the text with discomfort.

"And some of these," Iris continued. "Well, I've never seen anything like them before. But look." She brushed over a few paragraphs. "Do you notice anything unusual?"

"Like what?" Jake asked her.

"Like a pattern or any other similarities?" It was another rhetorical question. Both men waited for her to continue. "If you look at any language as a system," she explained, "there are certain levels and characteristics that define it — intonations, rhythms, lexical semantics, the basic rules of grammar." Her hands began to flutter as she spoke. "Anyways, what I'm trying to tell you is that I think all these languages are repeating the same thing over and over again. Like the Rosetta Stone — *on crack.* A key to translating some of the world's most secretive languages. All we might have to do is translate one of them."

"Which none of us can do," Cameron pointed out. "Right?"

She sighed. "Let me take another look."

Jake and Colonel Skull waited a few moments while she scanned over the pages a second time.

Come on, Iris. She thought to herself. *Think. There's got to be something here you recognize.* The languages were all too old. Many of them hadn't been spoken in centuries. And even though a couple of them could still be translated today, she was incapable of doing so.

"Hang on," she finally said.

Something caught her eye. The oldest language that she was fluent in — both the spoken *and* written form — was Tibetan. And in the center of one of the pages she noticed something familiar. *Sanskrit.* She thought.

"What is it?" Cameron asked.

"This one," she said. "It's Sanskrit. It's what the ancient Buddhist scrolls were written in before they were carried over the Himalayas into Tibet. I speak Tibetan," she proclaimed. "And the two languages aren't all that dissimilar."

"So, what does it say? Can you read it?"

"I'll try," she answered.

She bent close and traced under the script lightly with her forefinger, then stood back and shook her head. "I'm just not sure. It doesn't help that the ink is fading away."

"Try," Skull told her.

She bent down again. "I can't read the top part. But right here I think it says…, something about *the first journey*."

"What else?"

She hesitated. "Cameron…, I don't know. Even the little bit I think I recognize might be wrong."

Skull didn't say anything, but she could feel his eyes on her.

"The last line," she said. "I think this says, "*in the tongue of my messenger*."

"What the hell does that mean?"

"Why are you asking me? I don't have any idea."

"Wait," the colonel said quickly. "Jake, give me that page." He took the paper back from the Englishman and returned it to the stack.

"What are you doing?" Iris asked him.

"Hang on." He counted the top corner of each sheet of paper. "Seven. There're seven pages here."

Nobody said anything.

"Frank told me earlier," He continued, "that there are *eight* pages missing from the Codex."

"So, where's the last one?" Iris asked.

"Exactly," Cameron answered. "Where is the last one?"

"The friary," Jake offered quietly.

Skulls eyes lit up and he turned and grabbed Jake by the shoulders, but released quickly when Jake pulled back in pain.

"I just got shot there," Jake whined.

Cameron smiled. "Jake, you beautiful genius you. That's it." He turned to Iris. "You're brother's right. I realized it earlier. We need to find the first friary in the Czech Republic."

Iris didn't ask for a long explanation of how he figured that out. But she did offer another very valuable piece of information.

"When the STB was holding me hostage," she said. "I overheard one of the men say that they needed to go to some place called, *Brevnovsky*."

40

Colonel Skull dumped the motorcycle on its side just outside the front entrance to Brevnovsky Klaster. The early morning hour was beginning to brighten just slightly from the anticipated sunrise, but it would still be better than an hour before the morning sun crested the horizon. And so far the hailstorm had only lessened to a rainstorm.

It took little time back in Prague for them to define Brevnovsky. Iris had done a search on her Blackberry while Colonel Skull contacted Frank back in the States with a new assignment. As usual, Frank won the race against the amateur Google search.

Afterwards Iris had taken her brother back to Hotel Prague Castle on foot. An idea that Cameron was certainly not happy or agreeable with, but considering the possible urgency, Iris had been extremely insistent.

Before leaving however, Cameron had given the seven pages to her for safekeeping. They were useless to him, and maybe she could work out more of the translation once safe and warm back at the hotel. He had also thought about kissing her before leaving. But instead he had left it at just that — a thought.

In any case, Frank had quickly confirmed that the Brevnov Monastery was indeed the first Benedictine friary in Bohemia. It was founded just outside of Prague in 993 A.D. by Prince Boleslav II and the second Prague Bishop, St. Vojtech.

Frank had also pointed out that once Cameron reached the monastery he should try and get below ground. If the condemned monk had been held in confinement, it most certainly would have been underground somewhere.

Skull stepped over the BMW and quickly ran under an archway crowned by three statues. It had taken him about twenty minutes to ride there from the castle, which was about ten minutes to long. Had he not missed a turn at Dlabacov, he would have been there in ten. And now he felt even more urgency than before.

Crossing through to the inner garden of the monastery, he kept his movements to a minimum. Any noise that could be avoided, including footsteps, needed to be contained. As with all monastery's, this one too was inhabited 24 hours a day by the monks who lived there.

He stepped quietly onto a cobblestone street running through the center of the lawn. However, it was not a street intended for driving. Each side of the road had park benches placed every twenty feet or so for visitors to sit. And just up ahead of him, Colonel Skull could see a wooden sign poking up out of the grass.

He crept over to it. It was a directional marker for tourists. Arranged by navigational sequence, starting with north, each line on the marker gave the name and direction of a particular area of the monastery.

Cameron scanned over the information. Most areas of interest were down the path to his right, including restaurant Klasterni, followed by monk's quarters, the Church of Saint Margaret, and Therisian Hall. But the last entry on the sign is what particularly caught his attention. It was the words ROMANESQUE CRYPT, followed by a set of arrows — one pointing to the right, and the other pointing down.

Quickly he ran down the path, following each sign until he ended at the main entrance of St. Margaret's Basilica.

The crypt must be preserved underneath the church, he thought, reaching out for the handle. Surprisingly, the door opened — almost as though it had been purposely left unlocked for him.

Cameron pushed it open without stepping inside. The room was dark. Then as the door opened past its midpoint, a back-draft nearly sucked him off his feet and into the cathedral.

He caught himself on the doorframe.

What the hell was that about?

With his left hand he felt around his back for the submachine gun then slowly took a step inside. The room was deathly quiet and dangerously dark. Before continuing, Colonel Skull looked back over his shoulder one last time. An odd shimmer caught his attention and he paused temporarily.

He squinted and rubbed his eyes. "What the hell is that?" he asked out loud this time.

Slowly he retreated from the church and walked closer to the reflection. It was a small lake nestled some twenty yards east of the monastery. One edge of the basin traced the curve of highway 6 that he had just ridden in on. But with the surrounding storm, everything was wet, and he hadn't noticed that it was in fact a body of water.

The lake brought back many memories in Cameron's mind. Without haste, he abandoned the upcoming search of St. Margaret's Basilica and headed straight for it.

Four years earlier, during one of Nightcorp's slower periods, Cameron had been requested in Nova Scotia Canada to help NATO's Public Diplomacies Division Commander calm the public and explain why the world military was suddenly a common presence in the small maritime province.

Colonel Skull had found the assignment rather boring to say the least.

NATO command had intercepted a radio transmission describing strategic geometric landmarks placed throughout the countries landscape. As it turned out, a local land surveyor had indeed made some unique discoveries throughout the terrain regarding GPS coordinates of pre-Columbian monuments. However, nothing about his discoveries should have ever caused such uproar among world powers.

But Cameron had decided not to waste the trip. He'd checked himself into a hotel room later that afternoon and spent the next few days relaxing and doing the "tourist" thing. One venture in particular he'd found very intriguing.

It was a boat trip he'd taken to neighboring Oak Island. The Money Pit, as it's called, fascinated Cameron. It reminded him of his late-night documentaries that he loved so much. Except this time, he was actually there to see it.

The elusive treasure of the Money Pit and Oak island came with a fascinating tale, one that spanned hundreds of years, and came with everything that a good story should — mystery, fortune, betrayal and death. And one particular method of deterrent that Cameron never forgot.

A complex man-made trap had been constructed deep into a shaft in the earth. Coconut fiber mats, giant slabs of stone, and layered wooden planks all guard the secret of whatever lie at the bottom. But most interesting is the way that the pit had been purposefully flooded with seawater by means of underground tunnels and artificial swamps.

Some claim that it was pirates who put it there, while others suggest it was the Knights Templar. Either way, radiocarbon dating of artifacts is consistent with the 16th century.

And to this day, treasure hunters from around the world have *all* been unsuccessful at uncovering whatever lies beneath.

The Colonel stopped himself abruptly once reaching the outer edge of the pond. He looked down by his feet and could see by the outer bank that he was right. This was also manmade. *This is it.* He realized. *They flooded it intentionally. Used the elements to their advantage. The ultimate obstacle if you want to keep people out.*

There was no hesitation. He dove headfirst into the icy water fully clothed with the rifle still hung from his back. He swam out ten or twenty yards before sucking in a deep breath and diving below the surface. But the water was murky and dark. He couldn't see anything more than an arms distance in front of him.

Quickly he resurfaced and sucked in another few breaths, then dove again. Almost neutrally buoyant, Cameron hovered a few feet below the surface and looked in all directions for anything useful.

It wasn't until he was about to go for a

third breath that he saw it — a twinkling reddish-orange glow from across the lake. He came up for air again and gasped. His limbs were starting to shiver in the freezing water, but calmed slightly once his heart rate rose from paddling himself across the water to its far end.

Once he reached the opposite bank, he grabbed onto the shore to give his arms a moment of rest. Before letting go, he stuck his face underwater and looked again for the small glow. It was about 15 feet below him now, and 7 or 8 feet to his right.

Now or never, I guess. He thought, as he inhaled deeply and dropped again below the surface.

He tried to focus as the light drew nearer. *What is that?* He questioned to himself.

It got closer and closer with each pull of his arms until he was right on top of it. It was a small entrance to an underwater cavern.

He was starting to get short on breath again, but still he forced himself to swim in up to his waist to get a look inside. The orange light was still off in the distance. Much closer in front of him however, Skull could see how the small cave entrance opened up into a larger room. And more importantly, the room had an air pocket.

—

His forehead slowly broke through the surface until the frigid water drew a line across his upper lip. The only thought going through his mind right now was getting onto dry land as quickly as possible.

Unfortunately, even with all his training, and even though he might have felt like one at the moment, Colonel Skull was definitely no Navy Seal. His sea legs were limited to a 50-meter ocean swim with fins and a two-hour DVD on basic offshore lifesaving. And even both of those had been part of his indoctrination to Nightcorp, well over a decade ago.

Breathing through his nose, Cameron treaded the water and slowly rotated a full 360 degrees before swimming to a ledge inside the tiny grotto. The underground chamber, roughly 8 feet by 8 feet, was walled by hand-dug stones of various shapes and sizes. Whatever concrete or mortar had originally been used to hold it all together had since crumbled away, and the ceiling was concaved downward from centuries of heavy earth pushing down on it.

He lifted his chin out of the water, placed his hands firmly onto the dirt floor, and hoisted himself out of the water. The room above the waterline smelled of mold and decay, and the walls were damp along their bottom edges.

He rubbed his shoulders hard, then blew a warm breath into cupped hands and began removing his top layer of clothes. The wet fabric would only slow him from drying off, and one important thing that he did remember, was that cold water robs the body's heat 32 times faster than cold air.

Once stripped down to his boxers, the colonel quickly stuck his feet back into his boots and grabbed his rifle. He checked the magazine — only two rounds left.

He looked to his right. The orange glow that had led him there was nothing more than a flickering incandescence coming from an adjoined hall, yet it provided a ghostly radiance throughout the room — making his shadow dance and flicker dimly across the back wall. Although its source was still two distant to determine.

The rooms connecting corridor was narrow. And as Cameron moved to the doorway, he noticed streaks of burgundy trailing down each side. He touched one of the bloodshot veins and rubbed the substance between his fingers.

It's rust, he realized.

Years of moisture seeping through the walls from the flood water had eaten away the metal bars. He knew now that what he was standing inside was an 800-year-old prison cell — a dungeon — the last remains of an 11th century Benedictine misericord.

Along the wall to his right, waist height from the ground, was a faded crucifix that had been worn smoothly an inch deep into the wall. Most likely it had been carved out with a loose stone by one of the cells early inhabitants.

He glanced further over his right shoulder. Resting half-perched against the stone wall was what was left of the man's decayed skeleton. His left arm had broken away from the collar bone, as had the lower mandible of his jaw fallen from his skull. Suddenly a small cave rat emerged from the man's eye socket and scurried down through his ribcage and then across the toe of Cameron's boot.

Cameron flinched back a step. *How long had this monk been imprisoned to carve a crucifix that deep into the rock?* Then he found himself wondering if the man had even been justly accused.

As his mind pondered the fate of the pronounced monk, Colonel Skull shifted his gaze through the doorway. "Sorry friend," he said out loud. "But I'm not going to die in here with you."

The hallway beyond was lined with the same quarried stone as the cell. It stretched out in both directions. To Cameron's left the passage darkened. But off to his right was the amber glow that had guided him thus far.

The flame burned passionately inside the urn of a medieval torch — shamelessly devouring its fuel of animal fat in a steady inferno. But like the bars that once presided over the cell door, the torch was also falling victim to corrosion. It hung impotently from the wall, appearing as though the slightest breeze would blow it to the ground. But one thing was for sure. It had been lit recently.

Further down the passageway, two more torches hung. They were spaced apart from each other every 15 feet or so. In between them Cameron could see the dark outline of several more recesses in the wall. Most likely they were additional cell doors, but he told himself that somewhere in here there had to be a passage that the ancient monks used to access the dungeon. But then again — maybe not.

He looked again behind him then knelt to tuck one of the laces back into his boots. Suddenly he felt death in the air and he could feel the tiny hairs on the back of his neck rise up.

The submachine gun leapt to his shoulder and he pinned his side to the nearest wall

He assured himself that he was ready. *Come on you bitch. I know you're here.*

Nothing happened.

His nerves were definitely on edge, but he willed himself not to become jumpy. With only two rounds left in the rifle, he couldn't afford to take any impulsive shots.

Slowly he rose up and began creeping his way further down the stone corridor, stopping just before reaching the first of several interconnected chambers.

He took in a slow calming breath before poking his head around the corner, when a strange sound quietly reverberated from down the corridor to his left.

Again, the rifle came up quick—focusing itself blindly into the darkness. "I thought we weren't playing games?" the colonel called out.

The noise resounded again, but his question remained unanswered.

"Oh fuck this," he said in confidence. He reached out and tore the metal torch from the wall. Sparks of embers erupted from the fire as it protested its disturbance. Holding the flame like a true Olympian, Skull waved it into the depths of the passage.

"Caaammeronnn." The voice calling him echoed so softly that it was hardly discernible.

But instead of losing nerve and overreacting, Cameron stayed calm. He was back in focus—back in tune with his mind and body. A remembrance, not of his training, but of a Buddhist quote; *It is better to conquer yourself than to win a thousand battles. Then the victory is yours. It cannot be taken from you, not by angels or by demons, heaven or hell.*

A glowing ember from the fire above his head floated down in an unpredictable pattern. It landed softly on Cameron's shoulder, only to be quickly extinguished by his still damp skin. The flame was providing welcomed warmth over him. But more importantly, it revealed that beyond this doorway was not another small cell as he'd anticipated. Instead, it was a long and narrow tunnel that stretched farther than his light shown.

Above him, cobwebs clung to the low ceiling. The ones that didn't shrivel into nothing as the fire brushed across them, attached unshakably to his hair and face in a sticky web.

Skull ducked slightly and moved a few steps into the tunnel. Still the light from his torch only illuminated the walls a few feet in front of him, outlining the black void of the cave's artery in the shape of an arch.

He turned and looked behind him.

"Caaammerronnn," the voice whispered again.

He closed his eyes tight and shook his head. Was he hallucinating? The voice was ethereal, almost angelic. *Almost*, he thought, *like Kate's voice*. But without question, it was *not* the same voice that had come from the demoness Lilitu earlier.

Another proverb, although this one not from Buddha, suddenly came over him. *Be master of mind rather than mastered by mind.*

Cameron faced down the dark corridor once more.

Then, as if awaiting his return, another torch erupted to life in front of him. The tunnel lit up in a fury of bright orange, but there was no sign as to what, or who, had ignited it.

Cautiously Skull inched further down the passageway. Unlike the other corridor, this one descended deeper into the earth. It declined gradually, but at an angle nonetheless.

As he continued, one torch after another inflamed in front of him—seemingly matching the speed of his footsteps until the corridor finally revealed another hoard of granitic stones creating a wall at its far end.

He paused, expecting to hear the voice again. But all was silent, save the crackle of fire, the stirring of cold water, and the low-toned sound of his own laborious breathing.

He looked down at his bare legs. The far end of the tunnel had sloped below the waterline, leaving all but the tops of his boots submerged.

This passage was clearly the most shamed part of the ancient monastery. Hidden deep beneath the rest of the abbey and secluded even from the primary dungeon—all to hide the lone doorway harbored less than two steps in front of him.

—

The heavy breathing he'd heard moments ago did not belong to him. Drowned in the lifeless noises of fire and water, Cameron had mistaken the breathing for his own.

He let the barrel of the rifle hang loosely

in front of him as he inched towards the door. The sense of fear had diminished in him — replaced now by mental acquisitiveness and a morbid curiosity. Had harm been meant to come to him, why here? Why now? Why this way?

Slowly he leaned into the doorway. The room, another cell, was larger than the others. More the size of a bear cage than a man's. In its center was an enormous stone table, carved from a single piece of rock.

Along each wall, a ridge jutted out of the stone nearly a foot. Too high for a bench, it must have served as more of a mantelpiece. Perhaps a place for items like strands of rosary beads, vials of holy water, certainly a crucifix, and other such items to cleanse the mind and body of the fallen one.

The shelf outlined all but one section of the room. Directly across from him was what appeared to be a washbasin. The tub sat on its own pedestal, built directly into the wall. Above it, two small streams of water poured in from separate cavities to join each other in the small bath. From there, the water collected and overflowed into the pool which he was now standing in.

"The first journey," whispered the angelic voice.

Cameron spun his head to the back corner of the room but it was too dark for him to see anything. "What journey are you talking about?"

he asked.

The demoness stepped slowly from the shadows and revealed herself in the fiery light. "*This* journey."

Skull fought to resist her allure. Something in her voice lured him like the Greek Sirens who seduced sailors into shipwreck. "I know who you are, *Lilitu*," he said in confidence.

"Ah yes..., Lilitu," She said. "Referring to Lilith, Adam's betrayer, no doubt."

Cameron was confused and said nothing.

"Queen of the demons," she continued, stepping closer to the altar. "Or perhaps you speak of the Assyrian deity Alu."

A pain was forming and Cameron held a hand to his head. "I don't know what you're talking about."

"Yes, you do," she said. "In ancient Babylon, *Alu* is a demon. *Lilu* is the female form."

He rubbed harder on the side of his head, still trying to keep the rifle raised with his other hand.

"I have waited a long time for this day," she said, changing the subject and taking a step closer to him.

"Aahhh," Cameron moaned. Something was wrong. The pain in his head felt like a thousand knives slowly pushing their way through his brain—and it was worsening. "What are you talking about?" he tried asking as his knees began to shake and buckle. "What's happening?"

The demoness sashayed around the edge of the altar, brushing a gentle hand over its surface. A plume of dust rose up and surrounded her, further distorting her appearance. "Tell me…, *Cameron Skull*…, have you ever searched for *GOD* with such passion?" She cringed at the mention of the Holy Father. "Risked your life and your family? Crossed the seas? Abandoned your morals, to find *HIM*?"

He spat at her.

The demoness laughed. "Yet you have done all this and more to seek out what you once thought as evil." She glided forward, through the dissipating cloud of smoke, as if somehow suspended above the ground.

Be master of mind, not mastered by mind, Cameron ordered himself. He stood up straight. "Go to hell bitch."

Lilith's empty eyes grew wide, and for the first time, she smiled. "I shall," she whispered.

—

The phone sitting next to the bed in the hotel room nearly vibrated itself off the nightstand. Jake leaned over and checked the caller-ID. "It says James K," he shouted out to his sister.

Iris rushed out of the bathroom. "That's

General Kestner," she said, reaching out for it. "Give it to me. Hurry, hurry." She took the cell from Jake. "General," she said quickly into the mouthpiece.

James' voice was neither panicky nor calm. He spoke with a dull and emotionless tone — a tone which portrayed absolute devotion to the task at hand, both straight forward and blunt. "Where is Cameron?" he asked.

Iris glanced at the seven pages laid out on the bed before answering him. "A place called Brevnovsky Klaster. It's a monastery on the outskirts of town."

Again, to the point, the General asked next, "Jake?"

"He's here with me at the hotel."

In fact, General Kestner had been unaware of Colonel Skull's abandonment of Iris and her brother until this moment. "He went without you, or were you separated somehow?"

"No," Iris said. "He wanted Jake and me to wait for him here."

"That's fine," the General said. "I need you to do me a favor. Call Frank back in the states. Let him know that Colonel Skull has moved on to level three resistance. Tell him to have Ethan Price prepare for deployment. But also tell him that until further orders we will continue to follow NATO ROE's."

"Sure thing General," she said. "Is there anything else?"

"No," Kestner answered. "Just sit tight and keep yourselves locked up in your room. Don't do anything until you hear back from me."

"I won't," she promised. "But, General..."

"Yes?"

"What are you going to do?"

"Don't you worry about that young lady. I'm going to get our boy some god-damned backup."

41

It wasn't even a fight. Knowing that Lilith would expect him to raise the rifle, Colonel Skull instead dropped it to the ground and went for her wrist—quickly, efficiently, and directly. He pulled her arm downward and struck an open hand against the back of her elbow, catching the tendon precisely in the right place and hyper-extending it.

He then spun around behind her and landed another strike to a vital acupoint between the base of her neck and the inner curve of her shoulder. If delivered incorrectly, Cameron's attack could have done more harm to him then her. Acupuncturists use the same location on the body to release anxiety. But executed properly as he had just done, with the correct angle, direction and force on the nerves caused severe pain and physiological damage.

She dropped to her knees and the colonel immediately forced her face-first the rest of the way to the ground. He landed a knee on the center of her back and pressed his left forearm hard against the base of her skull, pinning her face under the water. "Antichrist my ass," he said firmly.

Her spine arched up under his weight as she tried to inhale. Bubbles rose up around her. Then she began to laugh. Even through the water Cameron could hear it. It started as a light amusement, almost an embarrassing admittance of defeat. But then it progressed. Steadily, her soft laughter turned to a deep bellow.

"What the fuck?" Cameron pressed down on her harder.

Suddenly she thrust upward, launching Cameron's 190 pounds into the air like a piece of confetti. He landed hard on his backside at the opposite end of the room.

"You are mistaken," Lilith said in a grainy savage voice. She slowly started moving towards Cameron who remained sitting in the cold pool of water staring at her wide-eyed. "Did you really think that all ended with John's bias vision he tells in Revelations?" she asked. "With *GOD* and that *worthless* angel Michael fighting the war in heaven? Your ignorance is vain, and it offends me."

Skull crawled backwards on his butt and elbows until his back pressed against the wall. "What the hell are you talking about?"

The demoness roared in anger. She continued towards him but her movements were no longer effeminate as they had been. She moved now in a feral, beastlike poise. "I should have been the chosen one," she announced. "I would have led the army of the damned into the netherworld. But instead…" She roared out again, shook her head and swiped a hand across the air in front of her. "*This*."

"But I thought…" Cameron began to say.

"ENOUGH," she yelled. "I will listen to this no more." She sprung at him. Her mouth was open, exposing the rows of sharp pointed teeth. Her hands became weapons of knifelike barbs and her eyes burned with a heinous inferno.

Cameron dove out of the way. The demoness hit against the stone wall and quickly turned, only to launch a second lightning fast attack.

Shit shit. Cameron thought, struggling to back away fast enough. Unable to rise to his feet, Colonel Skull crashed down an open hand beside him, sending a wave of icy water into the creature's face.

It held her back only a second, but it was long enough for him to scramble to his feet. He turned and ran, searching frantically for a weapon. But again the demoness was on him, digging a handful of claws into his back.

He screamed out and fell forward, landing back in the water. *I can't beat her*, he suddenly realized.

Nevertheless, he forced himself to roll over.

Again she was standing over him, panting heavily. She looked him in the eyes then lifted an arm above her head. "I shall be forever…"

Suddenly her eyes grew dark and heavy. Her arm lowered and she slowly sank to her knees in front of him.

Skull's right arm was still imbedded in her abdomen. A unique strike taught to him by an ex-member of the Russian Sambo Red Army — gigantic men who weren't satisfied with just tearing joints and breaking the bones of their opponents. But Cameron had only experimented with the move, successfully performing it only once before on a large block of Siberian ice. That is… until this very moment — when he perfected it.

Lilith's face went pale and her eyes met his as she sunk further into the water.

Cameron didn't say anything but he kept his gaze matched to hers as he ripped his hand from her belly — pulling with it a mess of blood, bowels and digestive organs.

She gasped, and then fell lifelessly onto him.

Cameron's head fell back and he sighed in relief. Then he pushed her off of him. He began to stand when suddenly the room shook violently, knocking him back down. *Earthquake!* He thought. The ground tremored and stones of all sizes fell from the ceiling. One rock the size of a baseball splashed hard into the water just between his legs.

"Mother fucker," he said out loud, heaving up and pushing himself towards the exit. "You've got to be kidding me."

He reached the doorway leading back into the tunnel when suddenly the shaking stopped. Unsure why, he stopped with it. No longer fleeing, he looked back into the cell. Lilith's body still lay face down in the water.

"Time to go," he had to tell himself.

Again, he turned for the door when another voice, this one not belonging to the demoness, echoed lightly through the room.

He listened close. The language was foreign. Where had it come from?

He looked around.

There was nothing.

Then the voice spoke again — softly but clearly. "Sa main derniere par Alus sanguinaire."

Cameron recognized it immediately from the context and accent. *It's Old French*, he realized. Then suddenly another frightening reality came over him. *I know what it means.*

He did not speak French. Not in any degree. But it was a sentence that he had read on paper more than once.

And the voice...? Was it who he thought it was? *Impossible.*

The voice repeated and he translated it quickly. What it had just said was frightening and he spoke the words out loud. "His hand finally through the bloody ALUS."

It was the first line of Nostradamus' prediction of the third and final antichrist.

Cameron listened for it again — his mind racing through what he had just heard. *His hand finally through the bloody Alus.* He looked down at his blood covered right arm. *ALUS*, he thought, *the ancient Babylonian word for demon.*

His hands began to shake, followed seconds later by his arms and legs. Equally overwhelmed, his mind flashed quickly through the rest of the prophesized quatrain. *He will be unable to protect himself by sea; Between two rivers he will fear the military hand.*

At the mercy of his bodies quivering, Cameron slowly turned back into the chamber. Once more he looked upon the stone washbasin against the rooms opposing wall. Again, he whispered the words out loud, "Between two rivers."

He suddenly realized that this was how the chamber had been flooded — how even the entire lake outside had been created — all from right here. Everything in the dungeon had been designed to do just that. Precise angles on passageways, staggered elevations, depths and pressures in rooms. All of it had been predetermined and engineered like this, centuries ago.

He stared at the two streams of water

pouring into the basin.

And then he knew.

Slowly, he walked past the body of Lilitu and over to the raised pool. He placed both hands on its outer rim, closed his eyes, and then bent over the water.

Taking in a deep breath, he opened his eyes and looked down at the reflection.

Between two rivers, he will fear the military hand.

42

The water rippled out from the center in all directions. The reflection of a man — not the man he knew as *Cameron Skull* — but a different man looked back at him.

He turned his head abruptly to look away. Despite the cold on his bare flesh, he felt himself begin to sweat. *What the hell is going on?*

Nervously, and *fearfully*, he returned his gaze to the water. Just as before, a face looked back at him. The reflecting apparition had his eyes, his nose, his mouth, his hair, but yet it did not resemble the man he knew. The image looking back at him had something deep in its soul that did not match his own. Something inside there was inhuman, something inside there was…evil.

"NO!" he shouted, and smashed a hand into the water.

The disruption in the pool distorted his image further, but it also revealed something else hidden below.

A tanned sheet of large paper rested in the depths of the tub. Timidly Cameron reached an arm in and grabbed for it. Lilith's blood washed off his hand and stained the water a crimson red as he pulled the page from it.

He held it before him. At first glance it was a bare sheet of parchment, all ink having long since washed away by its submersion.

But another fear came to him, one formed from a question posed earlier by the demoness. Had he ever ventured to such extremes to find God? The answer he knew was *NO*. But she was right. He had risked everything in search of Satan and his antichrist. And now here he stood with a new enlightenment. Everything had been predetermined. It had all been planned from the beginning. From the missing books to the cemetery angel, to his recent battle with Lilitu.

It had all been a test — a test for him. And… it was a test that he had unfortunately passed.

Lilith was not the antichrist. *HE* was the antichrist. The predictions of Nostradamus had been about *HIM*. She was just a tool from Satan to guide him here — a false prophet.

The paper shook in his hand and again he looked down at it. Glassy beads of water rolled down its surface. But under the shine of the water, something started to happen. Streaks of black ash began burning into the page. Even wet they left marks of charred script under the damp surface.

Skull's heart pounded against the inside

of his chest and he closed his eyes. Then slowly he reopened them and looked down at the page. Thin lines blazed across its wet surface and a form began to take shape. But it was not a text like he'd imagined, or like Frank had suggested it would be. Instead an image began to appear.

Lilith's body moaned off to his left as the post mortem residual air in her lungs escaped past the vocal cords. Cameron heard the noise but didn't turn. What he did not hear however was the slight stirring of water as the fingers on her right hand slowly reanimated.

Suddenly the muscles throughout Cameron's body contracted as if he were being electrocuted. His hands clenched the paper until it crinkled beneath his grasp and his eyelids pulled up in his forehead beyond the lashes.

Wanting desperately to look away — he could not. He was being held captive by his own body and being forced to stare upon the horrible image appearing before him.

Then the shaking started. And then came the burning. A terror unlike anything he could imagine coursed through his veins. He could feel his skin beginning to burn and the fluids that were trapped throughout his body begin to boil, as if he were literally being cooked from the inside out. A stream of urine trickled down his inner thigh, melting and cauterizing a line in his flesh until it hit the water surrounding his ankle.

The image in front of him somehow grew

brighter and even more horrifying, although it resembled nothing. Cameron saw nothing in the image. Not words, not a face, not anything — except for Hell itself.

He forced his eyes to the side and looked over his left shoulder. Lilith now stood, swaying lightly on her feet. Blood was dripping from her open wound and a foamy trail of saliva hung from her lower lip. She stared at him with disobedient intent.

Uncontrollably his eyes were pulled back to the page. The burning image spun and morphed and Cameron tried to cry out. But instead of a scream he managed the words, "Whhaaat…, what is this?"

"It is not for you," an animalistic voice answered.

From his rear, a low growl came from Satan's Beast. Cameron turned to her. She wavered in short motions like a pendulum. As did Poe's Pendulum of the Inquisition swing a heavy blade above the condemned until it slowly sliced through its prey, Lilith swayed on her feet creeping slowly towards him, preparing to slice through *her* prey.

An evil tore deep at his soul and Cameron fought desperately to escape it. Suddenly a thousand thoughts flooded his mind and he gently shut his eyes and replaced the thoughts with memories — his graduation from the School of the America's, Kendall's first birthday party, a midnight road trip with Frank to hit the opening day waters of Ten Mile lake, and then — his wedding day.

Kate's auburn hair had been kept down with a single cream-colored dahlia pinned above her left ear. She wore a strapless side-draped gown and held a clutched floral bouquet of snow white astilbes. She smiled at him.

Cameron inhaled deeply. He could almost smell the scent of her perfume in the air around him. "*I love you,*" he said to her in his dream.

She smiled at him once more. Then she leaned into his ear and whispered two soft words, "*My knight.*"

His eyes opened and he awoke with a new strength.

Turning back to the demoness, Cameron grinned. *It's NOT for me*, he realized. *The instructions are for the antichrist. And NO*, he refused to believe it. *I AM NOT the antichrist.*

That's when he realized it. Realized that there was something more — a deeper meaning behind the voice that had spoken to him. The prophesy — he had misinterpreted it.

Nostradamus had never tried to predict the third and final antichrist.

Knowing that he would never see the Kingdom of God while still on earth, Nostradamus had asked the Lord for a small glimpse into the future. He was asking God to let him see Heaven, not Hell. And God had answered, showing him the *Good*, not the *Evil*. The third prediction was not about the antichrist. It was about the savior. The guardian sent by God to defend man *against* Satan's antichrist.

Cameron was right that the prediction had been about him, but he was wrong in its meaning. Nostradamus was describing him, but describing him as the one to *defeat* the antichrist.

He almost smiled. Then he brought the sheet of parchment up to his chest and tore it in two.

Divided, the two halves of paper floated down to the water by his feet. They hovered on the surface for a few brief seconds before sinking slowly to the bottom.

Lilith roared out in anger and the earth again began to quake. Stones both small and large crumbled from the walls and ceiling, splashing into the water with explosive energy.

Cameron spun quickly on his left heel and shot towards the door. He stopped quickly and threw himself back when another giant rock shook loose from the ceiling and shattered in front of him. The boulder sent a wave of cold water and debris flying into his face and he had to wipe his hands across his eyes before continuing.

He reached the doorway and immediately turned back down the narrow tunnel to his right. But as the wall-hung torches had illuminated his journey down into the cell, they now extinguished themselves, one after another until the passageway was a treacherous shade of black.

He stumbled and had to keep a hand against the wall. The violent shaking around him was making it nearly impossible to maintain balance. And then another splash of water sprayed up at him, although this time not as intense as the last. Partially due to the stone being smaller than the last, and partially it was because the pool at his feet was now shallower — a clear sign that he was nearing the main corridor.

Almost there, he told himself.

Suddenly his right hand found a corner. The wall turned sharp to the right.

Yes!

He swung around the bend. Each step he took gradually increased in length until he found himself nearly at a sprint.

Then something grabbed him from behind. Two grotesque arms wrapped around his shoulders and pulled him hard to the ground. His chin struck against the rock floor and he almost lost consciousness.

Satan's beast was on top of him, tearing at him, avenging the desecration of her master's will. She clawed again at him with vengeance and Cameron had to pull the last of his strength to roll over onto his back beneath her.

At last he managed to catch one of her wrists. He held firm and tried to press her off of him. But her strength was incredible. She tore her arm loose and raised it high above her head. Then she released her talons and drove them deep into the side of Colonel Skull's throat.

He gasped for air. His eyes opened wide in astonishment and the demoness leaned down to him. Her forehead nearly touched his and her rotting breath exhaled into his open mouth.

She snarled. "Maybe God will forgive you," she said. "But you will never meet him to find out." She ripped her nails from his throat and reared her arm back again.

Cameron choked and coughed. Something had to happen—now!

Was it too late? Her arm pulled back an inch further, and then she released it.

Skull watched as it came down upon him. But his minds-eye saw it happen in slow motion. He flexed the muscles in his stomach, grunted in exertion and pushed up hard with his powerful legs. His body tumbled backwards over itself, sending the demoness flying over him.

Unsure how he did it, he sprang to his feet, almost feeling as though another pair of invisible hands was helping to lift him up. He ran up to the creature and was about to plant a booted foot into the side of her head when he was suddenly forced back. A giant chunk of stone broke and fell from the ceiling. It grazed the tip of his nose and landed in front of him with such power that the body of Lilith crushed and vanished beneath it. He kicked the rock anyways for good measure then turned and ran again for the small cell that he'd entered from. He ran harder than he'd ever run before — knowing that that was it. Lilith was gone but he still needed to escape. Her blood had splattered out in all directions when the immense stone pulverized her like a piece of raw meat. But he still had to get the hell out of this dungeon before it crushed him just the same.

With his eyes now fully adjusted to the dark he could finally start to see the faint outline of the doorway just a few short yards ahead of him.

He encouraged himself to run faster, but the shaking around him continued to grow worse.

Then suddenly the entire ceiling caved in

—

And the darkness consumed him.

43

The next time his eyes opened was into the bright sunrise of a Czech morning. It blinded him and he closed them tight again. But yet he could still feel that someone was pulling him from the debris.

"Where...," he began to say.

Suddenly a finger pressed into the open gash on the side of his throat and his eyes shot open in pain. He gasped for air.

"Shut your filthy American mouth," the man said in his heavy accent as he pressed a dirty finger harder into Cameron's open wound.

Cameron felt another pair of hands suddenly grab his other arm and pull violently.

"My leg," Cameron cried. "It's stuck."

"Cut it off," one of the men ordered without hesitation.

The sound of the blade being pulled from the man's sheath cut into Cameron before the steel ever could. It sent a painful chill up his spine and he started to fight for freedom. But the brute of a man held him, and Cameron was simply too fatigued and beat up to offer much resistance.

The big man walked over and kicked away a clump of dirt over Cameron's thigh then bent over and positioned the STB combat knife just below the joint of his knee. But before he broke flesh, the man turned. "Why don't we just kill him?"

Cameron inhaled loudly. Thoughts of Kendall flooded through his mind, but he hadn't enough strength left in him to escape. *I'm never going to see her again*, he thought, and a tear fell from the corner of his eye. He let out the breath and rested the back of his head against the dirt. Was this how it was going to end? Crushing Satan's beast and entombing her body under the same earth where Satan had possessed the Black Monk, only to be murdered by a pair of corrupt STB mercenary's.

Cameron opened his eyes once more. Then suddenly the man's head above him exploded and bits of skull and brain matter showered down onto the Colonel's face.

The second merc released Cameron's arms and sprang up. He quickly pulled the small double action Luger pistol from his belt and fired blindly.

Cameron couldn't make out what was happening. Shots were being fired. That was all he knew. His vision was still too blurred and his mind and body too weak to determine where the shots had come from or who was firing them.

He blinked a few times and tried to focus. But the sun was still blinding and a piece of the mercenary's exploded brain was threatening to fall off Cameron's forehead and into his left eye. He shook his head to remove it and again tried to focus.

Suddenly a familiar sound, *Whoosh, Whoosh, Whoosh,* bellowed deep overhead and the circular swirl of air from the helicopter's rotor came into view above him. Then the black silhouette of an American Apache Gunship blocked out the sun like a giant whale gliding through an empty sea.

Then a voice sounded from the copter's loudspeaker. "Drop your weapon and step away from the Colonel. You have *two* seconds to comply."

"They're not joking," Cameron said.

The merc looked at the Apache and all its weaponry before looking down at Colonel Skull. "They're bluffing," he said. "They won't shoot. Not while we're close together. They won't risk hitting us both."

Cameron gestured his head towards the attack chopper.

"One," the voice called through the speaker.

The mercenary looked back at the Apache. The chopper gracefully moved to its left, revealing a second helicopter, this one a Special Forces Extraction Black Hawk.

The Black Hawk was turned sideways, its gun door open. And from the open side door, the mercenary holding the tiny pistol at Cameron Skull looked up and could see the glare reflecting off the scope of Ethan Price's M91 sniper rifle.

"You better..." Cameron never got a chance to finish his sentence, and the man on the loudspeaker never gave the count of two. But at precisely the two second mark, Ethan Price pulled the trigger.

—

Kestner's team of EMT ground recruits wasted no time with Colonel Skull. Once freeing him from the collapse they immediately inserted a pair of small plastic tubes into his nasal passages to provide supplementary oxygen. Then they continued wrapping, probing and monitoring him—a blood pressure cuff around his left bicep just above the inflatable splint, a 12-lead cardiac monitor providing real-time 3D images of the heart, and his favorite, the bulky spinal collar that was securely fastened around his throat. As if his injuries weren't already bad enough, the collapse of the dungeon had also partially dislocated two of the vertebrae in his neck.

From there they air lifted him to Saint Anne's Hospital in Brno.

—

"Knock, knock," came a sweet voice from the door.

Cameron hit the mute button on his bedside remote for the hospital room's television then turned his head. Iris was standing there. She smiled and held up a small bouquet of flowers in her right hand and a small velvet box in her left. She walked it over and handed him the flowers first, then the small box.

"What is it?" he asked, looking down at it and feeling its softness.

She smiled and said jokingly, "Just something I found in the gift shop.

Cameron smiled back.

Inside the box was a silver bracelet. Etched on it were the words, *Min Cameron Vaktare*. He brushed his thumb across the engraving. But in the back of his mind he was almost upset with her. *Why would she give me...?* And then it occurred to him. *Iris doesn't know about my necklace.* A warm feeling of serenity came over him and he smiled. "What does it mean?"

"It means..." She leaned down close to him, a tear escaping her eye and she couldn't stop herself from crying. "I..., I thought I was going to lose you back there."

He was startled and pulled his head back.

"*That's* what this means?" he asked. "I thought I was going to lose you?"

Iris sniffled, smiled, wiped her eyes and pushed him on the shoulder. "No, you idiot." She smiled again, almost laughing at him. "I was just saying… what I meant was…" There was no sense hiding it any longer. "I was afraid of losing you."

"Oh," he said. "Sorry. I wasn't trying to…"

Again, she smiled. Earlier she hadn't wanted to admit to herself that her feelings for him were growing strong. But seeing him here in the hospital she could no longer deny it. She hardly knew him, yet — she was falling in love with him.

"So," Cameron said, smiling back at her. "What *does* it say?"

Before she could answer him, Cameron looked up at the tears still running down her cheeks. Then thoughts of his wife entered his mind, but not like they had ever done before. He saw images of Kate smiling at him, and of her holding their daughter, and holding his hand, and holding his face as she kissed him. But this time it was not the same kiss that she had given him a thousand times before. This time it was a kiss that spoke words, *My dearest Cameron. I hold our love with all my heart. It is the most beautiful and perfect thing I have ever known. You are my true love, and I know that God himself blessed us with our time together. And I thank him every day for letting me spend my life with you. You are and forever will be, my best friend and my knight. I love you.*

Cameron's lip quivered in sorrow. But deep down he knew that his vision of Kate was her way of asking him for peace. It was her way of telling him, *I know that you love me, as I will always love you. But you must let me go. To love another is not to love me less. You must live your life my dear prince. Be happy. For, our daughter needs a mother. You need a partner. Iris needs…*

"Cameron the Guardian."

"Huh?" He looked up at her.

"The engraving," Iris said. "It means… *My Cameron, my Guardian.*"

Epilogue

Benton County, Oregon — One Month Later

After a two week stay at Saint Anne's Cameron was finally released and cleared for relocation to Cedars-Sinai Medical Center in Los Angeles. Then, *finally*, two days ago he was sent home.

"So? You sure you're up to this?" Iris asked.

"Just shut the door behind you, alright." Cameron lightheartedly bumped her with his slinged arm then limped down his front walk.

Iris rolled her eyes before shutting the door and hurrying to catch up. "Is this how it's going to be the whole way over? You know it's like an hour and a half drive, right?"

Cameron graciously accepted as his lovely chauffeur held the passenger door of the Chevy. "I'm still just a little surprised..."

Suddenly a small head poked out from in-between the two front seats. "Hurry up Daddy." Kendall instructed happily. "We're going to be late."

He laughed and pushed her playfully on the forehead. "Get back in your seat you little rascal." He turned back to the front and leaned over the center console so he could see her in the rearview mirror. "You don't even know where we're going. And put your seatbelt on."

She huffed but did as she was told.

"That goes for you too, mister," Iris said, before shutting his door for him. She walked around to the driver's side and readjusted the seat before turning the key. "But she's right you know. We are going to be late."

Cameron slouched down in his chair and leaned back against the headrest. "What are they going to do? Start without us?" He closed his eyes as the truck began to back down the long driveway. A minute later and he was napping.

An hour after that his Chevy truck hit a pothole in the road, awakening him from his sleep. "Where are we?" he asked, blinking his eyes a few times.

"We've got about another 20 minutes till we get there," Iris answered.

"Get where?" Kendall asked from the backseat.

Her dad answered. "We're going to Portland, honey."

"Your dad's being modest, honey," Iris interrupted. "Some people want to give your daddy an award tonight at the Museum of

Science and Industry. Isn't that exciting?"

"It sure is," she answered. "What kind of award?"

"Don't you think it's a little strange," Cameron said, turning the conversation back to Iris, "that I'm being presented with an award for this?"

"Not at all. You're just upset that it's not some kind of military award, or something else like that."

"I am not," he argued. "It's just that... well... the Society for Historical Archaeology? Seems a bit out of my expertise, don't you think? I mean... what am I even supposed to say to these people? I don't even remember a lot of what happened."

Iris took her eyes off the road and looked at him. "It's the SHA Award of Merit. And don't forget, you're also being nominated for the AIA Gold Medal Award for Distinguished Archaeological Achievement." She returned her attention to the road. "They're both very prestigious awards. You should be proud."

"Yeah, I guess I am, but..."

She stopped him. "That underground dungeon that you uncovered, even though half of it is destroyed now, is over 800 years old." She paused and looked at him again. "*And* you found the seven missing pages of the Devil's Bible? Yeah, I'd say you deserve this award."

"Which reminds me," Cameron

continued. "Have you heard anything else from Kestner? The last time I spoke to him he said that the excavation was almost complete. Have they found anything else? A body? Artifacts? Anything?" He scratched the side of his head.

"Are you okay Daddy?" Kendall leaned forward and asked.

"Yeah, I'm okay, sweetie. Daddy's just got a headache."

"Still?" Iris asked.

"I can't seem to get rid of it," he admitted.

"When do you see the doctor again?"

He didn't want to talk about his head. "Tomorrow," he answered quickly. "So, getting back to the dig... What have they found? Any sign of Lilith?"

"Not that I know of," Iris said. "I think so far all they've uncovered is the main dungeon. They're trying to map out the ancient system the monks used to flood it."

They got off the freeway and crossed over the Ross Island Bridge.

"Are we almost there?" Kendall asked.

"Just about," Iris said, turning them left onto Grand Avenue. She looked briefly at Cameron who was still rubbing his temple. "I'm going to pull up and drop you two off. Then I'll go park the truck, alright?"

Cameron nodded. The ceremony was to take place outside the museum, along the bank of the Willamette River. He enthusiastically described to Kendall what they were about to be in for. The U.S.S. Blueback 581 Barbel-Class Submarine, moored there since her decommission in 1990, was providing the venue for tonight's affair.

"We're going on a submarine," she said excitedly.

"Well," he corrected, "we're not going *on* it. But we are going to go see it."

"But I want to…"

"I know honey. Next time, okay? But it'll still be fun." He did his best to turn around and look at her. "I promise."

She smiled.

"Okay, here we are," Iris said. "You two hop out and I'll meet up with you in a minute."

Kendall jumped out of the truck faster than her father did and ran up to help him as he eased his broken shoulder between the seat and the door.

"Colonel Skull — *SIR*." The man stood at attention with a hand raised sharp to his hairline.

Cameron recognized the insignia on the man's uniform right away. *Coast Guard*, he thought.

"Admiral Parks is looking forward to meeting you," the man continued.

Cameron's ears perked up. "The *Admiral* is here?" Quickly he began to straighten his collar and tidy up the waistline of his pants.

"Yes sir. And he's..."

Suddenly another man ran up, catching both men by surprise. He quickly attached a small receiver to the back of Cameron's belt and handed him a tiny beige colored piece of equipment. "Stick this in your ear Colonel. It's an audio transmitter. It'll let you hear yourself better when you get up to make your speech."

Cameron felt himself getting nervous. *What the hell am I going to say?* He looked around for Iris. She was jogging her way through the parking lot.

"All set?" the man asked, stealing Cameron's attention away from the beautiful blonde.

Cameron nodded then followed as the man led him down the set of steps to the submarine and the crowd of people.

Hands began to clap and people began to rise from their seats. Cameron, almost embarrassed, waved timidly before following the man's instructions and taking the stage behind the microphone. He placed both hands on the podium and looked through the lights at the crowd eagerly gathered around.

No words came out. At least not right away.

There it was again.

I swear I'm going to get rid of this thing, he told himself as he pulled the iPhone from his pocket and glanced down at the screen.

"Colonel," a man to his right said.

Cameron looked at him and then back at the phone.

"I've got to take this call," Cameron said.

The man's eyebrows stood up in confusion. "But…"

Cameron pushed his way off the stage, leaving the crowd of onlookers and amateur archaeologists equally confused. "James," Skull said into the phone. "What's up? I'm kind of in the middle of something right now."

"I know Colonel," General Kestner said back. "And I'm sorry to disturb you. But something's come up."

Cameron knew it must be serious. James Kestner never addressed Cameron as *Colonel* any more than Cameron addressed him as *General* — unless things were very serious.

"General," Cameron said. "What is it? Did our guys find the body?"

"Not yet," James answered.

Cameron frowned. "Well what then? I'm back home in Oregon. Christ, according to the doctor I shouldn't even be out of bed right now. There's no way I can go back to Prague for at least a…"

"This has nothing to do with Prague, or what you just went through," the General said dryly. "But unfortunately, I… no no, *WE…, your country*, needs you again."

"Why, what….?"

"Colonel," General Kestner announced loudly to interrupt him. "Take some time for yourself and Kendall. I'll have Frank start on pre-deployment Intel and Ethan will set up your credentials and ground command. But by this time next week I need you to have your gear packed. Make sure you bring both the day and night tactical entry kits and some climbing gear." He paused briefly. "Sorry Colonel, things might get a bit difficult out there. But we need you."

Author's note

Dear reader,

First of all, thank you for coming on this journey with me. I certainly hope that you enjoyed it. I did my best to try and tell a story that was both exciting and thought provoking.

I would like to start by saying that, although I have never visited any of the locations in this story, I tried very hard to accurately describe each of them. As well, much of the information provided in this book is based on facts. I spent many long hours and late nights researching. So to help you clarify the facts from the fiction, I will start from the beginning.

Facts

The Prologue: This is simply my interpretation and my spin on a real legend. The entire story of the possessed monk in Bohemia is the actual tale behind the creation of the Devil's Bible. And the name of the monk, Hermann Inclusus, is also real. His signature can be found in the necrology of the Codex.

The Codex Gigas: Also known as, The Devil's Bible. This book is absolutely real, and it is indeed kept at the National Library in Sweden. And yes, there really are pages missing from it.

Nostradamus: We all know who he is right? But along with the predictions, I want to point out that the astrological chart pictured in this novel is not a drawing that I made up. It is in fact a picture of the actual chart that Nostradamus created for King Rudolph.

The Lost Book of Nostradamus: Also a real book. And yes, it is said to predict the apocalypse. Here is one of the images from it.

(A Black Pope? You be the judge…)

King Rudolph: My accounts of him are also true. And he did bring the Codex to Prague Castle in 1594.

The Statni Bezpecnost: *WAS* a real organization in the former Czechoslovakia, but is no longer in existence. I simply brought them back.

Additionally: Much, much more in this book has truth to it, either in part or in whole — e.g. the cemetery outside the Sedlec ossuary containing earth from the Golgotha, and the story of Lilith.

I encourage you to research on your own any part(s) of this book that you are curious about.

Thank you all so much for your support.